A Mint C

# A Mint Condition Corpse

## By

## Duncan MacMaster

*Kirby Baxter Investigates : Volume 1*

## Fahrenheit Press

Batman schmatman, there's a new hero in town and he's kinda dorky...

Kirby Baxter went to Omnicon for the cosplay, the comics and the collectibles.

No-one was supposed to get murdered.

Get ready for a whole new kind of crime novel. The Dork Knights are rising and Kirby Baxter and his friends are putting the nerd firmly into noir.

Its all fun and costume changes at OmniCon until schlock horror superstar Erica Glass turns up dead. Fresh from a mysterious adventure in Lichtenstein Kirby Baxter soon finds himself up to his geeky neck in a deadly murder mystery.

Kirby must deploy his unique skills of deduction and detection before the body count rises and ruins OmniCon for everyone.

*To my parents Gordon and Pauline MacMaster who believed in me*

*even when I didn't believe in myself.*


*And Chris McVeigh and Fahrenheit Press, a publisher crazy*

*enough to give me and this book a chance*

VOLUME ONE

BAXTER BEGINS

ISSUE #1
KIRBY BAXTER'S PRECIOUS LITTLE LIFE

Even after two years, traveling first class still felt alien to
Kirby Baxter. He wasn't complaining; it just felt strange
walking off a trans-Atlantic flight and not feeling like he'd
spent the long hours wedged between a three hundred
pound block of ancient cheese, and a gorilla that had recently
run amok at the perfume counter of a discount store. Kirby
was surprisingly free of the cramps, and pins and needles
feeling that he normally associated with long flights. He even
scored some much needed sleep over the Atlantic
somewhere between Iceland and Nova Scotia, leaving him
fairly awake and coherent when he arrived in Toronto.

Gustav had reluctantly left Kirby alone to follow his
employer's carefully laid out plan. Gustav's part of Kirby's
plan was to collect their luggage from the 'Elite Class'
luggage pick-up, which Kirby hadn't even heard of before
this trip, and then collect the car from the rental agency.
Kirby's part of the plan was to first find Mitch and then
hopefully figure out some way to prepare his old friend for
his first sight of Gustav.

Kirby Baxter didn't know how Gustav felt about flying
first class since the man kept such things, like his feelings
over his sudden change in lifestyle, to himself. Kirby didn't
even know if the big man had slept during the flight since, as
far as Kirby was awake enough to see, he kept the same
vigilant position in the aisle seat next to him, eyeing everyone
and everything on the plane like he could see right through

them and straight to any of the felonies and misdemeanours they may have staining their souls or festering in their imaginations.

The food court that Kirby passed through on his way to the escalators was a parade of sensations. While the sounds of conversations, announcements and sales pitches danced circles around his ears, the smells of Indian tandoori, all-American hamburgers on the grill, and Italian pizza flew dizzying spirals around his considerably keen nose. Despite the crowd and the sensory overload, Kirby didn't worry about finding Marvin Mitchell Mandelbaum, AKA Mitch, AKA 3M, AKA That Little Bastard because, despite his height, or maybe because of his lack of it, the man had ways of making himself stand out in a crowd.

Kirby looked down from the top of the escalator and saw Mitch's sign poking out above the heads of the milling throng below. It was a piece of plain white Bristol board, with LORD KIRBY Q. FISTBOTTOM ESQ. carefully printed on it in block letters.

Mitch had officially made his presence known.

Kirby waved and caught Mitch's eye, the short man waved his sign in response. Mitch often described himself as "five feet and five inches of sexual dynamo," and whenever he did Kirby would ask where he kept two of those five inches. That question usually resulted in Mitch doing his patented flying kamikaze tackle/atomic wedgie combination. Mitch had sharp brown eyes that were always on the lookout for trouble and black hair in the style of a Brillo pad. He was dressed in his regular uniform of oversized black denim jacket; blue jeans that were too old to be trendy, and too worn to be retro; and a t-shirt adorned with a Lovecraft abomination pitching Cthulu Cola: the Elder God of Soda.

"Kirby!" called out Mitch.

"Mitch, you're a class act as always," said Kirby as he shook Mitch's hand.

"You don't like my sign?" asked Mitch.

"You misspelled my last name," said Kirby, "there's a

hyphen between 'fist' and 'bottom,' and my correct title is 'Grand Exalted Emperor of the Known Universe' not 'Lord.'"

"I blame it all on my dyslexia," said Mitch, "that's why I became a colourist instead of a letterer."

"Thank God for that," said Kirby. "I don't want to know what you'd do with 'Clark Kent.'"

Mitch couldn't hold his emotion or his sign any longer and leapt up to give Kirby a big hug.

"Damn it's good to see you buddy," said Mitch. "Two years is a long time, too long."

"Can't breathe," gasped Kirby at the little man's surprisingly strong squeeze.

"Sorry," said Mitch. "It's just been like forever since I saw your ugly mug. Cool jacket."

"I got it from an army surplus store in Switzerland," said Kirby, showing off what qualified as sartorial excess for him.

"Do the sleeves contain a bottle opener?" asked Mitch.

"Oh," said Kirby, his voice a sponge dripping with irony, "that's so original; I swear I never heard that one before."

"Everyone's a critic," said Mitch, "but I do dig the new ironic goatee, I guess puberty finally kicked in while you were away."

"So says the man who still wears footy pyjamas."

"That's purely a comfort thing."

"I'm sure it is."

"So, are you broke yet?"

"No," answered Kirby, "I've managed to avoid being a cliché." That cliché being the conventional wisdom that the overwhelming majority of record-breaking lottery winners like Kirby ended up broke within two years. "In fact," he understated, "I'm still pretty secure."

"That's great," said Mitch giving his old friend a friendly whack on the arm. "It's just that I saw you coming down with just your Con-bag and I figured you had to sell your clothes for your ticket."

"No," said Kirby, "Gustav's getting the luggage and the

rental car."

"Is he that guy you met in Frankenstein land?"

"The country's name is Lichtenstein," corrected Kirby, "and yes, he's working for me full-time now."

"Doing what?"

"He's sort of like a valet," answered Kirby, "and driver who does whatever needs doing." At first Kirby was unsure about Gustav's pledge of service once the mess in Lichtenstein had settled down, and back then part of Kirby sort of hoped that Gustav would lose interest and move on. Kirby at first underestimated the large man's skills as a driver, assistant and, more often than not, bodyguard, and Gustav quickly made himself indispensable. Where these skills came from was a mystery because the big man only told the bare minimum about himself to anyone, even his employer. All Kirby really knew about his sole employee was that he was an orphan from the Czech Republic, had been adopted by Irena Hacek's parents when he was a boy, spent ten years in the French Foreign Legion, then worked for a time as a policeman, and had met Kirby in the middle of the mess in Lichtenstein. Then Gustav, because of what Kirby did for Irena, felt compelled to act like someone out of a nineteenth century melodrama and become Kirby Baxter's strong right hand. Kirby was lucky to know what he did and only learned about Gustav's time in the Foreign Legion when he was helping him pack up his humble apartment to ship everything to what will be his new home in America, and found an authentic white legion kepi and dress uniform among his few possessions.

"He's your valet?" asked Mitch.

"It means more than just a guy who park cars at restaurants you can't afford to eat at."

"I'm not stupid," replied Mitch, "I just never tagged you to be the kind of person who would have a butler."

"Technically, he's not a butler. A butler works for a house and a valet works for a person. He works for me so he's a valet."

"Well," said Mitch; "thank you for plugging that hole in my knowledge oh great know-it-all."

"Thanks for having so many holes to plug."

"That phrase can be easily misinterpreted."

"Let's change the subject from your holes."

"Thanks for having me crash in your room," added Mitch. "My new boss doesn't believe in travel expenses for the star talent, let alone the colouring serfs like me."

"It's a suite," said Kirby, "you're getting your own bedroom and bathroom."

"I'm fighting the urge to hug you again."

"Don't," said Kirby, "I'm not being that generous; it's worth the money to avoid a repeat of our past roommate experiences."

"What do you mean?"

"Where can I start," said Kirby, "let's see, first, when you snore you sound like a choking elephant, and then there's the incident with 'Miss Kitty' at DragonCon."

"Don't remind me about that."

"You actually need to be reminded?" asked Kirby. "I thought that little episode in your sexual history was forever seared in your frontal lobe. You should be having screaming flailing post-traumatic flashbacks on a daily basis."

"You bastard," said Mitch as he picked up his old army surplus backpack, "I had carefully constructed a web of denial for that memory. Now it's back and making my balls retreat somewhere behind my nose."

"Then my work here is done," said Kirby. "Come on, Gustav will be here with the car any minute."

"I'm curious to actually see this guy," said Mitch as they stepped out of the terminal and onto the sun-baked sidewalk. "The news stories about the mess in Lick-en-whatever didn't have any pictures of him, and your description in the email was kind of vague."

"He's kind of hard to describe. There's our ride coming."

"Ooh," said Mitch, as he watched the car pull up to the broad glass doors, "a Mercedes, pretty swanky."

"Wait for it," said Kirby, having decided that a shock and awe strategy was the best way to introduce Mitch to Gustav.

"Wait for what?" asked Mitch before turning to see Gustav emerging from the car and blotting out the morning sun. "Holy flying shit!"

That reaction was a little extreme for someone seeing Gustav for the first time, but Mitch was never very good at moderating anything, including his reactions.

"Gustav," said Kirby, "this is my friend Mitch, who I told you about. Mitch, this is Gustav, who I told you about."

"You obviously didn't tell me enough."

Gustav shook Mitch's hand, making it disappear almost completely.

"Nice to meet you Gustav," said Mitch.

"Gustav," said Kirby, "could you please put Mitch's bag with the rest of the luggage?"

Gustav held out his hand and Mitch heaved his pack onto it like it was an offering to appease an all-powerful and potentially ill-tempered deity. Gustav took the offering, opened the back passenger door for them and took the pack to the trunk.

"OmniCon," said Kirby as he went inside the Mercedes, "here we come."

"Put that away," said Bruce Haring to his employer.

Erica Cross looked over the tabloid and wondered how the hell a paper like the Weekly Tattle got a picture of her hugging Brad Pitt, when she only ever met Brad Pitt once, at some charity event, and barely had a chance to shake hands, let alone hug, or have the passionate love affair that the tabloid alleged was currently breaking the hearts of both Angelina Jolie and Jennifer Aniston.

"That's all done with Photoshop," said Bruce, making her think for the millionth time that he could read her mind, "that's probably a picture of him hugging his aunt from Topeka, they then used a computer to slap your face on her body, because those are definitely not your hips, girl."

"Why would they want to do that?"

"Because you're young, beautiful and successful. That means that men want to have you and women hate themselves for wanting to be like you," added Bruce. "There's a lot of schadenfreude out in the real world and the people who make those rags make money from it."

"What is 'schadenfreude,'" asked Erica.

"It's a German word," said Bruce gently removing the copy of the Tattle from her hand and replacing it on the rack, "the closest translation is 'shameful joy.' It basically means that the people who buy these sorts of rags enjoy seeing people like you get embarrassed or shamed, whether you've done anything to deserve it or not."

"It's horrible."

"It sells millions of copies of trash like that every day and brings tons of traffic to websites too," replied Bruce. "My advice is to not even waste the effort ignoring it. It has nothing to do with you and everything to do with making some fat lady in a flower print muumuu and curlers feel better about her wasted little life by thinking you have been knocked down a peg or two." The pair walked across the arrivals area, past a short man with wild curly hair holding a sign reading LORD KIRBY Q. FISTBOTTOM ESQ and toward the car rental desk.

"I thought modelling was bitchy enough," said Erica, who was never comfortable in that world. Her oval face, scarlet hair, alabaster complexion and curvaceous figure made her stand out from the other girls, and standing out bred resentment if not outright hatred. Andi Stallworth was Erica's only true friend from that world, and Bruce knew that the thought of catching up with her made the discomfort of playing the pony in Max Cooperman's latest dog and pony show bearable.

"Besides," said Bruce, "in the long run I actually think it's a good sign."

"You think that is a good sign?"

"Remember Oscar Wilde?"

"Who did he design for?"

"Don't act dumb," said Bruce, "being a cliché does not become you."

Erica laughed. "I just couldn't resist poking you a little. What little nugget of wisdom did he give you?"

"Oscar Wilde said that the only thing worse than being talked about, was not being talked about."

"I just wish they were saying nicer things," said Erica, "I'd even settle for true things."

"That would mean giving that brute publicity," said Bruce, instantly regretting his words, "I'm sorry to even mention him."

"You're right," said Erica. "Besides, we can't just go around denying that he exists, or denying what he's done. That would be admitting that he has me running scared, and I'm not going to do that."

"That's my girl," said Bruce.

"You're the best assistant I ever had," added Erica. "You're also the first assistant I ever had."

"You're the best boss an assistant can get," replied Bruce, "I know how badly it can turn out, because I have worked for many. I once spent a week working for Naomi Campbell."

"You made it a whole week?"

"It's a testament to my skill as a model wrangler."

"Or your reflexes."

"It's most likely a little of both."

Erica laughed; Bruce thought it was good to see her laugh again, hopefully putting the business in California behind her. He was glad to have her out of Los Angeles and hoped that maybe she'd find a little more laughter in Canada. The simple thought of her seeing some old friends in the unlikely place of a comic book convention sounded like the perfect recipe for some peaceful fun.

He hated her.

He hated how good she looked coming off a plane even

though she was without make-up and was dressed in a baggy t-shirt and jeans. He hated how easily she made money. He hated the adulation of her that was all over the internet. He even hated the prissy little prig of an assistant she had.

He really hated how ridiculous he looked because of her. He was born and bred in Southern California and had no idea it got so bloody hot in Canada of all places. He was using the mini camera hidden in his ridiculously long coat to watch her, to capture her, to own her, because he figured that the security people in Canada weren't as permissive as their colleagues in Los Angeles when it came to strange men in ridiculous outfits wandering around airports with cameras.

She and her toady were leaving the little magazine stand and heading toward one of the car rental desks. It was time for him to get back to the hotel. He hoped he would have an easier time hiding among the freaks and geeks so he could get what he wanted out of her.

Andrea "Andi" Stallworth-Hack knew exactly where her husband was, and she didn't need to use the GPS or the maps on her iPhone to find him. She had studied the laminated floor plan that lay next to the complimentary stationary and had completely committed it to memory.

First stage: Andi left the hotel room and then turned right twenty paces to the bank of elevators, and called for what her husband called the 'Excelsior Express.'

Second stage: She rode the elegantly appointed Art Deco box down thirteen floors to the lobby.

Once in the lobby she reached the third stage of her journey by turning left and crossing a marble floor which was decorated with streamlined shapes ripe with the optimism of the future on the eve of the Great Depression, until she reached a pair of grey institutional metal and glass doors that had nothing to do with the rest of the decor. She went beyond those doors, showing her convention staff pass to the half-asleep security guard who barely noticed her presence, and walked along the well-worn beige carpet for about one hundred feet until she reached the final stage: inside the convention centre itself.

There another pair of inelegant metal and glass doors met her, with the words WATERLOO CONVENTION CENTRE etched into the glass. She then walked past the hundreds of vendors putting the final touches on their booths selling comic books, magazines, toys, DVDs and anything else that might remotely attract the interest of a collector. Then came the place the organizers called 'Artists Alley', lined on both sides with long tables and drawing boards. Past them were the comic book publishers. The displays for the independent publishers ranged from simple folding tables and few shelves of merchandise, to the slicker full scale booths decorated with professional looking company logos. Beyond them lay the 'booths' of the major companies, many of them as big as houses and decorated with a visual cacophony of so-called superheroes, super-villains, monsters, robots and scantily clad femmes fatale, all immortalized in their two-dimensional glory.

Then she reached the displays of the movie studios and television networks. They made the major publisher's booths look like elementary school science fair displays on photosynthesis constructed by slow children. The smallest studio rig was at least twice the size of the biggest publisher display and all were covered with images of their biggest stars in their even more two-dimensional glory.

She walked past those displays to a set of wide metal and wood doors marked ROOM B. The doors were propped open so the tech crew could wheel in the dollies loaded with equipment, and she had officially arrived at her destination.

"Did everything arrive in one piece?" asked Andi, her elegant accent gliding across the racket of construction.

"Yes, darling," said Henry 'H-Bomb' Hack, as he climbed down from his three-quarter complete stage to greet his wife with a kiss on the cheek, "are you feeling any better?"

"The headache's gone," answered Andi. "I took a long bath and it did wonders."

"You used a new scented soap today," said Hack inhaling deeply. He affected a more working class accent than his wife, though he had a similar upbringing of boarding schools and upper middle class respectability. While her accent was a slice from the upper crust, Hack's dwelled in an urban netherworld combining whatever parts of London and/or Manchester had the most street cred that week. "Very fruity, like an orchard."

"It worked better than the pills," said Andi.

"Will you be in any shape for the party tonight?" asked Henry Hack. His wife's migraines had a nasty habit of turning up at inopportune times. When they traveled together, which was rare lately, they usually had to book suites with two bedrooms; one for him, and one for Andi to spend quality time with her migraines. This trip had been worse than usual forcing Andi to spend the last two days and nights holed up in her room, unable to see anyone, not even her husband.

"I'll be fine," said Andi, "I wouldn't miss this party for the world." The upcoming party was a combined effort of the movie companies shilling films and TV shows at this convention, a little bit of friendly socializing before the convention proper when it would be a no holds barred battle for the attention of comic book, science fiction and fantasy fans, and a piece of their precious disposable incomes. This sort of convention was a new experience to Andi and her husband, having never organized a show for such people, but Henry jumped into the gig with his usual gusto, putting on a superhero themed version of his 'H-Bomb' dance party show for every night of the event. It wasn't the sort of job a celebrity DJ and promoter of Henry's level usually took on, but Andi knew he had his reasons and one of them was that they paid very well, and in advance. "Erica will be here, and it's been so long since we've seen her."

"Yeah," said Henry, "you two have a lot of catching up to do."

"I've been too long without any decent gossip," added

Andi, "and Erica always had a good ear for such things."

"Your ears aren't so bad yourself," said Henry leaning in to where she could feel his breath on her cheek. "The rest of you is pretty hot as well."

"Control yourself," said Andi gently pushing him away. He was right, despite being an 'old gal' of twenty-nine she could easily stride the catwalks of Paris again and show those scrawny teenagers a thing or two about fashionista ferocity. Her figure was long, naturally slender with matching legs, and the sort of features, a few inches on the feminine side of androgyny, that the cameras loved. One of her last acts as a professional model was to be a mentor and friend to the scarlet haired girl with the alabaster skin and wide green eyes that seemed able to reach through the cameras straight to the viewer. Through its combination of cruelty and inaccuracy the fashion industry had stamped an expiration date on Erica's beauty, even at the still tender age of twenty-three, leading her to pursue an acting career that brought her to this convention. "You know, it will be great to have Erica here, she's always fun to have around."

Andi looked around; scaffolding ringed the room, normally home to wedding receptions and upscale proms, while the technicians, most of them locally hired stagehands, draped them in coloured lights, projectors, and all manner of paraphernalia.

"Let me guess," said Andi, "the green lights are supposed to represent kryptonite?"

"I think they're supposed to represent the Green Lantern," answered her husband, "at least that's what I'm telling the folks from Warner Brothers. They're trying another movie, or a TV series or something like that."

Andi went to sit down on a long blue box, but Henry grabbed her arm and pulled her forward.

"Bloody hell?"

"Sorry darling," said Henry, "but that's not a regular box. Just touch it."

Andi let her fingertips just graze the box, and recoiled.

"It's freezing!"

"It's full of dry ice and liquid nitrogen," said Henry. "You would have frozen your poor little bottom off."

"Is this for the new cloud dance?" asked Andi as she watched condensation form on the blue plastic. The 'cloud dance' effect was one of the trademarks of her husband's music and light show. He had been working on a new variation of this effect for the OmniCon show for months, wanting to make the show special, even though most nights the crowd would be the sort of people who didn't normally attend his sort of show.

"The old smoke machine was getting a little too smelly," said Henry. "They were starting to give me migraines. Plus it's actually a little cheaper to do it this way."

"Why do you need so much?" The container was over ten feet long and five feet wide.

"There's enough for tonight," said Henry, "then there's tomorrow night, and two more nights after that. I have enough to not only give this place a floor of mist, but it's going to leak out into the main room."

"Won't it be chilly?"

"Folks will dance closer," answered Henry. "Plus, the organizers say they'll save on air conditioning. Apparently Canada has summer too my dear."

"You know," said Andi, "I think this is going to be a great time after all."


No vermouth.

No fucking vermouth.

Max Cooperman wanted to yell, he wanted to scream, he wanted to roar. He wanted to rip the bolted down furniture out of the arrivals area and swing it wildly at someone, anyone, everyone, but he couldn't. There was a time when he would have thrown a conniption fit that was visible from orbit over such an egregious injustice, but he couldn't afford to do that now.

He couldn't afford the lawsuits, the fines, and the pay-offs that he used to just laugh off as pocket change, anymore. It was his own damn fault that his plans for a mid-flight Martini had been ruined. He told that brain-dead lickspittle Weatherby that the only time the great Max Cooperman would fly commercial was if they were shipping home his corpse in a crate, and to do whatever it took to make sure the MaxCo Films corporate jet would take him to that goddamn geek festival in Canada or face his considerable wrath.

Weatherby did what Max ordered, but at what cost?

The plane's on-board bar, usually restocked with fresh bottles of the world's best liquor for every trip, was empty except for a twenty dollar bottle of vodka. All but one of the plasma screens had been stripped and sold, and the imported Egyptian cotton hand towels by the once gold plated, but now aluminum, sink, were replaced by a roll of goddamn paper towels from a goddamn Walmart. At first Cooperman wanted to throttle the uppity weed, but Weatherby explained, in that high-toned Boston drawl of his, that it was either those luxuries, or fuel, the company couldn't afford both. Cooperman was still wondering how he survived the damn flight.

"The car is here," announced Weatherby, earning a grunt from his boss, "and the luggage is loaded." Another grunt, as Cooperman wondered why the kid stayed for so long. He had worked as the film mogul's assistant for what would be six months next Tuesday, a record smashing survival time for anyone so deep in the maelstrom called MaxCo Films. It wasn't like the kid was without options, his family was the majority shareholder in one of the banks that MaxCo owed money to, and he had the sort of Ivy League pedigree that burned the ass off a self-made hustler from the Bronx like Max Cooperman. Weatherby could go anywhere, but he wanted to be in the movie biz, and judging from his refusal to quit and ability to avoid getting fired, he really, really wanted to be in the movie business.

Another point in the little bastard's pro-column was that

he hadn't been ratting him out to TMZ or Jackie Paine's Hollywood website like so many others before him.

Max slumped in the backseat and wondered why they weren't moving yet. He leaned forward to see the cause. There was a Mercedes blocking the Cadillac Escalade that Weatherby had finagled from the rental agency by using his own credit card. What looked like a bald Sasquatch dressed like an undertaker was putting a ratty looking backpack in the trunk, so Max fought the temptation to reach over Weatherby's shoulder and honk the horn. Max Cooperman was a big man, weighing in at over three hundred pounds, but where he had bulk, this behemoth obviously had real size and power on his side.

The theme song from Jaws started coming out of Cooperman's cell phone. Max fished it out of his pocket and saw that it was Laval.

"I don't like talking to you over the phone," said Cooperman, "meet me at the convention centre, I'll text you the time. Since you already look like a freak that lives in his momma's basement, you should blend right in. Yeah, that's right, I'm a fucking sweetheart, and don't forget that this sweetheart is paying you. So do as you're told and don't call this number again."

Cooperman hung up and his bulk seemed to melt into the seat a little. The Cadillac was moving now, gliding away from the terminal toward the city of Toronto, OmniCon, and yet another plan to keep everything from falling apart.

"No," said Fred Ashmore into his cell phone, "I haven't even landed in Toronto yet. How can I talk to Cooperman, he went on a different plane?"

Ashmore quickly shut up and listened; he always had to listen when his father spoke, whether the old man demanded the possible or not, you still had to listen. Ashmore Senior didn't have to listen to you; being listened to was a privilege, but listening to him was a sacred responsibility. Ashmore Senior also didn't have to understand what you were trying to accomplish; understanding your situation was also a privilege, but in his world, in which you lived at his pleasure, obedience to his commands was another sacred responsibility.

"I will talk to him at the hotel," said Ashmore, "we can settle all this then. He's skirting the edge of his option, if he's late by so much as a day our problems will be solved."

"Excuse me sir," said a pretty flight attendant with brown hair, "but you're going to have to turn off your cell phone, we're coming in for a landing."

"I have to go Dad," said Ashmore, "we're going to land in Toronto. I'll call back when I've got news–" Ashmore didn't have a chance to say 'goodbye' since his father had already hung up.

Ashmore turned off his iPhone, pocketed it, bolted back the last of his complimentary champagne, and passed the glass to the flight attendant with a polite nod. Inside his mind he was acting out a scene where he was finally telling off his parents, his aunts, his uncles and his cousins. He was telling them to shut the fuck up and leave him alone to do his business. In his fantasy he told them, in no uncertain terms and decidedly salty language, that he had rebuilt Atlantic Comics into a major player, after his great-uncle Smiling Sam and his cronies spent the 1990s and 2000s driving the company to the edge of bankruptcy. In his mind Ashmore was telling them that a big movie studio like Continental Pictures wouldn't even be thinking about buying Atlantic Comics if it wasn't for his work cracking the whip on the talent, getting the distributors and the shops off their broad behinds, and making the once struggling company a serious going concern.

Sure, it wasn't a perfectly smooth transformation, even Ashmore admitted, if only to himself, that he made some mistakes.

Chief mistake was Max Cooperman.

Almost two years earlier Max Cooperman swanned into Ashmore's office dripping honey and promising the moon.

Superhero movies were exploding in theatres all over the world, and Max Cooperman was looking for a comic book company that didn't already have a relationship with one of the major studios for his MaxCo Films. The other independent publishers had shown Max the door, but Fred was still relatively new to the business and didn't fully understand the producer's reputation.

Cooperman promised big money, he promised Fred Ashmore an executive producing credit, he promised Ashmore a spot right on the stage at the Kodak Centre when they collected the first Best Picture Oscar for a superhero movie. For all Ashmore knew there was something behind those promises. Cooperman's company, MaxCo, had produced movies that made money, movies that won awards, and a few that did both. What Ashmore didn't know was that it had been a long time since MaxCo released a profitable movie. In fact, MaxCo's business model centred on coming up with excuses to not release movies.

MaxCo would use money from outside investors to buy up independent movies, literary properties, and movie rights to comic book characters, and then sit on them. Max Cooperman would then take these properties deep into the world of Hollywood bookkeeping, just past the sign marked 'here there be dragons & madness,' where they were used to inflate the value of MaxCo's assets to attract more investors. Only in the real world they weren't doing anything, let alone making money.

Ashmore didn't know that then, and he let himself fall for all the smooth talk and mile high promises. He signed a deal giving MaxCo a shot at making movies based on Atlantic Comics stable of superhero characters.

That was a really big mistake.

That big mistake grew over time and became positively huge when Cooperman started to rush The Vengeance Sisters into production. That move was a disaster of positively super-heroic proportions, and it taught Ashmore exactly what a bastard Max Cooperman could really be.

Now Ashmore's family was on his back. The family had long treated Atlantic Comics as Great-Uncle Sam's occasionally profitable hobby but now they were viewing it as the ugly duckling that finally might become the goose that laid the golden egg. Cooperman had the power to wring that goose's neck and strangle Fred Ashmore's future with it. This weekend was going to be Fred Ashmore's make or break time.

Fred was going to make like he was happy, attend the press conference, the panel discussions, and all the other publicity crap, meanwhile, where and when people and their cameras weren't looking he was going to do everything he could to break this movie before a single frame of film was shot. He didn't know how far he had to go to do it, but he was perfectly willing to go there, if necessary.

Jimmy Madden paused from grumbling at the crew assembling his booth to ogle the long drink of water that passed by on the way to Room B. She was tall, lean, and in a pair of denim short-shorts and funky purple tights that worked on her if not anyone else. Her short and spiky blonde hair wasn't normally Madden's style, but for her he made an exception. Maybe what attracted him the most about her was the sheer lack of notice she paid him and his entirely impressive booth under construction.

She had what Madden's mother called 'an abundance of sass,' and that more than made up for not being his normal type.

"What are you waiting for," growled Madden at his crew, "a blessing from the Pope!"

The crew went back to work stacking his shelves with action figures, books and other merchandise. He made sure to remind them that most of that crap was, if not worth more than their lives, at least worth more than their collective asses.

He felt a buzzing in his pocket, it was his phone. He pulled it out of his half-size too tight jeans and checked the caller ID. It was LaGuardia, just like the airport, and why the hell was he calling him now.

"What the hell is it?" asked Madden.

"It's Kevin."

"Of course I know it's Kevin," snapped Madden, "there is such a thing as caller ID."

"Hey," said LaGuardia, "I'm on the plane; we'll be coming in for landing soon."

"Jeezus," growled Madden. "What the hell is wrong with your brain? I thought you were so worried about being overheard, and you're calling me with Ashmore there?"

"He's in first class," said LaGuardia, "he's got me stuck in coach."

"He's still on the same plane!"

"I'm pretty sure that someone heard us talking about the Wilco situation," added LaGuardia.

"You're being paranoid."

"You're not being paranoid enough."

"Now I know you're an editor," sighed Madden, "you're speaking in clichés."

"I'm telling you the truth," snapped LaGuardia.

"Why are you so certain?"

"I just saw on Twitter that Kirby Baxter's back from Europe, and he's going to OmniCon."

"So," asked Madden, "he's an artist, they go to conventions all the time. Doesn't he have money now; maybe we should invite him?"

"Hell no," said LaGuardia.

"Why not?"

"He's actually met Wilco," said LaGuardia, "in fact he knows him pretty well."

"Oh shit," said Madden.

"Yeah," said LaGuardia, "the one person on the whole fucking planet who actually knows the son of a bitch and has seen him in the past thirty years is going to be at the convention."

"This is going to be okay," said Madden. "It is an

invitation-only event and he will not be getting an invitation."

"What if he tries to interfere?"

"If anyone tries to interfere," said Madden, "I'll take care of it."

"I gotta go," said LaGuardia, "we're coming in for a landing."

"Just stay calm," concluded Madden, "everything's going to be all right."

All he got was silence, LaGuardia had already hung up.

"Fuck it," muttered Madden.


"I guess that business in Lick-en-whatever was pretty wild," stated Mitch, hoping to draw out more from his friend.

Kirby scratched the ash blond hairs of his beard and shrugged. "It was very wild."

"The European newspapers were all over you like the Hulk on a hissy fit," said Mitch.

"Yeah," said Kirby. "Maybe someday someone will tell what really happened."

"What did really happen?"

"I said someday," answered Kirby, "this is today, and today is all about OmniCon."

"Be that way."

"Don't whine," said Kirby. "Why don't you tell me what you've been up to?"

Mitch shrugged.

"The Ash-hole canned me about a week after he fired you," said Mitch. "After that I bounced around from company to company. Did some work for Marvel, DC, Image and Dark Horse. I became the town bicycle, everyone's had a ride."

Mitch was a colourist; it was his job to take black and white line art drawn by illustrators like Kirby and add colour to them. Mitch thought that description belittled his work and preferred to say that he brought drawings to life, which was actually more apt. Where others in his field took technology to the extremes, plastering the art with every effect their computers had stashed in their hard drive, Mitch was different. His training as a painter made him think of himself as more of a creative artist than a technician. He didn't just digitally paint the necessary colours and shades; he composed those elements in ways that made the art seem like it was about to take a deep breath and leap off the page.

That's why when Kirby had his pick of people to work with on Shadowknight, he chose Mitch over the older and more experienced colour artists. Even though Kirby was a rich man now, he still thought of those days as his personal mini golden age. He had his dream job, scripting and drawing his favourite title, he had a good team working with him and the sort of freedom one had when no one in authority could be bothered to interfere with what seemed an inconsequential endeavour.

Shadowknight used to be one of the premiere titles published by the Atlantic Comics Company, with a history going back to the dawn of the industry in the late 1930s. However, by the time the assignment landed on Kirby's drawing board it was a sinking ship, with dwindling readership, convoluted back-stories that didn't make a lick of sense to anyone, even the hardest of the hardcore fanboys, and an annoying sidekick called the Shadow-Squire that no one liked.

With everyone expecting the young unknown artist, literally fresh from the farm, to just fill in the contractually obligated issues until the company could quietly cancel the character's last remaining monthly book, they didn't bother him with their usual meddling. With no scripts coming in and no one telling him what kind of stories to tell, Kirby decided to do the sort of book he wanted to read when he was a kid. Kirby had The Jester, Shadowknight's arch-nemesis, blast Shadow-Squire into bits in his first issue, and then Kirby went to work straightening out all the story continuity problems left over from the 1990s.

Kirby's changes sparked better sales, and those better sales meant that a job that was only supposed to last a few months ended up stretching out to five years. Shadowknight went from the bottom of the superhero heap, to number two in sales, not just within Atlantic Comics, but in the industry overall. Movie studios started sniffing around the character, top talent started vying to contribute to the company's other titles and the publisher, the Atlantic Comics Company, leaped several spots up the importance ladder of the Ashmore publishing empire. Then everything fell flat on its proverbial face.

Fred Ashmore had been in the corner office at the Atlantic HQ in the Empire State Building for a little over a year. Fred had moved over from working in middle management of the family's gardening magazines to run Atlantic Comics when his great-uncle, the legendary Smiling Sam Ash, finally retired. He decided to celebrate his first anniversary as a comic book mogul by sitting down to an interview with a popular comic book podcast. The host asked how much he felt he owed to such a wonderful talent like Kirby Baxter, since his groundbreaking work on Shadowknight had sparked the company's renaissance.

That was the single worst thing to say to Fred Ashmore, especially the day before Kirby Baxter's exclusive contract was coming up for renewal.

Kirby showed up the morning after the podcast had been recorded, expecting to sign on the dotted line as he had done twice before, but an expressionless security guard named Reuben intercepted him at the entrance of the Ashmore Building. Reuben passed him a cardboard box containing his drawing gear and personal effects, and told him that he had less than one minute to vacate the premises, or he would be forcibly removed. Kirby's girlfriend, Zoë Wheaton, who never had good timing, decided that was also the perfect day to break up with him. The whole incident plunged Kirby into a deep dark funk. During the good times he had felt that he was finally master of his own fate, possibly for the first time in his life. Yet those times came crashing to a halt and

Kirby was left alone, unemployed, and knowing that no matter how hard he worked, how big his talent, or how loud the outrage from fans, he was still subject to the petty whims of those in power whether they knew anything about what they were doing or not.

Twenty-four hours later Kirby was walking alone on an empty street, when he found a five dollar bill, right below a flashing sign advertising a world record lottery called the Mega-Ball. Kirby doesn't know why he bought the ticket, he had never done it before, in fact, and he had never seen a number that big before outside of reports about government debt. Maybe it was the sheer ridiculousness of the situation that appealed to him and compelled him to buy the ticket, leaving the rest to end up, if not history, good fodder for the European tabloids.

"Ooh," said Mitch as something came to his mind.

"Ooh what?" asked Kirby.

"I just realized that we're in Canada!" declared Mitch.

"Yes," said Kirby, "Toronto is a Canadian city, that's why you needed a passport to come here."

"I know all about Canada!" snapped Mitch. "In fact, my folks used to take me to visit relatives in Montreal every summer, which is why I'm so excited. Did you know what the best thing about those trips was?"

"Family togetherness?"

"No."

"The exotic French-style charms of Montreal?"

"No."

"An attractive distant cousin with a taste for experimentation and low moral standards?"

"Definitely no," said Mitch. "Freezie Pops!"

"Freezie Pops?"

"Yes," said Mitch, "a plastic tube full of sugary chemical goodness that you put in the freezer. Once they're frozen and hard they are like frosty sugar orgasms in your mouth."

"You are opening yourself up to so many attacks," said Kirby, "I don't know where to take my first shot. You've literally stumped me."

"Grow up," said Mitch. "Freezie Pops are only available in Canada. You can't get them back home."

"There's probably a good reason for that."

"This is making me giddy with excitement," declared Mitch. "A top line hotel room, good friends and Freezie Pops. There is no way that this can be anything but the best time ever."

"I hope you're right," said Kirby.

"And let's not forget Dick."

"I hope you're talking about Dick Wilco?"

"Yeah," said Mitch.

"That's still just a rumour," replied Kirby.

"True," said Mitch, "but my source for that rumour is impeccable."

"Debbie the receptionist?"

"She's eerie when it comes to knowing what's up," answered Mitch, "she knew you were going to get fired before anyone else." That was true, however Kirby missed the message Debbie left and was thus unprepared for what was waiting for him. Kirby drove those memories from his mind to move on to more pleasant things.

"It would be good to see him again," said Kirby, remembering how his mentor brought him into the world of creating comic books. Before Kirby's grandfather introduced them, Kirby never really thought about where comic books came from, or who made them. He was an eight-year-old kid, and Wilco was already a legend in the industry, albeit an eccentric one and that legend literally kicked the doors of Kirby's imagination wide open.

"I want you to introduce me to Wilco," said Mitch, "because if you don't, not only will I never forgive you, I will give you a wedgie that may well prove lethal."

"Threat noted."

## ISSUE #2
## THE ROYAL TREATMENT

He parked his motorcycle a few feet into the alley. The position was just deep enough for him to see out, but anyone at the entrance of the Waterloo couldn't see him unless they went out of their way to look for him. He made good time, reaching the hotel before she and her toady got there. He had mapped out the best route the day before, just to make sure. That's why she was not going to get away, or ever get away from him; he was literally one step ahead of her all the time.

He took a deep breath and looked around. There was already a line-up in front of the convention centre. People were already camping out under the banner announcing that OmniCon was starting Friday, and it was only Thursday. Some were in crazy-ass costumes, some were playing board games and one guy had a little TV, an Xbox Kinect, and a sign advertising some sort of game tournament.

Weirdos.

Her toady pulled up to the front of their hotel in a rented Toyota Camry, like they were normal people, and Erica got out. She pulled out a bag from the back seat and talked a bit to Bruce before letting him drive away to the parking garage. He took careful aim at Erica, this time using his proper camera with the proper lens, and snapped a few shots. Her oval face, half covered by sunglasses and framed by scarlet curls filled the little LCD monitor on the back of his camera.

Someone came out of the hotel; a skinny bitch in a t-shirt,

cut-off shorts and purple tights wrapped around a long pair of legs. Erica turned, saw the skinny bitch and squealed in delight. Both women outstretched their arms for a big hug.

He snapped off some more shots. The long lens gave him a good look at the skinny bitch's face. There was something familiar about her. Something he'd have to look up once he got back to his own meagre room, his laptop and his files.

Six more shots of the two women hugging at the door, then half a dozen more of them making the usual 'it's been so long' poses, the 'how have you been' looks, then four shots of the group going inside the hotel.

He slipped the camera back into its case and snapped the motorcycle back to life. He had a lot to do this weekend, a lot to do.


"So," said Mitch as the Mercedes glided down Bay Street toward the heart of downtown Toronto. "What are you going to do?"

"At the convention?"

"No," answered Mitch, "with the rest of your life. What are you going to do with it?"

Kirby shrugged. "I really don't know."

"You always know," said Mitch. "I've never seen you without some sort of a plan. You don't need to work for a living anymore, so what will you do? Are you still going to work for that whole 'artistic fulfillment' thing, or will you become the male equivalent of Paris Hilton, only slightly skinnier?"

"I don't look good in a miniskirt," answered Kirby, "my knees are too knobby and high heels hurt my feet. So I guess I'll still work."

"Going to self-publish?"

"Yes," said Kirby. "I've got some stories that I want to tell, I want to tell them my way, and I can afford to do it in style now."

"That's your plan?"

"The plan is to go back to grandpa's old place," added

Kirby, "and work from there for a while."

"I love that place," said Mitch who, despite a childhood in the suburbs of New Jersey and what passed as his own form of adulthood in Queens, really took an old fashioned shine to the Long Island farm called Charlatan's Cove. Not just for the bucolic atmosphere found in an area of Long Island not yet swallowed up by suburban gentrification, but for the lighthouse, the wonderful magical lighthouse. The sprawling Victorian seaside farm had been the home of Kirby's grandfather, the late Albert Valentine, who toured the world as the magician The Great Valentino before retiring to the cove, expanding and converting the lighthouse building into a workshop where he designed and constructed illusions for other performers. The place always fired Mitch's imagination, literally a wizard's workshop, filled to the high rafters with exotic props and stage equipment.

"Need a colourist," asked Mitch, "preferably a live-in colourist with an office in your grandpa's lighthouse?"

"I'm going to go all black and white from now on," said Kirby with a grin. "Colourists are just too annoying to deal with."

"Very funny Mr. Dill-hole," said Mitch, flipping Kirby the bird.

"But I'm not going to rule out doing something for another company," added Kirby. "I'm still a silly drooling fanboy at heart after all, and there are a lot of characters I'd like to work on."

"Thinking about doing anything for Atlantic again?"

"I don't think Ashmore would let me," answered Kirby.

"The Ash-hole won't be there much longer, no matter what happens," added Mitch.

"What do you mean?"

"Ashmore's family wants to get out of the comic book biz," said Mitch, "and the word on the street is that their timing is perfect because Continental Pictures wants to buy the company and their superheroes."

"That's understandable," mused Kirby aloud, "comic book

movies are big business right now." When you looked up 'big business' in the dictionary of entertainment you found a photo of the very large and impressively built wrought iron gates of the Continental Pictures studio lot in Hollywood. Continental did everything big, spending more on an average movie than the gross national product of a third world country, and they usually got a return on that investment, not that any Hollywood studio would actually admit to making a profit on anything.

"That is," said Mitch, "until Ashmore somehow screws it up."

"He's not a raving incompetent lunatic," said Kirby.

"You're just feeling all forgiving because you're richer than he is now."

"Living well is the best revenge," said Kirby. "We're almost there."

Gustav turned the Mercedes around a corner and they saw the convention centre first. It looked like a massive rectangular pound cake made out of glass and criss-crossing steel bars.

"Look at the line up," said Mitch.

Kirby leaned over to look at the line in front of the convention centre. These were his fans, his community and his people. A tiny sliver of good feeling ran down his spine. After two years in the alien world of the rich and the famous, it was nice to be among those he had so much in common with.

"There sure are a lot of them," said Kirby.

"OmniCon's second only to ComiCon in San Diego now," said Mitch. "It'd probably be bigger if it stayed in one city instead of rotating all over the place."

"I like that about OmniCon," said Kirby, sliding back into his seat. "I like visiting new places. Remember New Orleans?"

"No," said Mitch, "and I still haven't figured out how the tattoo of Wolverine appeared on my ass."

"Depends on what genre you are." said Kirby.

"What genre?"

"If you're science fiction," said Kirby, "an alien did it. If it's fantasy, a wizard did it."

"If it's a mystery?"

"The butler did it."

"What genre was my trip to New Orleans?"

"Low-brow gross out comedy," said Kirby, "that means the drunk idiot did it."

"You've solved the case," said Mitch. "Thank you oh great detective."

"This is going to fun," said Kirby. "It'll be good to see some of our old friends again."

"I see those people all the time," said Mitch pointing out the window. "I'm more interested in seeing that blonde in the Power Girl outfit."

Kirby leaned forward and saw a young woman beautifully filling the tight, white and decidedly skimpy uniform of DC's Power Girl, posing for some pictures with others in the line, pictures that would, no doubt, be on the internet within seconds.

"You're going to need a ladder."

"I like that costume," said Mitch, "it contains no unpleasant surprises."

"It's definitely not like a furry cat costume."

"I hate you Baxter."

Madden peeked over the top of his copy of the Toronto Star at the crowd forming in front of the reception desk. So far, no sign of Kirby Baxter, but there was a pair of good looking women in line, one a curvy redhead, the other was the haughty blonde he saw earlier in the convention centre. They were chattering like a pair of cartoon crows, as bellboys – did people still call them bellboys – guided the people, now officially guests, from the front of the line to the elevators, wheeling polished brass plated carts loaded with luggage.

Madden had been watching the little parade from a surprisingly comfy blue lounge chair that sat a little to the starboard of the reception desk, nestled between a row of Art Deco columns that marked the way to the one of the hotel's more upscale restaurants. He wanted a cigarette, really wanted a cigarette. Too bad he had quit smoking, under the orders of his doctor and his wife Ginny, because his body was screaming for the calming effect of nicotine. Screw the chance of cancer, some chances were worth taking.

Then Kirby Baxter entered the lobby and, aside from the new goatee, he looked almost exactly the same as the last time they met. He was still a tall scrawny bastard with a long neck, and a narrow pecker head, flanked by big jug handle ears, making Madden think of a live action Ichabod Crane. If push came to shove, the shove could send Baxter into next week.

Madden couldn't remember the name of the short guy that came in with him, but he didn't look like much of a threat either. Baxter seemed calm and collected, but the short guy looked awestruck.

"Damn," muttered the short guy, "this definitely isn't a Motel Six."

"I love the decor, Mitch," said Baxter, "but it makes me feel under-dressed for the occasion."

"Think we should be dressed like him," said Mitch, nodding toward a young man in an impeccably constructed blue suit and slicked back hair who looked like he'd just stepped out of a sophisticated romantic comedy from the early 1930s. He went straight to the two good looking women. He was introduced by the redhead to the bottle blonde and they followed a bellboy to the bank of elevators.

"Somehow I think we'd still look like a pair of dorks," said Kirby.

"Speak for yourself," said Mitch, "I clean up very well."

"How do you know?"

"Mr. Baxter?"

Holy shit! thought Madden at what appeared behind Baxter.

The hotel concierge, dressed in an impeccably tailored

grey suit with gold keys pinned to the lapels, had appeared out of nowhere, followed by a bald behemoth in a black suit. That man was the very definition of massive, and he looked scary as hell too.

"Yes," answered Baxter. "I'm Kirby Baxter."

"My name is Stevens, and I'll be your concierge for your stay. I can handle your check-in to the Royal Suite directly," said the concierge taking out a small electronic box. "Please swipe your card to confirm your booking, and I'll take you right up to your suite."

"Shit," muttered Mitch, as Baxter fished a black plastic card from his wallet, "membership does have its privileges."

"Hey," barked a loud, yet, nasal voice, and everyone turned to see a squat fat man with a head like a cannonball topped by dyed black hair appear at the door. "Why should I have to wait in line? Don't you know who I am?"

"I know who you are," said Stevens the concierge, obviously unimpressed.

"Damn right you do," barked the fat man, "I'm Max fucking Cooperman!"

"Of course Mr. Cooperman," said Stevens with a smile, "but you're not booked in the Royal Suite. So I'm afraid that we are very busy and that you will have to wait a moment, someone at the desk will be with you in a moment."

"I don't fucking believe this shit!"

"Excuse me," said the one called Mitch taking out a small digital camera, "but your face is turning a stunning shade of red. Can I just get a picture of it for future reference?"

"If you don't put down that fucking camera the next picture it takes will be the inside of your asshole!"

"Gustav," said Baxter with a nod toward Cooperman.

The bald behemoth stepped forward, Max fucking Cooperman stepped back, his eyes suddenly much wider as if to take in the terrifying expanse that stood before him.

"Please Mr. Cooperman," said Stevens the concierge in the most firm, yet diplomatic, tone possible, "your stay here is a privilege, not a right. This rule is especially true after your behaviour during the film festival last year. So we must insist that you do not pester, threaten, or otherwise attempt to assault any of our guests during this stay, or we will decline your business. I believe you might be able to find replacement rooms at the Holiday Inn down by the airport."

Cooperman was about to say something, but Gustav simply shrugged his shoulders, illustrating their truly massive breadth, and the fat man stepped back. "Fine," he muttered, "I don't need this shit."

A young good looking guy in a suit came in carrying a briefcase.

"I got the car parked Mr. Cooperman," said the young guy.

"Shut the fuck up Weatherby," growled Cooperman.

"Come with me," said the concierge to Kirby and his company. "Your luggage is already on its way to the suite." The trio followed the concierge to the elevators. Mitch was muttering something about how he could get used to this level of service.

Madden slumped in his chair, with that gorilla hanging around Kirby, he'd have to be very clever and cunning to keep that skinny bastard from ruining his plan.

Devilishly clever.


"This is the express elevator to the Excelsior floor," explained the concierge as he led Kirby and company to the bank of elevators. A bellboy in a red uniform jacket nodded to the concierge and held open the door. "While you can access the floor with the other elevators, this elevator is exclusively for Excelsior floor guests. You can summon the express elevator, Mr. Baxter, by holding your key card to the scanner by the call button."

"Are you Kirby Baxter?" asked one of the elevator's passengers, a young woman who even without make-up seemed to glow with a beauty that almost made Kirby choke.

"Uh," said Kirby.

"He is Kirby Baxter," interjected Mitch, "and you're Erica

Cross. Page twenty-seven of last year's Sport's Illustrated Swimsuit issue."

"Yes I am," said Erica.

"You have a fascinating complexion," said Mitch, leaning on the elevator's tiger maple veneer in an attempt to appear suave.

"I'm really happy to meet you Kirby," said Erica, holding out her hand, "if I can call you that?"

"Yeah," said Kirby, imagining himself saying far more charming things, "sure."

"I guess you can say that I'm a bit of a fan," said Erica.

"Really?" Kirby was surprised, nay, shocked; even his overactive imagination never conceived of those words coming from the lips of a Sports Illustrated swimsuit model.

"I'm in the movie version of The Vengeance Sisters," said Erica zipping open her carry-on bag. "We start shooting this week, but when I got the part a few months ago I asked the publisher to recommend some books for me to read. The editor recommended the crossover you did with them and Shadowknight, and I have to say I really enjoyed the story. And I never really read comics before then."

"Oh," said Kirby, "you liked it?"

"Loved it," said Erica, pulling out the trade paperback edition of the comic from her bag. "Could you sign my copy, please?"

"Sure," said Kirby reaching into his jacket pocket for a pen, "I'd love to."

"Oh," said Erica as Kirby signed her book. "I'm being so rude, sorry Andi. Everyone, this is my friend Andi Stallworth."

"It's been Andi Hack for the last five years," said Andi flashing her blatantly expensive engagement and wedding ring combo.

"You were in the Pirelli Calendar five years ago," said Mitch. "I thought you looked familiar."

"You didn't recognize me with my clothes on," said Andi with a picture perfect smile.

"You had longer hair then," said Mitch, "it was a deep brown with auburn highlights."

"You know colours."

"It's my job."

"And I'd like you all to meet my assistant Bruce Haring," added Erica.

"Very pleased to meet all of you," said Bruce with a smile and a nod.

"Here's the book," said Kirby passing it back to Erica. "This is Marvin Mitchell Mandelbaum, his job actually does involve colours, and the tall guy is Gustav, he's my...well...I guess assistant is the best word."

Gustav nodded.

"You're the 3M in the credits?" said Erica, holding up the book and pointing to the list of names on the first page.

"Guilty," said Mitch with a smile.

"What was all the fuss going on out there?" asked Andi.

"Some guy was making a lot of noise," said Mitch, "and turning a particularly brilliant shade of red. Take a look."

Mitch held up his digital camera and put the picture of the enraged Cooperman on the little monitor, earning an embarrassed laugh from Erica.

"Oh my," said Erica. "That's my boss."

"Really?" asked Mitch.

"He's producing the movie," explained Erica.

"I've met him. To call him a Philistine," added Andi, "would insult the Philistines."

"Ouch," said Kirby.

"It's a job," said Erica, "at this stage of my career, I need all the jobs I can get."

"We're at the Excelsior floor," announced the concierge, and the elevator chimed.

"If this is your first convention," said Mitch, "then you're going to need experienced guides. So feel free to call on us for any help, we're staying in the Royal Suite."

"Really," said Erica, obviously impressed as the door slid open.

"It was the only one available," said Kirby as he stepped out onto the tightly woven carpet of the Excelsior floor. "But if you do need anyone...uh...well, you know where to find us."

"We might," said Erica as she stepped out of the elevator and looked at the sign showing where the rooms were. "We're down the hall."

"And we're up the hall," said Kirby, hoping he said something, anything, different, "I'll see you around."

"Yeah," said Erica, "you should come to the party tonight. I'll have Bruce send you the extra passes they gave me."

"It'll be a pleasure," said Bruce.

"That will be great," said Kirby. "I'll see you there."

They paused a moment, watching the two women follow the bellboy down the hall.

"If you'll follow me," said the concierge as a maid passed by the women, pushing a cart full of cleaning equipment.

"Sure," said Kirby, reluctantly.

"That redhead was warm for your form," said Mitch.

"You're delusional," replied Kirby.

"I could take the skinny one," said Mitch, "I'm not greedy."

"She's married," said Kirby.

"Really?"

"She said she was married and showed everyone her ring," explained Kirby, "but your attention was drifting to other places."

"Well," said Mitch, "there's always Power Girl. I won't use my awesome all powerful sex appeal to get between you and Erica so she can jump your bones in peace."

"She does not want to 'jump my bones,'" said Kirby, "and when did we go back to the nineteen twenties?"

"Twenty-two skidoo!" said Mitch.

"Not only do I think you said that wrong," said Kirby, "I'm pretty damn sure you don't know what that means."

"Supermodels date rich men," answered Mitch, "it's one of the immutable laws of physics, like gravity."

"She didn't know I was rich until you mentioned the suite," said Kirby, stepping aside to let the maid and her cart pass. He caught a strong smell of apples as she passed, an almost sickeningly strong smell of apples.

"She knew," said Mitch, "supermodels can smell money from miles away."

"All I can smell are apples," said Kirby shaking his head. "Do you smell that?"

"A bit," said Mitch, "but not all of us are part bloodhound. Her choices at this convention are you and that movie producer."

"That Cooperman guy doesn't have all that much money," said Kirby.

"How do you know that?" asked Mitch, always enjoying the little 'insights' of his friend. "You only just met him."

"His Rolex watch is a fake," explained Kirby.

"Now how did you spot that?" asked Mitch, knowing that Kirby had to give the full explanation in order to be happy.

"I saw that the second hand ticks like a regular watch," said Kirby, "the second hand on a real Rolex does a smooth sweep around the watch face."

"Here are your key cards," said Stevens the concierge, passing a black plastic card to each of them. "You just swipe them over the black panel on the door to enter the room."

"Thank you," said Kirby as he took his key card and nodded to Gustav, who opened the door.

"The Royal," explained Stevens the concierge as he guided them into the suite, "has four bedrooms, each with their own full en suite bath, two half baths adjoin the main lounge, here, and the private sitting room. There's also an in suite kitchen, and a chef can be called from any one of our restaurants on request—"

"That's the biggest flat screen TV I've ever seen," exclaimed Mitch standing in awe before the broad black slab.

"There's a similar one in every bedroom," added Stevens. "Now remember, if you need anything, I'm a phone call away, just pick up any room phone and ask for Stevens."

"Thank you," said Kirby, slipping Stevens a tip that earned a wide smile and the concierge glided out of the room.

"I need more friends worth a few hundred million bucks," said Mitch to Kirby.

"Actually," said Kirby, "that situation's a little different now."

"I thought you said you had held on to your lottery money?" asked Mitch.

"I did," said Kirby, "but a couple of investments I made while I was overseas turned out really well."

"How well did they turn out?"

"They turned out crazy kind of well."

"Did I ever tell you that you're my most favourite friend in the whole wide world?"

"I don't like to make a big deal about it."

"It explains why that model was so hot for your bony bod. You're practically spraying hot money musk."

"Grow up," said Kirby.

"And don't get so tongue tied around women," added Mitch. "You've got a lot more going for you than you ever did when you got involved with Zoë."

Mitch saw the hurt look cross his friend's face and decided to change the subject.

"Why is Gustav looking into every room and closet?" asked Mitch.

"He's just making sure the suite is secure," answered Kirby. "It's a habit he got into after a rather unpleasant incident in Paris."

"I'm not complaining," said Mitch, "I guess the last thing you want is to get caught up in that sort of craziness again. Wow, a man can really get used to living like this."

"Don't make me have Gustav guard the minibar."

"According to this," said Mitch holding up a laminated card from the table, "the bar is complimentary with the room. This means you already paid for it."

"While I may have already paid for your drinking binge,"

said Kirby, "I'm not paying for your rehab or for any damage. So don't break anything, or bring home any strays that haven't had their shots."

"I'm going to forgive you for that snide remark because there's a frigging pool on the balcony!" said Mitch. "This is a sweet suite."

Kirby sat down on the couch, and realized that it was one of the most comfortable pieces of furniture he ever sat in.

"I love this place," said Mitch, "it's like I'm playing a rich guy in a movie."

Gustav emerged from the last room and nodded.

"We have the all clear," said Kirby. "So I'm going to have a shower."

"Good idea," added Mitch. "I'm going to have one too, in my private en suite bathroom, then I'm going to go for a swim, then I'm going to pick up the phone and ask Stevens for Freezie Pops."

"Don't abuse the concierge."

"Come on," said Mitch, "when's the next time I'll have a chance to have a luxury hotel concierge hop to obey my every whim?"

"Okay," conceded Kirby, "just this once. But just get an address to the nearest store; you can get your precious frozen whatever-you-call-them yourself."

"When did my relatives all become goddamn psychics," growled Fred Ashmore as he turned off his cell phone. "I'm not on the ground five goddamn minutes, and they're all riding my ass like I'm the town donkey!"

Kevin LaGuardia shrugged.

"What the hell do you know?" he growled at LaGuardia.

"This is a nice suite," said LaGuardia, hoping to change the subject from the career destroying disaster called The Vengeance Sisters movie.

"Do you know why they call this the Excelsior floor?" asked Ashmore.

LaGuardia shrugged again.

"Because we're on the goddamn thirteenth floor," snapped Ashmore, "that's why they call it the Excelsior. These hotel people are all freaking superstitious, and they feel that they have to hide it from everybody."

"I didn't know that," said LaGuardia, knowing how much that bit of local trivia must burn a superstitious man like Ashmore, who once had a conniption fit when the painters put a ladder in front of his office door. "I always thought they just skipped thirteen and called it the fourteenth floor."

Ashmore paced the room like a caged lion that had just downed fifty cups of espresso. "I guess they think they're special or something."

"This is much nicer than my room on the tenth floor," added LaGuardia. Ashmore didn't give a flying fiddler's damn how nice LaGuardia's room was, or about how the company's senior editor had to share it with two other editors and three of the company's staff artists crammed in there like immigrants in steerage hoping to catch a glimpse of the Statue of Liberty through a dirty porthole. Ashmore had more important things to do. Chiefly he had to save his own ass.

Ashmore sat down on the sofa and took a deep breath. Cooperman was in this hotel, he had left a message for the fat bastard at the front desk, which put him in a quandary. He didn't want to wait for Cooperman's reply, because that gave the fat bastard all the power and any delay had the potential to cost him more than a fortune, but hunting down and confronting Cooperman had its own perils. The man had a terrible reputation and an even worse temper. Cooperman's rages were legendary; one such tantrum, aimed at a poor filmmaker who had refused to sell Cooperman his movie at last year's Toronto International Film Festival, almost got the movie mogul charged with assault. The only thing that kept Max Cooperman from ending up in a Canadian jail was a flurry of phone calls from many of the prominent American politicians from Cooperman's speed dial list, and a cash payment to the poor filmmaker with the wrenched neck who was almost as obese as Cooperman himself.

"Boss?" asked LaGuardia.

"What?" snapped Ashmore.

"I have to go see how the booth's setting up," said LaGuardia, "I'll see you later."

"Yeah," said Ashmore, "you've got things to do, and I've got things to do."

Ashmore got to his feet.

"I'm going to have to nut up," said Ashmore, "or I've got to shut up."

With that he strode out of his room and into the hallway.

Kirby felt good to have the long plane ride scraped off him.

The shower was divine and though it took longer than he originally planned, it was well worth it. His jet lag was gone and he felt fresh and alert. He also felt like a Coke Zero and some ice. Mitch suggested calling the concierge and Gustav offered to fetch it for him, but Kirby opted to do it himself. Partly because he felt it was good to do simple errands on his own, also he wanted to go for a walk and stock up on fresh air before inhaling the reconstituted air of the convention floor.

The door clicked shut behind him as he stepped out into the hallway.

"Kirby Baxter?" drawled a voice behind him with a broad Boston accent.

Kirby turned to see Jim Madden in all that passed for his glory.

"Jim," said Kirby, "what a surprise." Madden owned one of North America's largest retail websites specializing in all sorts of collectibles, from comics, to toys, to celebrity autographs. He was a stocky fellow, built like a football player who had given up on training in favour of beer and burritos, and he wore his thinning hair long and pulled back into a ponytail.

"It's good to see you," said Madden holding out a hand, which Kirby shook. "I thought you were still in Europe."

"I just got in today for the convention," said Kirby. Madden smelled like hotel shampoo, at least three layers of Axe body spray, and nerves, so Kirby decided to push a button. "I heard you scored some original Dick Wilco art and are going to auction it off here."

"That?" said Madden forcing nonchalance. "That's nothing more than a silly internet rumour."

Then why are your eyes darting to the right as you speak? thought Kirby, so he decided to push the button again. "Really, I didn't see anything online about it."

"Some anonymous dick made an offhand comment on a fan forum about how I could get stuff no one else could, including Dick Wilco stuff," said Madden. "Before you could say 'The Flash' it had gone full blown Chinese whisper into people saying that I actually had some Dick Wilco art, and people are jumping on it like it was the gospel from on high."

"Really," said Kirby. "Crying shame, I'd actually love to get some original Wilco art."

"Yeah," said Madden, "wouldn't everyone. I'd love to chat some more, but I really gotta go."

"I'll see you on the floor," said Kirby.

"That would be great," said Madden as he headed for the elevators.

Now Kirby was certain that the rumours were true and that Madden was up to something. Exactly what that something was eluded Kirby at the moment. This certainty went beyond the little physical cues Kirby observed, it came from cold hard experience. Kirby and Madden had run into each other dozens of times at various conventions and industry events, and this was the first and only time that Madden didn't try to hustle some original artwork or autographed books out of Kirby for him to sell on his website. He was usually relentless on that quest and often went beyond just asking. One of Madden's more infamous tricks was to hire people, usually attractive young women, to pose as penniless fans, who just happen to have multiple copies that need autographs as well as sketchbooks for some complimentary drawings, but he never let a chance meeting pass without at least trying to score something.

At least he never did until now.

Maybe it was the surprise of seeing Kirby after two years away, maybe it was the stress of keeping this alleged auction of Dick Wilco art a secret, but why play coy with a known Dick Wilco fan that had more money than a Kardashian, and infinitely more taste?

Kirby knelt down to tighten the laces on one of his high-tops when he heard: "What are you doing here?"

Kirby knew that voice too and looked up for a confirmation. It was Fred Ashmore, the less than great man himself.

"I'm here for the convention," answered Kirby. "What are you doing here?"

"Business," said Ashmore, "important business."

"That's great," said Kirby, trying to choke down the nasty imp that wanted to rub his new wealth in Ashmore's face and realizing that without input from that nasty little imp, he really didn't have any reason to talk to Fred Ashmore. "I'm staying in the Royal Suite."

"Really," said Ashmore with a hint of jealousy that was so damn sweet to Kirby's nasty little imp. Kirby could see that something else was eating at Ashmore, and it had to be something big.

"It's a great room," added Kirby. "It's so big, I'm thinking about throwing a party for some of the industry folks and internet people." Kirby realized that little idea just came straight from the imp inside him, and the fact that it sounded like such a good idea worried him slightly. "It would be a good opportunity for me to catch up on things, let the fans know what I'm up to, and such."

"What have you been up to?"

"I've been up to lots of stuff," said Kirby, "too much to tell here, really."

"Then maybe we should meet later," said Ashmore.

"I'd love to," added Kirby, letting the imp run free. "Maybe you can come to the party? It will be a lot of fun, and I'm sure the reporters would love to ask you about Shadowknight's sales figures."

"I'm sure they would," said Ashmore. Then his cell phone rang. "Sorry, I'd love to catch up and all that, but I really got to take this call."

"No problem," replied Kirby heading to the elevator. "Have a fun convention."

"I know I put those passes somewhere," said Erica as she went through her carry-on bag.

"Try your purse," said Andi taking a seat by the wide

bedroom window.

"Right," said Erica, as she put down her carry-on bag and picked up her expansive purse. "This could take a while."

"How many did you get?"

"Four," answered Erica.

"You," said Andi, wanting a cigarette, but fighting the urge so she fished out her iPhone, "Bruce, and your boyfriend—"

"I don't have a boyfriend," answered Erica.

"What about that photographer in Los Angeles?"

"Chaz," said Erica, "we're not going out anymore."

"I never liked the look of him," said Andi. "Henry said he was the living proof that you really can judge a book by its cover?"

"Chaz was all cover," said Erica, "no book."

"So I guess you can spare two invites," said Andi scrolling through the info on her iPhone, "that covers the skinny guy and the midget. I think I can find one for their pet gorilla."

"Oh Andi," said Erica, "you can be so mean sometimes."

"A-ha!" exclaimed Andi shooting an arm in the air in triumph.

"What is it?"

"The skinny guy, Baxter," said Andi. "I thought there was something familiar about him, and it has nothing to do with comic books."

"What is it?"

"He was all over the European papers about a year and a half ago," said Andi showing a newspaper's website on her phone's monitor.

"Is that in German?"

"My German's a little rough, but it says that Baxter and that big guy helped the police catch a murderer," said Andi.

"Get out of here," said Erica, her hands plunging deeper into her purse, "he's a comic book artist."

"It's true," answered Andi turning over her iPhone to show Erica a photograph of Kirby Baxter, dressed in a suit that looked like he left the hanger in, shaking hands with a man in an much more elegantly tailored outfit. "Here he is getting a medal from the Prince of Lichtenstein himself."

"That's a surprise and a half."

"It also says he's rich."

"How rich can he be?"

"Obscenely."

"I figured he has to be rich to be staying at the Royal Suite," said Erica, "but he seemed so normal."

"Famous last words," said Andi, putting her phone away.

"Geeky, but a normal kind of geeky."

"Are you telling me that there are degrees of geeky now?" asked Andi.

"I have to get the full story of him catching a murderer out of him tonight," said Erica.

"I'm sure you'll get it out of him," said Andi. "Men tend to do whatever you ask for."

"You've been reading the tabloids again."

"I've got to read something while I'm waiting in airports."

"I thought you liked traveling," said Erica. "Oh, wait, I found them," she added, pulling out the two extra passes.

"It's lost some of its glamour," replied Andi, opening her own little purse and pulling out one of her extra passes, "I spend half my time following Henry from one party hot-spot to another. That means a lot of airports, a lot of hotels, a lot of going into clubs through the back door, and a lot of time stuck in hotel rooms with migraines. The rest of the time I just stay home."

"What about your plans to settle down and open your own club in Miami?"

Andi waved her hand. "Staying in one spot isn't in the cards. Besides, Henry says that clubs come and go, especially with today's economy, and that if he's going to stay on top he's got to stay on the move."

"I'm not an expert, but I think there's a contradiction somewhere in that saying of his."

"Henry's deal is music," answered Andi as she passed Erica the extra pass, "not lyrics."

"Bruce," called out Erica.

"You rang Madam," replied Bruce as he appeared at the door.

"Could you please take these to Mr. Baxter and his friends in the Royal Suite?"

"No problem," said Bruce, taking the passes.

Silence held sway for a beat and then Andi said: "Enough of my petty miseries. Let's talk about yours."

Erica paused. She had something she wanted to talk about, something that made her miserable, but didn't want to burden her friend with it.

"I'm just working my ass off," said Erica flopping on the bed. "Becoming an actress is a lot harder than my agent implied."

"You're working, that's a lot better than most actors just starting out."

"Let's see," said Erica, counting off on her fingers, "so far I've done one low budget horror movie playing a model chased by a killer in a clown mask; one guest spot on a sitcom, playing a model; and now this part playing a superhero, who works as a model by day."

"It could be worse," said Andi.

"I've got a lot riding on this movie," said Erica, "and I'm really freaking out about it. I let on that I'm enthusiastic, but I'm really scared. I don't know anything about whether the script is any good or not. I know nothing about the director, and the more I learn about the producer, the less comfortable I am with this whole damn thing."

"As long as you get paid," added Andi, "you can afford a little discomfort."


It was a rare event for Max Cooperman to find someone more full of shit than he was, but when it did happen he would sit back and savour the moment.

"The script for this project," said Markus L. the director of The Vengeance Sisters, "has touched a part of my soul."

"Sure," said Max looking over the man who would bring

his movie to life. The life-bringer's real name was Mark Lewis, but such a banal name just wouldn't fit so he changed it to Markus L., and with that name came a new image. A few tattoos, an ironic moustache, and a head carefully coiffed to look uncombed, and voila an artiste had been born. His biggest credit so far had been a music video for some kiddy pop singer, no one could remember which one because they all pretty much looked and sounded the same. "It's a really touching script."

"I feel it in here," said Markus, holding his hand over his heart. "I think my artistic vision can elevate this film above its bourgeois and banal roots in the so-called comic papers."

"I've been looking over your pre-production material," said Cooperman, as he patted the hefty binder on what remained of his lap, "it's very impressive. I really think the headquarters for the sisters is really first rate. How's the construction going?"

"We will be ready to shoot by Monday," replied Markus L., "though—"

"Though what?"

"Well," shrugged Markus. "The unions are starting to poke around. Apparently they don't like you shipping in a construction crew from another city. In fact we're all a little confused about that."

The crew building the elaborate sets was non-union, which was rare but not unheard of. Cooperman had trucked them in from Montreal. Now industry people considered that an unheard of move, especially in a city literally teeming with experienced movie and television crews. The fact that they all spoke French and so few spoke more than a few phrases of English had made communication tricky.

"Tell those shit-heels from the union to go fuck themselves," commanded Cooperman, "it's just that easy, and use those exact words." Cooperman had to have some of his own words with the head of the union because in movies, as in life, timing is everything.

"The schedule's going to be a little tricky," added Markus

L., pulling a sheet of paper from his own attaché case.

"It's simple," said Cooperman, "Sandy Doyle won't be free from her TV series until next week, so just shoot around her with Erica Cross and the stand-in."

"It's unconventional," said Markus.

"That's the beauty of being an independent filmmaker," said Cooperman, "you are not bound by those bullshit conventions."

They were having this little meeting in a booth in the back of the Carnival Room, a hotel bar decorated like it was Mardi Gras every day of the year, but without the drunken girls doffing their tops for beads. The décor – shiny baubles and gaudy looking masks covered the walls – making it look like someone had covered every surface in glue, dragged in a second hand parade float from New Orleans, and then lobbed in a hand grenade.

"Another potential problem," added Markus "is that we still haven't cast our Dr. Zardoz."

"Don't worry about that," replied Cooperman. "His scenes don't get shot for another three weeks, and the right actor can just jump right in." Cooperman was still negotiating with Christopher Walken and Ben Kingsley for the part of the mutated mad scientist, but he was stalling at making any sort of final agreement with either one of them. Cooperman was stalling because both Walken and Kingsley had worked for MaxCo Films in the past and knew how the company operated. This meant that they spurned his offer of only a share of the box office receipts and insisted on MaxCo paying them their standard fee in full, and up front. If Cooperman's master plan was going to work out he couldn't afford to make that sort of deal.

"It seems a little 'seat of the pants,'" said Markus.

"If I wasn't always right," answered Cooperman, "I wouldn't be rich. Now why don't you talk to the publicity people about what you're going to say at tomorrow's presentation?"

Markus nodded. Cooperman dismissed him with a wave

of one hand and signalled the waitress with the other.

"Vodka Martini," ordered Cooperman. Technically it was still fairly early but the sun had to be over the yardarm somewhere. He decided to linger at the bar for a while and make a few calls on his mobile and avoid going back to his suite. That dingus Ashmore knew his room number, and had already left a bunch of messages for him, no doubt wanting some way out of their deal. Well, a deal's a deal, and if they wanted to make Max Cooperman fuck off into the sunset then they were going to have to pay.

"Cooperman!"

Damn it!

It was Ashmore; the bastard had to be part goddamn bloodhound.

"I've been looking all over for you," said Ashmore as he crossed the bar.

"I'm a very busy man," answered Cooperman taking the Martini from the returning waitress and dropping an American twenty on her tray. "Keep the change honey."

"We're supposed to be partners," said Ashmore, his arms crossed and his long narrow horse-face pinched up in a vain attempt to look stern.

"And we are partners," said Cooperman. "The movies I'm going to make with your company's characters are going to be huge."

"I find that hard to believe," said Ashmore.

"Why?" asked Cooperman.

"I've actually read that piece of shit you call a script."

"Listen," said Cooperman, "I know the movie business, you don't. Now I really gotta go."

Cooperman made his way to the door, but that bastard was still on his tail.

Twenty bucks.

That's what it took to get the dishwasher to leave the door propped open so he could get in. There were no security cameras in this part of the hotel, because the powers that be in the hotel didn't figure that there was anything down here worth stealing. It goes to show what they knew, but he knew better.

The dishwasher only spoke rough broken English, so he just pointed down a grey cinder-block hall, and said: "There. Green box. Green box."

He nodded and passed the dishwasher another ten. The dishwasher nodded and stuck a little wooden peg under the door to keep it from locking.

"Green box," repeated the dishwasher.

"Green box," he answered with a smile.

He went down the hallway. A florescent tube flickered above him. He reached a pair of loose swinging doors, and he found his prize.

It was kind of a green box. Actually, it was a great big green bin sitting under a chute that he knew went all the way up to what the hotel liked to call the Excelsior floor.

Yes, at the Waterloo, the rich people's garbage got its own special bin. Wasn't that so goddamn precious.

She hadn't been there long enough to contribute to the contents of the bin, but her neighbours had. To accomplish his mission he needed knowledge, the sort of knowledge one found only in the trash.

Something sure stank like hell. It was sweet, past cloying and into nasty, yet familiar, like hearing a voice-over on a commercial and kicking yourself because you know the voice, but you couldn't place the name of the actor if your ass depended on it.

He held his breath and drew closer. He timed out the maid service and had another hour before the next round of bags get dropped down this special golden rich bastard garbage chute, so it was safe to stick his head in. He snapped on some gloves before he reached in to see what was in those bland white bags.

He paused. So that was the source of the smell. He could see what it was, and that it was really there in front of him, but he could come up with no conceivable reason for it being there.

He took a picture. He took several pictures, including close-ups.

This was information, very special information.

He didn't know exactly what it meant; only that it was so strange it could turn out to be useful in his mission later, very useful.

Six pack of Zero, check, courtesy of the convenience store across the street. It was on the elevator ride down that he realized that he might have to pay with his credit card because, despite his wealth, he didn't have the right kind of cash on hand. Lucky for him, the hotel's front desk was more than willing to exchange some of his Euros for Canadian dollars before he went out and embarrassed himself. Stevens the concierge offered to get the soda for him while exchanging the cash, but Kirby politely refused; the discipline to at least do some things on his own had survived the elevator ride.

Now that he was back on his floor, he had to get the ice.

Kirby noticed that the signs on the Excelsior floor were engraved brass, polished to a mirror's sheen, and not the plastic and wood laminate on all the other floors. This floor had three ice machines, one on each end, and one in a little room in the middle of the hall, just two doors from the elevators. That was Kirby's target.

The machine was a squat chrome behemoth that sat humming in a little rectangular room, wedged next to an electric blue pop machine. The buzzing florescent lights above the ice machine put a hint of blue in the machine's white surface. A stack of thin blue plastic buckets sat on top of the machine, wrapped in clear plastic. Kirby was in the midst of unpeeling one when he heard voices in the hall outside.

"Listen you stupid piece of shit," growled a voice that seemed familiar, then Kirby remembered; it was the angry movie producer with the fake Rolex named Cooperman, "you try to break our contract, and my lawyers will sue you, your family, and all their stupid magazines into the goddamn Stone Age. That's the beauty of contracts."

"You can't play these sorts of games!" said a second voice, and Kirby spotted that one instantly; it was Fred Ashmore.

"I play these sorts of games all the time," said Cooperman, "because I always win these sorts of games. The Vengeance Sisters are going to start shooting Monday, and there's not a damn thing you can do about it."

"I'll find something to do about it," declared Ashmore. "As God is my witness, I will not let you film a single damn shot!"

Cooperman laughed. Not a jolly laugh, but a cruel, nasty, poke a stick in your eye when you're down, kind of laugh.

"'As God is my witness?'" laughed Cooperman. "What is this, a remake of Gone with the fucking Wind? Why don't you just tell your family that they're bent over a barrel and their pants are down, so they better relax and take it with a smile, or else it's really going to hurt!"

"Go to hell Cooperman," growled Ashmore, "go to hell."

"I'll save you a seat," said Cooperman.

Footsteps went in opposite directions. Kirby waited a moment, because he didn't want to run into either of them.

After half a moment of silence, Kirby stepped out into the hallway and walked back to the Royal, the bucket of ice in one hand and the six-pack in the other, and knocked on the door with his foot.

Gustav opened the door. Kirby thanked him, and passed him the ice and soda, and Gustav disappeared into the kitchen with a nod. "Hey," cried out Mitch through the open balcony door amid a flurry of splashing, "the water's beautiful."

"I'll be there in a second," said Kirby. "I just got some ice."

"There's an ice machine in the fridge," said Mitch, appearing like a drenched gnome at the balcony door in his swim trunks and bath towel. "Plus, you just missed your girlfriend's assistant."

"She's not my girlfriend," said Kirby as he headed to his room. "We only just met, and we're not in the fourth grade anymore."

"Accept your fate," said Mitch, "rich men and models are made for each other."

"What did Bruce want?" asked Kirby, making a point of showing Mitch that he remembered the man's name.

"He dropped off some invites for tonight's party," said Mitch. "There will be music, dancing, networking and, if you're a good boy, some bone jumping."

"You are a douchebag," said Kirby as he emerged from his room in his own swim trunks. They, and a towel, had been neatly laid out and were waiting for him when he went into his room. Thank you Gustav.

"Sheesh," said Mitch, "two years of high living and you still look like Skeletor after a month in Somalia."

"I may not have six-pack abs," said Kirby, "but at least I'm not sporting a mini-keg."

"What took you so long?"

"I ran into some people," said Kirby. "Plus I overheard Ashmore and that movie producer having an argument in the hall."

"Ooh Hollywood gossip," said Mitch, "fill me in while we swim."

ISSUE #4
DINNER & A SHOW

As the elevator glided down from the Excelsior floor Kirby decided that when he moved back to his grandfather's old farm he was definitely going to put in a pool, possibly an indoor one. He could afford it, and thanks to that relaxing afternoon splashing around the suite's small private pool, it no longer seemed a decadent luxury, but a vital necessity.

"How many restaurants does this place have?" asked Mitch. Gustav passed him a brochure. "Thanks big guy. Let's see, they've got a really fancy French place, an Italian eatery, a steakhouse and an Asian restaurant."

"What kind of Asian?" asked Kirby. "It's a big continent."

"According to the brochure," answered Mitch, "a little bit of everything. 'The Pagoda Room menu offers the best of Chinese, Indian and Thai regional cuisines.'"

"That sounds interesting," said Kirby.

"Part of me says I should suggest we go to the expensive French place," added Mitch, "in keeping with my position as your official mooch."

"And that position's duty is to get as much out of me as possible," replied Kirby.

"Exactly," said Mitch. "But right now, I'm craving a steak."

"Actually," said Kirby, "that sounds like a good idea."

"Shall we give The Western Grill a try?"

Kirby looked to see if Gustav wanted that too, and the big man nodded.

"It's unanimous."

"Now as your official mooch," added Mitch, "I am compelled by my duty to order the most expensive piece of meat they have."

"You really enjoy me being rich," asked Kirby, "don't you?"

"Almost as much as I would enjoy being rich myself."

"I've always respected your honesty," said Kirby as the elevator glided to a stop. "It's the only thing about you I respect, but it's a kind of respect nonetheless."

"Hey," said Mitch as they stepped out of the elevator.

"Hey what?" asked Kirby.

"Hey," replied Mitch; "as in, isn't that Molly Garret by the door?"

Kirby looked across the lobby and through the crowd of early arriving conventioneers. It could only be Molly by the revolving door, she fit the description perfectly. She had Molly's petite build, taste for black clothing, and the sort of wild black hair and oversized eyes you normally only see in Japanese anime.

"It is Molly," said Kirby. "Hey! Molly!"

No response, she just kept heading for the revolving doors.

"She's got her headphones on," said Mitch. "Go get her."

"Why me?"

"Look at my stubby legs," said Mitch, "your gangly pins are twice my length, and Gustav would either scare her or accidentally step on her."

"All right," said Kirby. "I'll get her. You two wait here for me."

Dammit, she was already on the other side of the revolving door, forcing Kirby to zip around the milling guests, narrowly dodging a trip over a cosplayer's homemade Dr. Strange cape as he dove out onto the street.

Molly Garret had to get out of that hotel room.

Air laden with car exhaust and tobacco smoke from Toronto's furtive fugitive smokers was an improvement from the little two bed hotel room that was currently housing Molly and six other female artists, writers and editors. It could have been okay, Molly had survived it before, even enjoyed it as a form of urban camping, but Emma, a junior editor pushed Molly over the edge. Emma had purchased, then broken, a bottle of perfume that claimed to be Chanel, but smelled more like it washed ashore out of the English Channel. The lesson learned by everyone staying in that room was that the products sold by street vendors never matched what the labels said, in quality or odour.

Molly's thumb danced around her old iPod looking for something new to listen to once 'Caribou' by the Pixies faded out. She thought about listening to some of the comic book themed podcasts, because some of the people behind them were going to be at OmniCon, and she thought it might be good to brush up on a few.

"Molly!" said a voice from behind her. She turned around to see the crowd already lined up in front of the convention centre.

"Molly!" said the voice again, and she saw a hand with long fingers at the end of a long skinny arm poke above the crowd.

Molly popped the headphones out of her ears. The voice sounded familiar.

A skinny head with unruly hair on the end of a long neck popped up this time.

"Molly!" cried the head.

"Kirby?" asked Molly. That face was the last one she expected to see, especially with the stubbly attempt at the goatee.

Kirby slid between some costumed Star Wars Jedis arguing over the second trilogy, and skid to a halt in front of her.

"You really need to turn off the headphones sometimes," said Kirby. "I've been chasing you down the block."

Molly jumped up and wrapped her arms around him and squeezed as hard as she could.

"It's so good to see you," she said. "It's been too long." Molly hadn't seen him since she saw two security guards toss him a box, and then 'escort' him out of the building, they didn't even have a chance to say goodbye. She tried to call him, worried, and left a message with Zoë that he never got, and the next thing she knew he was rich and going into self-imposed exile in Europe. His absence and the strange news stories about him on European websites took her worries about him and gave them steroids. But now he was back, she finally released him from her hug, and he smiled at her.

"It has been too long," said Kirby.

Molly kicked him in the shin.

"Aaaaw!"

"Damn right it's been too long," growled Molly. "It's been what, almost two goddamn years and not a peep." She smacked Kirby on the arm. "Haven't you heard of Twitter, or Facebook?" She smacked his arm again. "Hell, I'd have even settled for something on goddamn MySpace."

"Agh!" said Kirby hopping on one foot and trying to dodge her blows and failing. "Okay, okay!"

"Well?"

"Well what?" asked Kirby. "Things got a little hairy while I was away, and I felt I had to keep a low profile."

"There is email," said Molly, whacking him on the arm one more time with her small fist. "You're supposed to be my friend!"

"If I'm supposed to be your friend," admitted Kirby, "then why won't you stop hitting me?"

"I'm trying to teach you a lesson," said Molly starting to laugh.

"Lesson learned," laughed Kirby then he opened his arms and gave her a hug.

"Is this a 'good to see you' hug," she asked, "or a 'please

stop hitting me' hug?"

"It's a little of column A, and a little of column B."

"It is good to see you, even if it's only to beat you."

"At least I learned my lesson before you hit me with your purse," said Kirby.

Molly laughed and looked down at the big faux leather sack she called her purse. When they first met Kirby had remarked that it actually weighed more than she did.

"Good point," said Molly, "it is qualified as a lethal weapon."

"Where are you going?"

"I was going to find some place to eat."

"Come on," said Kirby with a nod. "We're having prime rib on me. Not literally on me, but you get the picture."

"Who's we?" asked Molly.

"Me, Mitch, you remember Mitch?"

"It's impossible to forget Mitch."

"And Gustav," added Kirby.

"Who's Gustav?" asked Molly as they started walking back to the hotel.

"You're going to need some preparation for meeting Gustav."

"Why?"

"Trust me," said Kirby, "I'll try my best to explain him on the way."


"By the way," said Erica as her fork speared an orange segment off her room service plate, "your little app helped me find a great pair of shoes a couple of days ago. I'll show them to you later."

Andi just sat there, staring at her chicken salad in silence.

"Andi?"

"I'm sorry," said Andi. "I'm just letting my mind wander."

"Where are you wandering?"

Andi exhaled and leaned back in her chair.

"Wandering nowhere," replied Andi, "and I'm getting there very slowly."

"Come on," said Erica, "I've got a penny for your thoughts."

Andi sighed.

"This whole gypsy life is getting to me," said Andi. "Plus, I have suspicions."

"Suspicions?"

"I think Henry is cheating on me."

Erica's fork fell on the plate with a clatter.

"No," gasped Erica, "it can't be. Henry's crazy about you."

"Henry's crazy about the idea of me," said Andi, "I'm not so sure that he's all that crazy about me personally."

Erica pushed her plate aside and reached across the small table to hold her friend's hand.

"Don't talk like that."

"I'm not being just paranoid," said Andi. "I've seen all the classic signs. He's become so secretive lately, he's always going on extra 'business trips' without me for vague reasons, taking strange gigs, and then there are the emails."

"You've read his emails?"

"Not really, but he's made up a bunch of those free email accounts," continued Andi. "Why would he do that if he wasn't doing something he wants to hide from me?"

A tear ran down Erica's porcelain cheek.

"Now I'm ruining everything," said Andi, taking a deep breath. "We have to get ourselves together. We've got business tonight."

Erica squeezed Andi's hand. "I hope everything works out for you, because you and Henry are made for each other. I hope that this is nothing but needless worry."

"You're a hopeful person, aren't you?"

Even though there were only four of them, the hostess – dressed like a western saloon showgirl – took one look at the motley crew and brought them to a table for six at the back of the room. The motif of the restaurant was the sort of Old West envisioned by someone who had never made it farther west than the Hudson River. The eatery's pine plank walls were decorated with lassoes, hats and cattle skulls, while the air smelled like meat on a campfire. At one end of the room was an open kitchen where a band of chefs toiled over massive grills that erratically spurted fire like gaseous dragons. Gustav took out the chairs and guided everyone to their seats, he put Kirby with his back to the wall, and then Gustav took the seat between him and the aisle. Molly sat across from Kirby, and Mitch took the seat across from Gustav, creating a somewhat lopsided appearance to the table in terms of height.

A waitress – dressed like a pin-up cowgirl in a cut-off calico shirt and denim skirt that was just short enough to attract male attention, but not enough to make the Rodeo Grill the hotel's equivalent of Hooters – appeared and distributed menus among them.

"What have you been up to?" asked Kirby after thanking the waitress.

Molly had to tear her wide eyes away from Gustav to answer. "Oh," she said, "I'm still writing for The Vengeance Sisters monthly book. Ashmore wants me to participate in the panel they set up to hype the movie, tell the internet people that I'm excited for the project, I love the whole thing, and tell the fanboys that they're wrong to hate the movie before it's even made. He even got me invited to some movie party tonight hoping to impress me to go along with all this crap."

"We're invited to the same party," said Mitch, "we can all go together."

"That's a great idea Mitch," said Kirby, who had been wondering if he could get Gustav to trade his invite, even though he knew the big man enjoyed meeting new people, "but what's with the 'all this crap' talk Molly?"

"Do you remember that script that used to float around the office?" asked Molly, leaning in as if letting them in on a conspiracy.

"The Vengeance Sisters TV pilot from the nineteen eighties?" asked Kirby. "The one that never got made."

"And for good reason," added Mitch.

"Yep," answered Molly.

"What about it?" asked Kirby.

"That's the script they're using for the movie," said Molly.

"Get out of here," said Kirby. "That script was a joke and a really bad joke too. It had a musical guest appearance by Milli Vanilli."

"And the plot was about brainwashed break dancers," added Mitch.

"The producer literally paid pennies for it," added Molly. "Hired some gag writer to update the slang, and toss in some boob and dick jokes, and that's what they're going to film."

"Didn't they know that the same people who remade Knight Rider," said Kirby, "passed on that script?"

"I don't think they care," said Molly, "because it's actually better for MaxCo if the script is a stinker."

"What do you mean?" asked Kirby.

"Don't you read Jackie Paine?"

Kirby shrugged.

"Have you ever looked at Hollywood's Paine?" asked Molly.

"Is that some sort of internet gossip site?" asked Kirby.

"Do you live in a cave?" asked Molly, feeling insulted. "Now I should whack you with my purse. It is not about gossip, it's about business."

"Hollywood business?" asked Kirby. "I thought Hollywood's business was gossip."

"Yes it is," said Molly, "the site is all about who is screwing who, but on a corporate level."

"What does Jackie Paine say?" asked Mitch.

"That this whole movie deal," continued Molly, "is all part of a big plan to screw Atlantic Comics for millions."

"I'm going to need some more explanation."

"Max Cooperman is a big independent producer," explained Molly, "two years ago he made a deal with Atlantic Comics to make movies based on their characters."

"That's not hard to believe," said Kirby, "everybody's

doing comic book movies these days."

"If Cooperman made a movie based on one book within two years," continued Molly, "he would get to keep control of the movie rights to all of the Atlantic Comics characters for another two years."

"I think I see where this is going," said Kirby, "Continental Pictures is looking to buy Atlantic, and if Cooperman still owns the movie rights to the one thing Continental really wants, they will have to pay him off and pay him off big."

"So you're not a complete ignoramus," said Molly, amazed.

"I knew Ashmore would screw everything up somehow," added Mitch. "I told you so!"

"I overheard Ashmore and Cooperman arguing in the hall when I was getting ice," added Kirby. "I wasn't sure why they were arguing, but now it makes sense."

"They're both on your floor?" asked Molly.

"Kirby sprung for us to stay in the Royal Suite," said Mitch with some pride, "on the Excelsior floor."

"Lucky bastards," said Molly. "The company pretty much ordered me to come here, but I had to pay for my own room. Of course the only way I can afford it on my salary is to share."

"Who are you sharing it with?" asked Kirby.

"Just about every woman working in the comics industry is in my hotel room right now."

"Really," said Mitch, arching his lewdest eyebrow, "are you all trying on each other's clothes, frolicking in your nightgowns and having pillow fights?"

"Can't you see from the tree outside?"

"Is it that crowded?" asked Kirby.

Molly nodded.

"I have an extra room at my suite," said Kirby, "you can stay there."

"Are you serious?" asked Molly.

"It's no problem," said Kirby, he always enjoyed Molly's

company, especially when she wasn't savagely beating him for being an insensitive clod who doesn't know how to use email, "it has its own bathroom and all that, so you won't have to share with Mitch, but the hotel has a very strict 'no beating the host' rule."

"I can live with that," said Molly, "within limits. Thank you; that will be really great."

"Hey," said Mitch, "what about my plans to turn the suite into our swinging bachelor pad?"

"Is that why you packed an ascot and a smoking jacket?" asked Kirby laughing.

"Were you going through my luggage?" asked Mitch in mock offence.

"Now I'm definitely moving in," said Molly, "someone's got to keep an eye on you guys, and I don't think I can leave Gustav as the only grown-up in the place."

"At least I'm not the one cruising supermodels," said Mitch.

"What supermodels?" asked Molly.

"Say," said Kirby, "isn't that LaGuardia?"

"The airport or the editor?" asked Mitch.

"The airport," said Kirby, "turn your head and look."

Molly and Mitch turned to see Kevin LaGuardia standing tentatively at the entrance of the restaurant. Kirby waved, LaGuardia waved back and then left.

"He's gone," said Kirby. "What's up with that?"

"Probably doesn't want to piss off the Ash-hole," said Mitch, "he was always nervous about his job. He just didn't have the nerves to work as a freelance artist back in the day."

"Poor guy," said Molly, "he just doesn't know that pissing off Ashmore is the most fun part of the job."

"Maybe Dick Wilco will take a shot at Fred while he's here," said Mitch. "He kind of put the hex on the whole Ashmore family when he and Smiling Sam had their big split in the eighties."

"What are you talking about?" asked Molly.

"There's a rumour," answered Kirby, happy that they

weren't talking supermodels, "that Dick Wilco is going to participate in some sort of auction at this convention."

"But the auction is a secret," added Mitch.

"Wait a minute," said Molly, "your only reason to come to this convention is because you think Dick Wilco might be here?"

"It's more of an excuse than a reason," replied Kirby. "I was already planning to come back this summer; I just did it a couple of weeks earlier and stopped at this convention to see if I could find him."

"It sounds like a stupid rumour," said Molly, shaking her head. "Dick Wilco hasn't made any sort of public appearance in decades. You're the last person in the industry to actually talk to him, and even you haven't seen in him in, what, seven years?"

Kirby nodded. "It's been a little over seven years." Wilco had visited the farm, unannounced, to congratulate him for his work on Shadowknight. He refused to stay for dinner, or even a drink, just shook his hand, told Kirby that he was the best choice for the job, and scurried off into the night. It was a classic Dick Wilco move, carefully designed to maintain the mystery that surrounded him since his disappearance from public view.

"However," said Kirby, "rumour or not, there's no harm in trying, and I also get to reconnect with people and end my two years of silly self-imposed exile."

"Cheers to that," said Mitch.

Molly then turned to Kirby.

"Now what's all this about you 'cruising supermodels?'"

"Waitress," called out Kirby, "I'm ready to order."


"Indian food?" asked Madden as he entered the Pagoda Room. "I hate Indian food." The decor was a masala of decors from all over the exotic east. Indian elephants, Chinese dragons and Japanese temples all jostled for attention in the crowded colourful murals that lined the walls.

"They serve Chinese food here," said LaGuardia, "everyone likes Chinese food."

Madden shrugged.

"What's wrong with the steak place?" asked Madden.

"Baxter's there," said LaGuardia.

"So," said Madden, "if anyone asks, you're just selling me some art. That is what you're doing."

"That freak has ears like a bat," said LaGuardia, "I don't like talking business around him."

"Does he really scare you that much?"

LaGuardia nodded.

"Then I guess we're going to have to do something about him," said Madden, before turning to the hostess in the red faux silk dress. "We'd like a table for two please."

"What do you mean?" asked LaGuardia.

"Now you're not scared of being overheard?" asked Madden. "If you're going to be paranoid, be consistently paranoid."

They took their seats, took their menus, and when they were finally alone Madden laid down the law.

"Our buyers are going to arrive tomorrow," said Madden. "We can keep them away from Baxter, that's not very difficult."

"Some might want to see him," said LaGuardia. "He is the resident expert on Wilco and his work."

"Why would they want to waste time on Baxter," said Madden, "when we're going to give them Wilco himself?"

"He still might–"

"We have a lot of money riding on this," said Madden, "and a lot of shit if it doesn't go through. If Baxter causes trouble I'll take care of him."

"How?"

"Not here," said Madden, "we'll talk in my suite later where the walls don't have ears."

"Mr. Laval is here to see you," said Weatherby.

Cooperman didn't even look up from his room service

dinner of boneless skinless grilled chicken breast and salad sans dressing of any kind. The fact that he ordered a meal according to the diet laid down by Mrs. Cooperman was a sign to Weatherby that the big man was in a sour mood. When he was feeling good about things he was all about bloody steak, French fries that were greasier than a crooked agent and saltier than a sailor's language, and a wad of chocolate ice cream the size of Weatherby's head for desert. Those were times he felt indestructible and master of his own fate. Diet times were anxious times. If Cooperman was anxious, Weatherby was terrified.

"Send him in," grumbled Cooperman.

Weatherby nodded and stepped aside to let Laval in. The man himself was shorter than Weatherby had imagined, with wide shoulders and a thick neck supporting a hairy bowling ball of a head.

"Bonjour," said Laval, with an accent that dripped slush from the backstreets of Montreal from every syllable. He pulled a pack of cigarettes from a pocket in his denim jacket.

"This is a no smoking room," said Cooperman, enforcing another dictum from his wife, another sign that the man was under stress.

"Aren't they all nowadays," replied Laval with a Gallic shrug, slipping the pack back into his pocket.

"Have a seat," said Cooperman pointing to a chair. "We have to talk."

"Your instructions were pretty clear," said Laval.

"I want to make sure that nothing was lost in translation," said Cooperman. "This whole job is all about timing."

"You want it done on Tuesday," said Laval, "it'll be done on Tuesday."

"Not one day earlier," said Cooperman, "and not one day later."

"I'll do my part right," said Laval, "as long as you do your part right."

"What do you mean?"

"Come on," said Laval, "half now, half when the job's

done."

"That wasn't part of the deal," said Cooperman, a blatant lie, but the man never missed a chance to bluster his way out of paying money.

"Don't bullshit me Anglais," sneered Laval. "No money, no job."

"Fine," sighed Cooperman, "you'll have to come back tomorrow."

Laval stood up and leaned over the small table.

"I don't like games," said Laval, "even when I was a kid, I was all business. Now the deal is three quarters up front."

"What!"

"That's the cost of trying to play me like I was one of your Hollywood buddies," growled Laval.

"You don't know who you're dealing with!"

"I know exactly who I'm dealing with," replied Laval, cold as ice. "I read up on you. I know that if something was to happen to your little movie before Tuesday, you'd be righteously fucked up the ass."

Weatherby could see his boss' face turn red. The man wanted to scream, to yell, to just explode, but he couldn't.

"Have the money tomorrow," said Laval, "first thing in the morning, as a sign of good faith. Failure to show this good faith will lead to some costly penalties."

"Fine," said Cooperman, his voice a low growl.

Laval smiled and walked right out the door as if he were a much taller man.

Cooperman let his fork drop on his plate, then he picked up the plate, studying it for a beat. Weatherby knew what was coming, and his body tensed.

"Get rid of this shit!" screamed Cooperman before letting the plate smash against the wall.

"So," said Molly, "who is this supermodel Kirby's chasing?"

Kirby felt his face get hot.

"It's true?"

"No, it's not," pleaded Kirby in his own defence. "We just

met this morning."

"Who is it?" asked Molly.

"Erica Cross," answered Mitch. "She was warm for Kirby's form."

Molly burst out laughing; her tiny fist rapped the thick wooden table with enough force to make their glasses shake.

"Hey," said Kirby, forced to defend his honour and fragile ego, "it's not that unlikely. I am rich now, that can definitely lead to dating out of one's league."

"League," said Molly, "or species?"

"Besides," added Kirby, "we're not dating. We only just met. This is all wild speculation by the overactive one track imagination of one little troll." Kirby then pointed an accusing finger at Mitch.

"As your official mooch," said Mitch, "it's my official duty to do what I can to ensure that you lead the sort of insanely decadent lifestyle that rich men like you are supposed to live."

"Official mooch?" asked Molly.

"That's my new calling," said Mitch, "my most sacred vocation."

"Nice to know you've finally found your niche," added Molly.

"It's a tough job," replied Mitch, "but someone has to do it."

"I wonder if I can find someone else for the job," thought Kirby aloud.

"Are you taking applications?" asked Molly.

"Hey!"

"Isn't that Bruce?" asked Kirby.

"Who is Bruce?" asked Molly.

"He's Erica's assistant," said Mitch as he turned around to see Bruce Haring being lead through the restaurant by the hostess. "Hey, Bruce!"

"Oh," said Bruce, "hello."

"Why don't you join us?" asked Kirby.

"Sure beats a table for one," said Bruce. The hostess gave

Bruce a menu as he sat down. "Quite an entourage you have around you now Mr. Baxter."

"This is Molly Garret," introduced Kirby, and Bruce shook her hand.

"Pleased to meet you," said Bruce.

"She's the current writer for The Vengeance Sisters comic book," added Kirby.

"For now," said Molly, "I'm trying to get fired."

"This is news to me," said Kirby.

"I got an offer to do Wonder Woman for DC," answered Molly.

"I could go to the movie panel tomorrow," offered Mitch, "and ask a question that gives all the credit for the book's success to your writing."

"That would be great," said Molly, "it worked for Kirby."

Bruce gave his order to the waitress and passed her the menu.

"By the way," said Kirby, "how's Erica?"

"She's having a little girl time with her friend Andi," answered Bruce, "which is really good for her."

"What do you mean?" asked Kirby.

"Well," said Bruce, "a big reason she took The Vengeance Sisters movie was that it got her out of Los Angeles for a while."

"How come?" asked Kirby.

"The tabloids don't have this story yet," said Bruce, "which is amazing considering the amount of spying they do on her, but she has a stalker," said Bruce.

"Ah," said Kirby.

"It started a few months ago," continued Bruce, "with a few gushing messages on her Facebook page. We thought it was just a fan with no off switch, but then it got creepy. Emails started coming, with pictures of her attached. We're not talking about magazine clippings, or stuff off the web; I'm talking about pictures of her at home and on photo shoots. She'd change her email address, get a new security system, but they just kept coming."

"Things got even worse?" asked Kirby.

"How did you know?" asked Bruce.

"You can't keep secrets from Kirby," said Molly. "He's a mind reader."

"What?"

"I'm not a mind reader," said Kirby with a shrug, "my grandfather used to be a stage magician, and he used to do a mentalist act. He taught me how to do a thing called a 'cold reading.' Basically, I take things like micro-expressions, body language, and other little clues people have and use them to put together a picture of what they're thinking about, and use that picture to pretend like I'm really psychic. It's a glorified party trick."

"It's a much less disgusting act than the lunch trick," added Mitch.

"Wow," said Bruce, "you had me going for a second, I won't ask about the lunch trick. But you were right, things did get worse. In fact, a week ago someone tried to burn down her house."

"That's terrible," said Molly.

"The cops were looking at her ex-boyfriend," said Bruce, "but I don't think he did it."

"How come?" asked Kirby.

"He's a douchebag," said Bruce, "not a psycho. He won't do anything that might mess up his hair."

"The police don't have any other leads?" asked Kirby.

Bruce shrugged. "Not really," he added, "I really shouldn't be talking about this. It's bad enough having that creep in her life, giving him fifteen minutes of fame would be worse."

"Our lips are sealed," said Kirby.

"The last thing I'd want to do is upset a beautiful woman," added Mitch.

Molly laughed, "But you don't mind annoying them."

"Or boring them," added Kirby, "or embarrassing them, or disappointing them–"

"What did I do to deserve this mistreatment?" asked Mitch.

"Do you want me to get the list?" asked Molly and everyone laughed.

ISSUE #5
PARTY TRICKS

Kirby spat out the toothpaste, slipped his toothbrush back into the holder and looked himself over in the mirror. He regretted doing that, seeing his every imperfection in glaringly specific detail. To him, it looked like his eyes, ears and nose were just too big for the rest of his head. Despite the combing and chemical interventions, his hair was a mess, and not the sort of fashionable mess that was all the rage with the kids these days. It was just a plain, simple, ordinary mess. Even his goatee, a relatively new development, looked like a mistake.

It was an old joke in his business that comic book artists tended to draw their heroes to look like themselves. Kirby felt he was the exception to that rule, having yet to draw anything with a superhero that looked like an under-stuffed scarecrow. For years he drew faces for a living but never drew his own, or even wanted to.

Kirby stepped back from the mirror, he hated the damn things and swore to not let the damn things dictate things to him again. He fought the temptation to do some sort of self-affirmation like a self-help guru, he just had to remember that he had literally millions upon millions of reasons to be confident, and mirrors could go get stuffed.

"HOLY CRAP!" cried out Molly from the other room.

Kirby knew that meant Mitch had done something. He silently thanked the powers that be for making Mitch such a great distraction, and he stepped out into the living room.

He saw Molly first. She was wearing a little red dress and

Kirby stopped for a beat to admire just how damnably cute she looked in it, but he couldn't linger too long because he had to figure why she was laughing so hard.

Kirby looked over, and couldn't help but start laughing himself.

"What?" asked Mitch, resplendent in a powder blue leisure suit; with matching powder blue shirt, complete with lapels that could have been used as glider wings; powder blue patent leather dress shoes; and powder blue belt. Mitch had also slicked down his normally anarchic curly shag into a sleek hair helmet.

"Where the hell do you find these outfits?" asked Kirby. This was something that Mitch had done at every convention or major gathering. He'd show up to some panel discussion, industry party or interview dressed in some of the most eye-bleeding outfits Kirby had ever seen. There was always a method to his madness. The outfits were always composed around a single colour, from a chocolate brown tuxedo with matching shirt and tie or a completely lime green business ensemble, to the powder blue abomination he wore in front of them.

"I got it all from the internet," answered Mitch with an impish grin. "You have to search the whole world over to put together a fine ensemble like this."

"My eyes hurt," said Molly between giggles. "If my make-up runs I swear the next colour you'll be wearing will be blood red."

Gustav entered the room looking, as always, like Gustav, but even he did a double take at the sight of Mitch.

"I just can't decide if you've topped yourself," said Kirby, "or if you've hit a new low."

"I like to think that I hit new heights in the field of sartorial splendour," answered Mitch. "Besides, check out how tight my ass looks in these pants." Then he leaned forward and jutted his backside out like a presenting baboon. "Is this turning you on Molly?"

Molly couldn't speak, only attempt to croak some threats

between laughs while propping herself against the couch.

"Feel free to jump me," said Mitch, "all I ask is that you don't muss the Jew-fro. It took more work to tame it than it took to put together this outfit."

"Put that thing away," said Kirby trying and failing to fight the urge to laugh.

"Damn you Mitch," said Molly, "I should kick that tight little ass of yours right now. Why can't you be more like Kirby? He manages to clean up pretty well without being a sin against good taste and the laws of nature."

"Thank you," said Kirby, "you're looking very nice yourself tonight."

"Why Mr. Baxter," said Molly in a faux southern belle voice, "aren't you the old honey-dripper."

Kirby tried to keep his face from matching her dress, and failed.

"That's the sort of move you need to put on your supermodel," said Mitch, giving him a hearty pat on the back.

"You might have a shot," said Molly, "according to the gossip sites she's got low standards, and Gustav can scare away the stalkers or paparazzi."

"You two should grow up and quick," said Kirby, "we're going to be outnumbered at this party, so let's show these Hollywood folks that we are capable of behaving like civilized people."

"Yes Dad," said Mitch.

"Cause if you don't," said Kirby in a mock threatening tone, "I'll put you over my knee."

"That sounds like an invitation," said Molly.

"Now some of our friends are in the convention centre," added Kirby, trying to change the subject before it became any more embarrassing, "setting up their booths so, if we leave now, we can pay them a visit before going to the party."

"Ooh," said Molly, "a chance to rub it in their faces that we're partying with the rich and famous."

"That's the mature attitude to have," said Kirby.

There was no sign of her yet.

He had managed to slip into the convention centre pretty easily. There was only one security guard watching the 'Staff Only' door, and that guard wasn't watching it very well. He wore grey overalls, the universal uniform of someone who was supposed to be there for some reason, and had a little laminated card clipped to the collar. The card didn't say that he was supposed to be there. In fact, the card said his name was Heywood Jablowmee, and the picture in the corner was of Elvis. The security guard didn't even look up from his magazine and just nodded as he walked past.

No one inside the main room of the convention centre noticed him either. They were all too busy setting up their tables and booths full of all kinds of crap for sale. None of their silly immature nonsense remotely interested him. All he wanted was a nice quiet spot to watch from.

He found it nestled between a large contraption covered in cardboard cut-outs of movie actors playing dress up and a bank of plasma screens formed into a massive black monolith. He put down the black plastic toolbox and looked around. His new position had an excellent view of the entrance to Room B, which Henry Hack had turned into party central for the convention. From here he would be able to see anyone coming in or out.

So far, there were only a few last minute members of the DJ's technical crew leaving Room B, getting thanks from Henry 'H-Bomb' Hack as they left. Then some other people entered the convention centre. They weren't his target but some tall skinny geek, a powder blue midget, a cute girl in a red dress with big eyes that were visible without his telephoto lens, and what looked like a shaved gorilla in a black suit. He didn't take out his camera; they didn't look remotely important, though they were dressed better than the booth workers.

He slipped back into a dark corner.

He had to wait, and watch.

"See anyone we know?" asked Molly.

"There's Teddy," said Kirby.

"Which Teddy?" asked Mitch, "I know five guys and one girl named Teddy."

"Teddy Ricci," said Kirby, "over by his booth."

"Hey," called out Molly, "Teddy!"

"Molly?" asked Teddy as his head popped up from behind his front table. "Get down here."

"This is really impressive," said Kirby as they approached his booth. "It's like you brought the whole store with you." It was true, the 'booth' was a series of long tables laden with merchandise, surrounding four ten foot high walls lined with shelves, each lined with hardcover and trade paperback editions of all the top comic titles. If history was anything to go by, within those four walls were even more spinner racks, wire metal shelves, and display tables, themselves laden with merchandise. Teddy was the owner and chief executive officer of one of the largest online retailers of trade paperback and hardcover edition comics in the world. Ricci's online store didn't sell individual monthly issues of comics, or what the fans call 'floppies,' but only the larger collected editions, and if his online store didn't have it, or couldn't get it, it did not exist.

Teddy himself was one of those persistently happy people, always quick with a smile and ready for a good time. He was stout in every sense of the word, with a taste for loud Hawaiian shirts, and jeans, and he kept his brown hair in a loose shaggy heap. He was happy to see Kirby and came out from behind the table to give him a bear hug that lifted him off the floor.

"Damn Kirby," said Teddy, "it's good to see you."

"It's good to see you too," replied Kirby. "You obviously remember Molly, and Mitch."

"Love the suit Mitch," said Teddy, "you've made polyester fashionable again."

"And this is Gustav," said Kirby, "he works for me."

"Great to meet you Gustav," said Teddy as he shook Gustav's hand. "How did you end up working for Kirby?"

"It's a long story," said Kirby, and Gustav nodded.

"Well," said Teddy, "it's great to see all of you. And to answer your question, I didn't bring the whole store with me, at least not my American one. What you are looking at is the beginning of my new Canadian online store."

"Really," said Kirby, "you're expanding?"

"I'm expanding in all directions, and not just around my waist," added Teddy. "Despite the recent economy, I've been going great guns. There are a lot of trade-waders in the world, and a lot of them look to me to find what they can't find anywhere else."

"That's great news," said Kirby.

"I'm not as rich as you Kirby," said Teddy, "but I'm working on it."

"That's okay, I could use more friends with money," said Mitch.

"No moonlighting as official mooch," replied Molly.

"The correct term is mooch-lighting," said Mitch.

"What are you two on about?" asked Teddy.

"Mitch has a new career," said Molly, "as Kirby's official mooch."

"Maybe it is a good thing that you're doing so much better than me," said Teddy.

"Is the Luau Room going to be open at this convention?" asked Kirby.

The Luau Room was a long running convention tradition that Teddy had arranged with convention organizers. Basically it was a fully stocked bar set up by Teddy inside his little mini store, exclusively for artists, writers and people involved in organizing the convention, decorated with a selection of Hawaiian themed kitsch and a selection of tropical drinks being served regardless of the setting or weather. It became the after hours socializing spot for folks in the know, and a great place and time to catch up with old friends and acquaintances.

"Not yet," said Teddy, "it will be open tomorrow night. I couldn't help but notice how gussied up you guys are. I mean Kirby and Gustav are gussied, Molly just had to show off her normal hotness a little more than usual—"

"Please," said Molly, "you're embarrassing me. Keep going, my self-esteem needs it."

"—and Mitch is dressed like Gainsborough's Blue Balls."

"We have been invited to party with some of the movie people," said Mitch.

"Oh," said Teddy, "the joys of being rich and famous."

"Mitch and I just lucked into the invites," said Kirby, "Molly's going to be there on business."

"Save some starlets for me," said Teddy, "and bring some down to the Luau Room tomorrow night. After a few Margaritas, a lot of women mistake me for a young Mel Gibson without the drunken racist ranting."

"Wood grain alcohol can do that," said Mitch.

"Excuse me," said a British accented voice behind them, "but are you Kirby Baxter?"

Kirby turned to see a man with dyed blond hair moulded into spikes like a hedgehog.

"Yes," said Kirby.

"Henry Hack," said the man, "you met my wife earlier."

"Oh," said Kirby, "yes, you're Andi's husband."

Kirby introduced Henry to the group, and was impressed that the Englishman managed to meet Gustav without the usual expression of surprise.

"Are you going to the party too?" Henry asked Teddy. "I have a couple of extra passes."

"I'd love to," said Teddy, "but I have too much to do to be ready for tomorrow. Maybe I'll catch your opening night show."

"We'd love to have you," said Henry before turning back to Kirby and the others. "Perhaps your group would like a little tour before the show?"

"That would be cool," answered Kirby.

"Since this is a comic book convention," said Henry as he led them into the party room, "we've gone with a superhero theme."

The theme wasn't visible at first, but Henry took out a small black pad and pressed his thumb on the touchscreen. Instantly the main lights went down and digital projectors kicked on, bathing the once blank walls with the symbols of famous superheroes. This sparked some impressed 'oohs' and 'ahs' from Kirby and the others.

"Glad you like it," said Henry. "The studios with movies to promote at the convention each have a dance party for one night of the convention. We have the projectors rigged to show their movie posters on the different nights."

"It looks great," replied Kirby.

"That's just the beginning," said Henry, "how about a little preview of what I have planned for opening night." Hack hit another button, vents built into the DJ platform opened and the floor was instantly flooded with a white mist.

"Oh," said Molly, "that's cold."

"It makes people dance closer," said Hack.

"You must have insulated your fans really well," said Kirby, "to get them to move that mist so quickly and yet so quietly."

"You know a little about stage-craft?"

"My grandfather was in show business," answered Kirby. "I used to help out in his workshop where he developed illusions for stage magicians."

"Then let me give you the complete insider tour," said Hack, and with another click on the black pad the dancing superhero symbols disappeared, some fans kicked in and the mist retreated.

Hack gestured Kirby to follow him up onto the DJ platform.

"It's quite a system," explained Hack as they walked up onto the high platform, "I designed the whole works myself."

"Is this where you keep the dry ice?" asked Mitch from below. Kirby and Hack turned to look over the back of the DJ booth to see Mitch by a wide blue metal and plastic box.

"Yeah," said Hack, "that's a deep freeze. We need so much for the parties it would be a real pain in the ass to be running back and forth with my suppliers all weekend."

"It must be positively frigid," said Mitch, his hand hovering above the blue box, "I can feel it from here."

"I used it to freeze a can of lager in twenty minutes," said Hack. "Damn can burst open."

"I thought I smelled beer," said Kirby.

"Before the show I take a block out of the deep freeze," explained Hack pointing to the various apparatus from his perch, "I then put it in the cooler there and when I need the mist I tell the computer, the computer then tells some gears to dump the dry ice into the water tank, and to kick on the fans."

"Simple but effective," said Kirby.

"Building and programming everything wasn't that simple," said Hack. "It took a lot of trial and error to get everything to work smoothly, which isn't easy when you flunked math like I did. I'd have had better luck letting the wife do it, but the old ego wouldn't let me."

"Is that a Mac set-up?" asked Molly leaning over the railing of the elevated DJ booth and pointing to a bank of computers and monitors.

"Yes," said Hack. "All the music is digitized meaning the only disc this jockey actually uses is the disc on the hard drive. I can use the main control board to handle everything directly, or use an app on this mini tablet to handle pre-programmed effects and playlists."

"Good if you need to go on a pee break," said Molly.

"Molly?" Kirby suddenly noticed that she wasn't actually on the DJ platform, yet had somehow gained the height to lean over the railing. "How are you able to reach the booth?"

"I'm sitting on Gustav's shoulder," answered Molly rather matter-of-fact. "I only needed one."

Gustav's hand appeared over the railing and waved.

"Please," said Kirby, "Gustav isn't a ladder, and he isn't a carnival ride."

"You're no fun at all," sniped Molly.

"That's the sort of thing Mitch would do," replied Kirby.

"Now you're just being mean," said Molly.

"It's all clear," said Weatherby as his head darted from side to side, reminding Cooperman of a meerkat scouting for predators on some basic cable nature show.

"Fine," said Cooperman shoving him aside and going through the door of the convention centre. Cooperman's main concern wasn't predators, but nuisances. He knew Ashmore would be at the party, but he also knew that Ashmore wouldn't risk any sort of public blow-out in front of a crowd of important industry people, among them a detachment from Continental Pictures. The real danger lay in the space between Cooperman's hotel room door and the door to Room B. So he had Weatherby go ahead of him, checking around every corner and behind every plant for any sign of that rat-faced little bastard.

At first Weatherby tried to act nonchalant, but the closer they got to the convention centre, the more he began to act like a reject from a commando movie. Ducking, weaving and skulking, Cooperman was certain that the little bastard was deliberately jerking his chain.

Despite the late hour people were still milling around the place, setting up booths, stocking shelves and rigging up elaborate displays. MaxCo's booth was a tad small and bland by comparison, but it wasn't like he was going to piss away good money after bad, whether he had the bad money to begin with. It had a couple of mock up posters for The Vengeance Sisters movie hanging on it, but neither was bigger than the MaxCo company logo. The publicity department or, to be more exact, the few that had survived the recent layoffs, and their unpaid interns, had designed the cardboard cut-out of Max himself to be both thinner and taller than the real thing.

"Hello Max," said a voice from behind the cut-out. It was that bastard Ashmore stepping out from behind Cooperman's cardboard doppelgänger.

"Hello Freddie," replied Cooperman, with a totally insincere smile, "how lovely to see you."

"I'm sure it is," said Ashmore. "I tried to visit the set and I wasn't allowed to enter the lot."

"Of course you weren't allowed in," said Cooperman, "it's still under construction."

"I'm credited as an executive producer!"

"So is my niece Debbie," said Cooperman, "and she's not allowed in either. Child labor laws forbid it." Cooperman had made extra sure that Ashmore would be banned from getting anywhere near the sound stage, even to the point of bribing the security guards. The last thing he wanted was to give Ashmore the chance to do any mischief that might delay the start of principal photography and Cooperman's big day of victory.

"Mr. Cooperman," said Weatherby. "They're starting the party." Music was pumping out of the door and wafting across the convention centre.

Cooperman took a deep breath. "We have to be all smiles," he said.

"I know that," said Ashmore, "I just want you to know that I'm on to you."

"Then join the crowd," said Cooperman, "meanwhile, I've got a party to go to."

"So," said Molly above the din of the music, an impish smile on her face.

"So what?" asked Kirby.

"Where's your new supermodel girlfriend?"

"You have a weird way of showing gratitude to someone who took you out of your cramped little ghetto and gave you a place to stay," replied Kirby.

"You said I couldn't beat the host," said Molly, "but you

said nothing about a little light ball busting."

"Damn, I knew I forgot something. I really need a lawyer for that sort of thing."

"Besides, I'm dying to meet her, and I'm sure you're itching to see her again."

"She seems very nice," answered Kirby, refusing to rise to her bait. The introductions at the party had come fast and furious, including the director whose name was Markus L. and, while Markus tried to hide it, Kirby saw many signs of drug intoxication, and then he met the film's publicist whose name was Debbie. She was all smiles and immediately reintroduced Kirby to Max Cooperman and Fred Ashmore. Max Cooperman didn't appear to remember their meeting from this morning, just muttered a hello and scurried off to talk shop with the president of a Canadian movie distributor. Ashmore was only five per cent more polite before he went off in pursuit of some folks from Continental Pictures. There were people from other companies promoting movies at OmniCon, some he had actually met before at previous conventions, and a few were even fans of his work. However, there was no sign of Erica Cross or Andi Hack.

"I'm sure you're all bated breath waiting for her to show up, so you can fall on your knees and declare yourself her love slave."

"You are a lightweight," said Kirby, "half a beer and you're talking crazy."

"And you're smitten," said Molly, making a 'kissy-kissy' face.

Kirby couldn't help but laugh. "Smitten?" he asked. "What is it with you and Mitch talking like rejects from Turner Classic Movies?"

"You are in deep smit," said Molly, her voice turned sing-song, "drunk on love."

"Why don't you try to land yourself a director?" asked Kirby as he scanned the crowd. Few were dancing, most were in tightly packed clusters, engaged in deep conversation. Mitch was one of the few dancing, kicking up his heels with a publicist's assistant from Continental Pictures. Gustav was standing by the door, next to one of the convention's official security guards, watching everything and everyone.

"You mean The Vengeance Sisters auteur Markus L?" asked Molly. "I don't like stoners and I don't think I'm his type."

"Too short?"

"No."

"Too pushy?"

"No."

"Too needy?"

"No."

"Too neurotic?"

"No."

"Too—"

Molly's small hand clamped itself on Kirby's mouth.

"Don't make me beat you and stuff you in that freezer," said Molly.

"So I can't say 'Too violent?'"

Molly laughed.

"Where's that buffet table?" asked Molly. "I'm starving"

"You ate a steak bigger than Gustav's head," said Kirby, always amazed at tiny Molly's massive appetite, "you poached half my fries and then had that 'death by chocolate' dessert."

"What can I say," said Molly, "I have the metabolism of a hummingbird. Since there are no giant flowers filled with my weight in nectar around, I'm going to have settle for some of those little sandwich thingies."

"Do you want to dance?" asked Kirby just as the music shifted to a deafening crescendo to illustrate that either Kirby Baxter or the universe had dreadful timing.

"What?" she asked, yelling to be heard over the din.

"Do you want to—?"

"I'll be back in a second!" yelled Molly. "That sandwich platter is calling my name."

Molly vanished among the shifting lights and milling crowd. Kirby took a sip of his drink and remembered that he never really liked the taste of beer, even the expensive imported stuff.

Kirby looked over the crowd again. Ashmore and Cooperman were keeping their distance from each other. Ashmore was in intense conversation with someone from Continental Pictures. Cooperman was on the other side of the room, holding court with Markus the director, and Weatherby the personal assistant, and all three men seemed to be vigorously texting people, possibly each other in an attempt to communicate over the loud music.

Still no Erica.

Kirby looked up to see that Hack wasn't at his control booth. Kirby turned to see that he was with one of the clusters of very important people, somehow engaged in verbal conversation despite the music. The Englishman excused himself from the conversation, pulled what Kirby realized was an iPhone from his pocket, read something off the screen, typed something short in response, changed the app, and then pressed some sort of virtual button. The music's volume descended from a deafening roar to a lower rumble. The projected logos stopped dancing on the walls and ceiling, and the moving lights all stopped spinning and aimed at the main door.

The double doors swung open revealing Andi Hack and Erica Cross. Andi Hack was in a candy apple red minidress, matching shoes, and black tights, with her short hair slicked down she looked like the cover of a fashion magazine from Swinging London of the nineteen sixties. While Andi looked good, beautiful even, Erica looked radiant. She wore a green dress that accented her scarlet hair, which hung around her shoulders in waves, and her pale luminous complexion. She practically glowed with a light of her own.

The crowd seemed to part before them and Andi strode across to her husband, while Erica walked straight across to Kirby.

"Would you like to dance?" asked Erica.

Kirby took a beat to pick his jaw up off the floor, and said: "Yes."

The song ended and Erica stepped back.

"Thanks for the dance," she said. "I have to go talk to some people, but I would like to talk to you later."

"Sure," said Kirby, still feeling the touch of her hand on his, even though she had let go.

As he watched Erica step away he smelled Mitch's cologne creep up from behind him.

"You dog," said Mitch.

"Where's Molly?" asked Kirby.

"She's somewhere," said Mitch, "probably seething with jealous rage."

The music had shifted from the hardcore dance music to softer atmospheric tones, and the lights had gone up. More people gathered in different clusters, some no doubt wondering about the identity of the dork who just danced with an angel.

"She's not feeling jealous rage over me," said Kirby, shaking his head, "especially over a dance."

"For a man who is literally famous for being observant," said Mitch, "you can be completely clueless about women."

"This from a man," said Kirby, "who is famous for being clueless."

"At least you didn't get boner," added Mitch. "Nothing ruins your cool more than a public boner."

"I'm going to kill you Mitch," said Kirby, "with my own bare hands. Not only can I do it, I'm pretty sure I'll get away with it."

"You'll have to catch me first," said Mitch. "I can be quite nimble when I have to be, then you have to face the police."

"Remember," said Kirby, "I'm rich and white, I have ways to get out of trouble."

"Good point," said Mitch, "there's Molly over there."

Molly approached, making sure to swallow the last of her

little sandwich before speaking.

"I guess Mitch beat me to the punch with you dancing with Erica Cross."

"And he threatened to kill me," replied Mitch.

"Everyone's done that to you," added Molly, "and yet you're still alive."

The double doors swung open, revealing a tall blonde in a short blue dress.

"I've seen livelier funerals," declared the tall blonde, her voice loud and sharp enough to pierce the wall of music and slash right across the room.

"Sandy?" said Cooperman more surprised than pleased. "What are you doing here?"

"That's Sandra Doyle." declared Molly.

"Who is Sandra Doyle?" asked Kirby, watching the new arrival glide across to hug Cooperman and kiss the air next to each of the producer's cheeks.

"She's on one of those teen soaps," said Molly, "you know the kind of show where they have twenty-five-year-olds playing sixteen-year-olds with lots of money, and someone has a pregnancy scare every second episode."

"She's the one they cast to play the other Vengeance Sister?" asked Mitch.

Kirby nodded.

"I was able to clear my schedule," continued Sandra Doyle, "so I caught the first plane out of Los Angeles and came here. Did you know that there are a lot of funny looking people outside?"

"They're setting up for a comic book convention," said Cooperman, "we're doing some promotional stuff tomorrow, but we hadn't planned on you being here now."

"Well I'm here now," said Sandra.

"That's wonderful," said Cooperman without much sincerity. "We'll get you a seat at the panel tomorrow. Weatherby, get on that."

"I'm already on it," said Weatherby dialling his mobile.

"Where's my new 'sister?'" asked Sandra.

Bruce stepped up beside Kirby.

"This isn't good," he said.

"What do you mean?" asked Kirby.

"She was gunning for Erica's part," explained Bruce, "and word is that she can be six kinds of bitch when she doesn't get what she wants."

"Hello," said Erica coming from the bar with a tropical drink in hand, "I'm so pleased to meet you."

"I'm sure you are," replied Sandra. "So Max," she continued, "she's pretty enough, but was she a good enough lay to be worth the lead role?"

Kirby saw Erica's mouth open, and her eyes widen in shock.

"Don't be coy girl," said Sandra, "I've read the websites, you gotta give head to get ahead."

Erica's arm jerked, and her drink shot out of its glass and straight into Sandra Doyle's face.

"You bitch!" screamed Sandra, the tiny paper umbrella hanging from her long hair.

"I'm the bitch?" asked Erica backing away from Sandra. "How dare–"

Sandra stormed off, swung open the big double door and disappeared into the convention centre.

"Oh my God," muttered Erica, and Kirby could see that she was horrified at what just happened.

"Sandy!" called out Cooperman as he followed Sandra out the door.

All eyes were on Erica, whose alabaster face was turning red. Andi was coming across the room to her.

"Ladies and gentlemen!" called out a voice over the loudspeaker. It was Bruce, and all eyes turned to see him on Hack's DJ platform.

"For your entertainment," said Bruce, "we are pleased to present The Amazing Kirby Baxter!"

"Oh shit," said Kirby.

"Sorry about this," said Bruce, taking Kirby's arm and

leading him away from the DJ platform, "but Erica needs a distraction." Hack had rushed back to his control panel and aimed some of the lights at Kirby, making him the centre of attention.

"What do you expect me to do?" asked Kirby.

"Do one of those tricks your grandfather taught you," said Bruce, "I'm sure you can think of one quick, because the show must go on."

"Ah," said Kirby, "I'd like to do a trick for you, where I will make you believe that I have the power to read minds."

"Which one?" whispered Mitch. He had done this at industry events before. Usually with a lot more preparation.

"Get a deck of cards," said Kirby.

"Can I get a deck of cards?" Mitch asked the crowd.

Someone tossed Mitch a deck, still in the wrapper, which was perfect for Kirby. That was because all card companies packed them the same way, and Kirby had committed that way to memory before he had mastered the alphabet, and he had mastered the alphabet very young.

"Thank you," said Kirby. "Now I would like a volunteer from the audience."

Bruce took Erica by the hand and brought her forward. "Trust me," whispered Bruce, "this will help you."

"I want this lovely young lady," said Kirby, remembering the patter his grandfather taught him, "to pick a card. I don't want her to tell me which card it is. In fact, I will be outside this room while she picks it. And to make it even more challenging, I am instructing this lovely young lady to pick a card and while I'm in the next room, she is to give that card to someone she trusts. The rest of the deck will then be distributed to the other party guests. I will then read this lovely young lady's mind to find out, not only the card, but who is holding it."

"Do you remember how to do this one?" asked Mitch.

Kirby shrugged. It had been a couple of years since he tried this particular trick, but he literally had decades of practice. He spent every summer of his childhood at

Charlatan's Cove, studying, practicing and learning. Critics and fans praised Kirby's skills at seeing and interpreting tiny subtle details, skills that his grandfather taught him while teaching him tricks like this.

"Bruce," said Kirby, "I need you to keep an eye on the door to make sure for everyone that I'm not peeking. Mitch, when all the cards are distributed, I want you to knock on the door."

"I got it." Mitch knew exactly what he had to do.

"Can he really do this?" asked Andi Hack.

"Let's just say," answered Molly, "that when it comes to Kirby and cards, I would never play poker against him."

"I'm so sorry," said Bruce as he led Kirby through a side door leading to a white painted concrete hallway. "It's just that that bitch ambushed Erica."

"I understand," said Kirby. "Make sure the door is shut tight."

"You don't want to peek?" asked Bruce.

Kirby shook his head.

"Then how do you do the trick?" asked Bruce.

"I'll read their minds," answered Kirby with a wink before taking a deep breath.

Mitch knocked three times.

"Okay," said Kirby. "We're ready."

Bruce opened the door.

"Everyone is ready," said Mitch.

"Erica," said Kirby, wondering where the confidence in his voice came from, "take my hand."

Erica took his hand, and he let a finger drift toward her wrist, being careful not to be too obvious. The other party guests had lined up in front of Hack's DJ platform, each holding a card with the face pressed against their chest.

"Look into my eyes," said Kirby. "The eyes are the windows to the soul, and they will tell me what the card is and who you gave it to."

Her eyes twitched, a slight smile flashed on the corner of her mouth, then vanished. All the signs were in place.

Kirby looked over the crowd. He checked the usual suspects and paused.

Kirby's eyes narrowed, he studied the people standing in line very carefully, making sure that his finger remained on Erica's wrist.

A double game, he thought.

He led Erica across to the end of the line. Andi Hack stood stock still, fighting to keep her face a blank slate, which was always the biggest giveaway.

Down the line he went with Erica, holding her hand, trying to keep its soft delicacy from distracting him.

Two spots from the end of the line was Henry Hack. His face was a mask. He was good, but not that good.

Kirby placed his free hand on Henry's shoulder and said: "She first gave Andi a queen of hearts, but then you talked Andi into trading it with you."

The crowd erupted into applause as Henry held up the queen of hearts.

"Incredible," said Henry. "Absolutely incredible."

"The incredible Kirby Baxter everyone," called out Bruce. "Let's give him a hand."


"After Sandra showed," said Erica as she and Kirby stepped out of Room B and into the convention floor, "I thought I really blew it." Most of the workers were gone, and the last of the party guests had parted ways. "Thanks for coming to my rescue."

"It was nothing," said Kirby, trying to keep from blushing. "As much as I'd like to take credit for it, it was Bruce's idea. He found out I knew some tricks."

"You still stepped up," said Erica, "and played my hero beautifully."

For the first time in his life Kirby felt like saying 'aw shucks' without any irony.

"It's an old trick," said Kirby.

"You must tell me how you did it," said Erica.

"A magician must keep his secrets," said Kirby, "because

if you knew how I really did it, all the amazement would be gone because it's really pretty simple."

"I can understand that," said Erica. "I have an early day tomorrow, so I have to say goodnight."

She kissed his cheek. His cheek felt like it caught fire.

"Goodnight Kirby," said Erica.

"Goodnight," replied Kirby.

As Kirby watched her glide across the convention centre he felt Mitch's presence, or to be more accurate, his cologne, appear beside him.

"Would you like some alone time?" asked Mitch.

"Go bite yourself Mitch," said Kirby.

"It is kind of unfair," said Mitch, "she goes and starts the mower, but then doesn't cut the grass. Ain't that a woman for you?"

"I'm going to have Gustav break both of your legs," said Kirby, "and he'll do it for me, don't ever doubt it."

"Come guys," said Molly from her perch on Gustav's shoulder. "We have a big day tomorrow."

"He's not a ride," said Kirby, before turning to his valet. "You really shouldn't let her do this."

"I'm too drunk to walk," declared Molly, "and the temptation to finally be tall is just too much. Now mush!"

The corner of Gustav's mouth twitched slightly upward, which was as close to a laugh as his stony face ever let loose in public.

Kirby was about to say something, but something else caught the corner of his eye.

"What was that?" asked Kirby, as he looked over at a bank of dark plasma screens.

"What was what?" asked Mitch.

"I thought I saw something over there," said Kirby.

"Whatever it was," said Molly, "it's gone now. And I do believe I said 'mush!'"

They all walked, or rode, back to their suite, Kirby still feeling the warmth of Erica's lips against his cheek.

Kirby stepped out of the shower. As usual Gustav had come in the night before and laid out everything Kirby would need in a neat row next to the sink. Shaving cream, deodorant, toothpaste, toothbrush and a bottle of talcum powder. The deodorant was an extra strength brand made for athletes, not that Kirby was particularly athletic, it's just that crowded convention floors tend to get very hot very quickly and the ventilation is never what it should be. That meant that Kirby, like any man in a similar situation, had an expiration date. The talcum powder was there for similar reasons, making sure his nether regions didn't become 'never' regions.

Kirby was able to dress very quickly without hunting through his luggage, having pre-chosen his softest and lightest pair of jeans – which also had a couple of extra pockets – and a t-shirt with the cover art for Kirby's best-selling Shadowknight issue printed on the chest, for Gustav to lay out for him next to his toiletries. The Shadowknight t-shirt was just in case he ran into Ashmore again. Kirby wasn't by nature a petty man, but he wasn't above enjoying a little pettiness when he thought it had been earned.

Kirby stepped out into his bedroom, the curtains were wide open and the morning sun peeked from between the high buildings. He woke up extra early, wanting to get to the convention floor before the crowds got too thick and once there reconnect with old friends, and hopefully score some sweet deals. There had always been things he wanted to buy at conventions, but couldn't afford, but the situation was extremely different now, and damn it he was going to indulge himself for a change.

Gustav, ever the model of efficiency, had also pre-packed what Kirby called his 'Con-bag.' When Kirby had first told Gustav about the Con-bag back in London the big man nodded and asked Kirby for the bag and a list of what he needed in it. The Con-bag itself was Israeli army surplus, could be slung over the shoulder and, for its size, had an interior capacity second only to Doctor Who's Tardis. Kirby had a variety of pencils; pens; and black, red and metallic Sharpie markers; tucked into the bag's heavy cloth hoops which had originally been designed for rifle bullets. Kirby packed the pens, pencils and markers for impromptu sketches and autographs on any material and in the most visible colours available. Kirby Baxter may have been out of the comic book game for two years and wasn't attending the convention in any official capacity, but still had fans, and was also a fan himself. Inside one of the outside pouches were a small travel toothbrush, a mini tube of toothpaste and a small bottle of mouthwash, for freshening up after meals. In another outside pouch were three small plastic tubes, one held aspirin, another held antacid tablets and another contained a dose of pink all-purpose stomach remedy. Con-food wasn't exactly great food, or even good food, but the combo of mystery meats, grease and preservatives served by vendors at the convention centre was both Kirby's opiate and his kryptonite.

Inside the bag's main area was a brand new sketchpad for giving away sketches for fans and for trading sketches with other artists, an autograph book, a camera with two fresh batteries and two extra memory cards in reserve in a zippered inside pocket. The other inside area kept several cloth shopping bags, tightly twisted into narrow tubes. The plan was for Kirby to call Gustav to come collect whatever he bought and take them back to the suite to prepare them for shipping back to Long Island. Kirby had suggested that the big man take the weekend off, but Gustav considered any duties not involving the sort of trouble they encountered in Europe a holiday.

Kirby slung his Con-bag's long strap over his shoulder and put on his best sneakers. They were relatively new, that meant that they both looked good and smelled good, but he made sure they were well broken in long beforehand. He had once made the mistake of wearing new, fresh off the shelf, sneakers to DragonCon in Atlanta and his feet were ready to fall off before the first day was done. Never again, that's why he bought these sneakers several months in advance and carefully prepared them for the occasion.

Kirby's plan was to let everyone else sleep in, catch some breakfast in the hotel's ground floor coffee shop and use his VIP pass to slip in before the official grand opening so he could spend some time reconnecting with friends before the chaos of the day kicked into high gear. He opened his bedroom door and stepped into the suite's main living area. It was quiet, with sunlight creeping across the floor from the wide bank of windows overlooking the balcony. Kirby scribbled a note on hotel stationary telling the others to have room service breakfast on him and meet him on the floor when they were ready, and he left it on the table.

Before he opened the door to leave, he turned and looked around at the sheer grandness of the suite. A tiny part of him, dwelling deep inside, still refused to believe that this was his life now.

Kirby checked his teeth in the washroom mirror; clean, white and not a stray fleck of food in sight. He snapped his mini travel toothbrush back in its holder and tucked it and the mini tube of toothpaste back in the side pocket of his Con-bag. Breakfast had been simple and light, he wanted to be nimble on his feet. He had people to see, things to do, and he couldn't afford to be weighed down.

He had just stepped into the far stall to get rid of some of the morning's coffee and closed the door when the washroom's main door opened.

"Do you have it?" asked a voice. The accent sounded French Canadian, pronouncing 'have' as 'av' and 'it' as 'eet.' Kirby froze in place, standing above the toilet with his fly halfway down. Something about this was making him tense.

"I have it," said another voice that Kirby recognized. It was Max Cooperman, but for the first time Kirby heard what sounded like nerves jangling in his voice. Kirby heard paper being passed.

"Do you want to count it?" asked Cooperman.

"I will trust you that far," said the French accented voice.

"Remember," said Cooperman, "you have to get the timing just right."

"I know my job," said the French accented voice. "You just remember your part of the job, and don't fuck it up. You go first."

Kirby heard Cooperman muttering something to himself, then footsteps, and the washroom door opening, then closing.

He peeked a little out of the washroom stall and caught a glimpse of the other man washing his hands in front of the mirror. He only saw the face for a second before he retreated back into the stall. Then he listened to footsteps, then the door opening and closing. After a second Kirby accepted that he was all alone in the washroom, and he stepped out of the stall.

What was that all about?

"Welcome to OmniCon," announced a voice over the loudspeakers. "The special panel for the upcoming Vengeance Sisters movie will be at eleven thirty on the main stage in Room A. The first round of the cosplay pageant will be in Room B, at two thirty this afternoon, with music provided by the 'H-Bomb' Show. Have fun everybody."

Kirby got in early thanks to his VIP pass, and he and Teddy Ricci watched the crowd roll in.

"Looks like a good crowd," said Teddy.

"Yeah," said Kirby. The incoming horde was the usual opening day hardcore fans. Some were in costume, either for the competition or just to show off, and some of the others were dressed in their most comfortable and practical travel clothes.

"Let's hope they all brought cash," added Teddy. "Baby needs a new pair of shoes."

"And by 'baby' you mean favourite hooker?" asked Kirby.

"Good thing my wife's back in Chicago," said Teddy, "so she doesn't have to hear you dip into the blue ink."

"What have you heard about some Wilco art being up for sale?" asked Kirby.

Teddy shrugged. "Just some rumours," he said, "but no one who is supposed to know what's happening is admitting that they know anything, so everyone else doesn't know anything for certain."

"What were we talking about again; I kind of lost the plot somewhere in there?"

"I don't know anymore," said Teddy. "It's really early and I was up late last night, though I was not up as late as you. How was your first Hollywood party?"

"The music was loud," said Kirby, "most people just talked the sort of business that I know nothing about, but there were a few bright spots."

"I know that," said Teddy with a leering grin, "I know all about that."

"Why are you talking like that?" asked Kirby.

"Talking like what?"

"Like that guy in the Monty Python sketch," said Kirby, "all 'nudge, nudge, wink, wink, say no more.'"

Teddy Ricci's impish smile grew as he took out his laptop, clicked on his web browser and clicked to a bookmarked website.

Kirby almost fainted.

"What the hell!"

It was a gossip website, and beneath a photo of what looked like Kirby Baxter and Erica Cross in a passionate clinch was the headline: GORGEOUS GLAMOUR GAL GLOMS GEEKY GAZILLIONAIRE.

Kirby felt his face start to burn.

"Put that away," he said.

"I was thinking about printing it on a t-shirt," said Teddy.

"Don't give Mitch any ideas," pleaded Kirby. "Oh jeez."

"What's your problem?" asked Teddy, "I know you like to keep your private life private, but right now you are the King of Stud Mountain."

Kirby leaned on the counter and breathed deeply.

"I had my money on you scoring pretty well," continued Teddy, "but this is quite literally a home run hit right out of the park."

"Nothing happened," said Kirby. "She just kissed me on the cheek to thank me for doing some magic tricks at the party."

"Sure, I'm sure some tricks and magic were involved," said Teddy with a knowing wink. "Nudge, nudge, wink, wink, say no more."

"This is terrible," said Kirby.

"What's so terrible?"

"She's a good person," said Kirby, "she's really nice, and she's under a lot of pressure, especially from these tabloids."

"I get it," said Teddy, "you don't want these things ruining any chance you might have."

"I don't have a chance," said Kirby, "I just don't want to see anyone get hurt."

"You might get hurt," said Teddy, "if Molly sees this picture."

"She knows what really happened because she was there. In fact, she literally had a bird's eye view of the whole thing," said Kirby, then he paused for a beat, "and besides, why would she care?"

Teddy Ricci just shook his head and said: "Sometimes my dear boy, you can be a pretty dull pencil when it comes to the women closest to you."

"You're the second person who said something like that

to me this weekend."

"Who was the first?" asked Teddy.

"Mitch."

"He'd know," said Teddy.

"Know what?" asked Kirby.

"I live in a different city," said Teddy, "I only talk to you guys through the internet, and at conventions like this, and even I know that Molly's been sweet on you for years."

"Sweet on me?" asked Kirby. "Am I trapped in some old fashioned romantic comedy from the fifties?"

"Even Gidget and Frankie Avalon know she likes you," said Teddy. "Come on, I've seen you tell people what they are thinking just by looking at them, and you still can't see that because she's right in your blind spot."

"She's not really interested in me," said Kirby.

"The signs were definitely there."

"What signs?"

"Remember how much she hated Zoë?" asked Teddy.

"Everybody hated Zoë," said Kirby. "I believe Mitch said that I should stick with our own kind. He even did a song about it at my birthday party."

"Mitch didn't like Zoë because Zoë didn't understand us and looked down on us," said Teddy, "however Molly despised Zoë. I'm talking teeth-grinding daggers out of the eyes snap into a full blown catfight if she had the chance kind of hate. Women can be very territorial, they don't like outsiders in their territory, and Molly's territory includes your skinny backside."

"I think you're seeing things that aren't there," said Kirby.

Teddy shrugged. "I think you are so good at seeing the minuscule that it's keeping you from seeing the obvious."

"And you've obviously got some customers," said Kirby, cocking his head to the people gathering around Teddy's booth. "I need to go for a walk."

Kirby stepped away from Teddy's booth and sauntered across the convention floor. Convention goers milled around him, each one looking for their favourite artists, characters and merchandise. Some were in costume, and Kirby noticed that some of those people looked really good in their outfits. Some others really should have gone for Jabba the Hutt over Poison Ivy. Kirby's head was swimming, Teddy had to be busting his balls over Molly, he just had to be. Sure, Molly did hate Zoë, but there were a hundred reasons for Molly to hate Zoë, and none of them involved her having any serious feelings for Kirby. Teddy had to be just playing a silly game to embarrass him, he had to be, no matter what the little signs that Kirby normally trusted screamed at him.

A bump and a quick apology from a passing Cobra Commander snapped Kirby out of his reverie, and he suddenly became re-aware of the world around him. He caught the smell of a brand of cologne that reminded him of old leather and that smell meant only one thing to him, Kevin LaGuardia was here.

Kirby turned to see LaGuardia, the editor, not the airport, talking to a tall thin man in a long coat and fedora pulled low over his head, and a bottle of Pepsi in his right hand. "Hey," said Kirby waving, "Kevin."

"Oh," said LaGuardia, "hi Baxter." LaGuardia then tapped his companion on the arm, and the man shuffled off into the crowd.

"How are things going at Atlantic?" asked Kirby.

"What?" asked LaGuardia, watching his companion disappear into the throng. "Oh, right," he said, "I'd say things were all right, but that wouldn't be the truth."

"Then how are things," asked Kirby, "for real?"

"Things are pretty tense," answered LaGuardia, "Ashmore's family is riding his ass to sell the company, and you know what happens when a company changes owners. They break out the new brooms and nobody knows if they're going to get canned or keep their job."

"That does sound pretty tense."

LaGuardia shrugged. "The funny thing is that we've all got to be smiles and sunshine for The Vengeance Sisters panel, but that sucker could sink us."

"So those rumours are true?"

"Worse than true," replied LaGuardia, as he checked his watch. "If the sale doesn't go through, things could be a lot worse than just uncertainty. Sorry, but I got to go. I'll see you around."

"Sure."

"You have the entire run?" asked Kirby.

"It's all here," said Doug, from Toronto's Silver Snail comic shop. "Every Denny O'Neill and Neal Adams issue of Detective Comics."

Kirby leaned over and flipped through the contents of the row of long boxes. Every issue seemed to be there, carefully wrapped in Mylar bags.

"They all seem to be here."

"They're also in mint condition," said Doug. Then he shrugged. "Okay, the twelfth and the seventeenth are more near mint, but you really can't get much better at the price we're offering."

Kirby looked over the price tag. It was reasonable, especially in the light of Kirby's financial situation. As he studied the boxes he calculated the cost of shipping them to Charlatan's Cove and realized that even then it was still a good deal. He was still going to haggle a little, because that was all part of the fun.

"Okay," said Kirby. "It's all very interesting."

"I can make it more interesting," added Doug with a wink as he put some comics on the counter that Kirby was very familiar with, "I have ten mint condition copies of Shadowknight number 534," that was the issue where Kirby snuffed out the venerable hero's rather grating sidekick, which marked the beginning of the book's renaissance, "and some autographs might get you an extra ten per cent off the whole deal."

"I think we have a deal," said Kirby, pulling one of his autograph pens from his Con-bag.

"If you're staying in the Waterloo we can have these boxes

sent to your room," offered Doug, as Kirby signed the ten issues, "save you the hassle of lugging them around."

"I have someone coming down to pick them up," said Kirby, as he passed over the signed issues with his credit card. "You can't miss him."

"Aren't you Kirby Baxter?" asked a voice from behind him.

Kirby turned and found himself looking at a vaguely familiar face.

"We've never met," said the vaguely familiar face, a mid-sized man wearing horn-rimmed glasses beneath unruly blond hair, "but I'm a big fan."

Something clicked and Kirby now recognized the visitor.

"You're Grant Upton," semi-asked Kirby.

"That's right; I guess my reputation precedes me." Upton came out of Silicon Valley, and the reputation that preceded him everywhere he went was of a comic book super-fan with a passion for rare pieces and the cash, courtesy of his software empire, to back it up. He was probably one of the few people attending the convention who was richer than Kirby himself.

"What brings you here?" asked Kirby. Collectors of Upton's stature usually had the mountain brought to them instead of coming to the mountain themselves.

"Oh," said Upton, becoming uncomfortable. "Business. I had some business here in Toronto, and I decided to pop into the convention and see what's happening."

"That's good," said Kirby.

"I'd love to finagle some original art from you," said Upton, "there's a wall in my office that really needs one of your Shadowknight sketches."

"I'll see what I can do," replied Kirby as Doug passed him back his credit card.

"I also heard that you're an expert on Dick Wilco," said Upton.

Kirby shrugged. "I guess you can say that."

"Is it true that you actually know him?"

"Yes," replied Kirby, "he was a friend of my grandfather's, and he taught me how to draw when I was a kid."

"Oh, really," said Upton.

"Grant," said Madden who suddenly appeared beside Grant Upton. "I have those pieces you were looking for."

"What?" asked Upton.

"You should come and see them," said Madden in a voice heavy with meaning.

"Oh, right," said Upton. "I'll see you later Kirby."

"Sure," said Kirby as Madden ushered Upton away, wondering what that was all about.

"So it's not a problem to get these wrapped and shipped?" asked Kirby.

Gustav nodded as he put the last long-box on the dolly provided by the concierge and snapped a bungee cord in place to keep them locked in. Kirby had gone a little nutty with the shopping in the last couple of hours, but even the stingier imps of his nature were telling him that for the first time in his life he really could afford more than all he ever wanted.

"There you are," said Mitch as he appeared, dressed in jeans and a black t-shirt with the face of Boris Karloff from The Mummy emblazoned across the front. "I've been looking for you for over an hour."

"We do have phones," said Kirby pointing to the little disposable one clipped to his belt which he bought for the trip, "you could have called."

Mitch shrugged. "I could," he said, "but then I wouldn't have run into Teddy Ricci."

"Shit," said Kirby.

"Relax," said Mitch, "I didn't get it printed on a shirt. The line in front of the t-shirt printer's a little long right now."

"Gee thanks," replied Kirby.

"So," said Mitch, adding weight to every letter of every word, "have you seen Molly yet?"

"No," replied Kirby, "I'm assuming that she's getting

ready for the movie panel."

"Yeah," added Kirby, "I'm sure that's it."

"Yes, it probably is."

"How about your supermodel girlfriend?"

"Erica is not my girlfriend," said Kirby, "and we are not back in the sixth grade, even though you could pass for it."

Mitch smiled and an exasperated Kirby turned back to Gustav. "You can take those back up to the suite; we'll wrap them up for shipping later."

Gustav nodded, Kirby thanked him, and the big man wheeled the dolly to the exit.

"I noticed that TMZ called you the 'Geeky Gazillionaire,'" added Mitch as Gustav left.

"Yeah," said Kirby, "so what?"

"I always had you down as more of a dweeb than a geek," concluded Mitch.

"You're too kind."

"You should pop down to artist's alley," said Mitch, "there are guys you've idolized your whole life who want your autograph now."

"So that's how I finally achieved the admiration of my peers."

"Face it," said Mitch, "you're a rich, talented comic book artist who has a real life supermodel with a bad case of the screaming thigh sweats for you. You're living the dream of every man."

"And yet I have to put up with you?" asked Kirby.

Mitch shrugged. "It's your cross to bear that we live in the age of snark against the more fortunate. I blame the internet."

"I blame that deep down, you're a little asshole."

"Guilty as charged," said Mitch, "by the way, I got a line on a source of Freezie Pops."

"It's nice to see that your life's dream will finally be fulfilled."

"I'm going to slip out this afternoon and pick up a box or two," said Mitch, "then I have to figure out how to ship some home to New York."

"Don't even think about sneaking those leaky things into my boxes," declared Kirby. "Remember, Gustav has skills, very scary skills."

"Note taken." Mitch checked his watch. "The Vengeance Sisters panel will be starting in a bit. Let's go get a good spot. Maybe we'll catch a good catfight."

"Molly and Erica?" asked Kirby. "Now you are dreaming."

"Actually I was thinking about Erica and Sandra Doyle," answered Mitch. "I wonder what Freud would say about that little slip."

"He'd probably diagnose you as being completely full of shit," said Kirby, before giving Mitch a friendly clip on the ear.

ISSUE #7
POST PARTY DEPRESSION

"Goodnight everybody," announced Henry Hack from his DJ platform.

The music hit a deafening crescendo then started to fade. The crowd cheered and clapped and some fans kicked in and began blowing out the fog which carpeted the floor. The doors opened and people, many in costume, started milling out onto the main convention floor.

"Did you see your little supermodel friend?" said Molly, her voice poking through the curtain of sound that still hung over his ears.

"No," said Kirby, "she's been in interviews all day." It was good that Molly was talking to him again. He hadn't seen her all day and was worried that she was avoiding him. She was in her semi-official Con-uniform; a t-shirt showing the comic book versions of The Vengeance Sisters, loose-fitting black jeans, and black and white checkered high-top sneakers.

"I talked to her a bit before the panel," said Molly. "She saw the picture and hoped you weren't embarrassed."

"According to Teddy Ricci I'm the 'King of Stud Mountain,'" replied Kirby. "But I was worried that the whole business might hurt her feelings."

"She told me it wasn't the first time that happened," said Molly with a shrug, "in fact, she said the paparazzi do that to her all the time. Exaggerate a hug here, a kiss on the cheek there, or just plain Photoshop something together, and then they have a wild romance to write about."

"Now I know how she feels."

"The whole thing has shattered what little faith I had in the tabloid media," added Molly as they stepped out onto the convention's main floor. The big windows and skylights were all pitch black, and the whole area had that sickly pale appearance from the massive banks of lights hanging from the high ceiling.

They walked in silence for a moment, the murmur of the thinning party crowd fading around them.

"I'm sorry I've been a jerk today," said Molly.

"What do you mean?"

"I've been avoiding you," explained Molly, "when I first saw that picture on my laptop this morning I got all pissy. Probably the hangover talking, because I was actually there and saw the whole thing–"

"You did have a bird's-eye view," added Kirby.

"Yeah, I did," replied Molly, "then, after I talked to Erica at the panel, I ended up feeling like an ass."

"Why would you feel like an ass?"

"I just did," said Molly, "mostly because I did avoid you this morning over that picture, and after I realized what an idiot I was, I avoided you because I felt bad for avoiding you like an ass."

"Well, we're here now," said Kirby.

"Yes," said Molly, "and I–"

"Aloha kiddies," said Teddy Ricci, resplendent in an ocean blue Hawaiian shirt and bright green Bermuda shorts, as he came from behind his table to take both of them by the arm. "You're just in time, the Luau Room is open for business."

"That's great," said Molly, lacking her usual excitement for the Luau Room.

"It sure is," said Teddy as he pushed open the curtain of bamboo chains at the entrance of his makeshift little tavern.

"You've really outdone yourself this time," said Kirby.

He had outdone himself. The room itself was more like a high-walled cubicle with a series of wood and canvas panels formed into a rough square. The panels were then plastered with travel posters of Hawaii, plastic coconuts and faux tropical foliage, including paper flower leis hanging from a coat rack. Four folding tables lined the walls, with little hula-dancer lamps on them, giving the place a pale orange glow. The tables were full of familiar faces, mostly other artists, writers and editors, sipping tropical drinks and talking shop with a handful of the convention's top organizers. Don Ho music played low from an MP3 player plugged into some speakers at the bar.

"The blame falls on Keith over there," said Teddy pointing to a skinny guy in a mostly greenish Hawaiian shirt tending bar. "He's my website's regional manager and his girlfriend teaches set design at Ryerson's theatre school. She got the panels and the furniture, and then we raided some thrift shops for the rest. Mind you, moving the shelves full of merchandise in and out is a bit of a hassle, but it's worth it."

"This is impressive," said Kirby.

"Time for you two to get lei'd."

Teddy Ricci pulled a pair of paper flower necklaces off the coat rack and draped one each on Kirby and Molly. "Come and have a drink. Keith makes a bitching Mai Tai."

"Sure," said Molly, sitting on a stool at the bar. "I need to catch up on my alcoholism."

"At least you'll be a cheap drunk," said Kirby.

"What does that mean?"

"I have luggage that weighs more than you," said Kirby, "and my shaving kit can hold more booze than you."

"That sounds like a challenge," said Molly, waving to Keith the regional manager/volunteer bartender. "Let's have two of your Mai Tai things here. And what do want Kirby?"

"Very funny," said Kirby.

"I have to get off my feet," said Molly. "After the panel Ashmore and Cooperman had me doing interviews with every podcast and website that wasn't deemed worthy of talking to any of the movie's stars. I have to admit that, after that panel, doing the interviews was kind of relaxing."

"Yeah," said Kirby, "I got the feeling that their movie set is not going to be a happy place to work."

"Nowhere near," said Molly. "The moment the cameras were off, Ashmore and Cooperman were ready to kill each other, and you could catch frostbite from the vibes coming off Sandra Doyle when anyone showed any attention to Erica."

"I could see it from the audience," said Kirby.

"So," said Teddy Ricci, "did you have a chance to talk to your new supermodel friend?"

"No," said Kirby.

"I did," said Molly. "Managed to get a few words with her before the party but it wasn't much because she was whisked off for an interview with Entertainment Tonight Canada."

"Canada has its own Entertainment Tonight?" asked Teddy.

"Apparently," said Molly.

"What do they cover?" asked Ted.

"I guess they spend a lot of time stalking Christopher Plummer," said Kirby.

"Christopher Plummer is Canadian?" asked Molly.

"Yeah," said Kirby, amazed that someone didn't know that simple fact. "How can someone know so much about show business and not know that Christopher Plummer is Canadian."

"I always thought he was like British or something," pleaded Molly in her own defence.

"Really?"

"I thought he was Australian," said Teddy with a shrug.

"I feel like I just walked into a Philip K. Dick novel, nothing makes sense anymore," asked Kirby.

"Have a Mai Tai," said Keith.

"Then take either the red pill or the blue pill," said Teddy with a laugh.

"Maybe you should have used Shatner," said Molly, taking a sip of her second drink of the night.

"What?" asked Kirby, still nursing his first.

"For your Canadian actor reference," said Molly. "You should have used William Shatner."

"That was almost an hour ago," said Kirby.

"Sorry I'm late," said Molly, "I spent some time lost in the wonders of these Mai Tais."

"Shatner's Canadian?" asked Teddy.

"Don't you start," ordered Kirby.

"You should keep this Keith fellow," said Molly. "The world needs good bartenders."

"He's not a bad manager either," added Teddy, "but don't tell him I said that. He might ask for a raise."

"Where's Mitch?" asked Molly.

Kirby shrugged.

"I don't know," said Kirby. "It's not like him to skip a session at the Luau Room. It gives him a chance to wear his lucky shirt."

Molly shuddered. Mitch's lucky shirt made Teddy's look positively demure. The front was your standard conglomeration of palm trees on a pale blue background, but the back was what made it special. Mitch had painted the back of the shirt himself with his airbrush kit, carefully composing colours and lines to create the unforgettable image of Princess Leia, in coconut bra and grass skirt, dancing the hula next to a ukulele-playing Mr. Spock, in his original series Starfleet uniform shirt and grass skirt, while the Death Star hung in the sky with a flower necklace around its equator.

Yet there was no sign of Mitch or his shirt.

"Hello?" asked a voice from the door.

"Come on in," said Teddy. "All are welcome here on the island."

Andi Hack's head popped in through the bamboo curtain.

"Hello Mr. Baxter," said Andi as she saw Kirby at the bar. "Have you seen my husband?"

Kirby shook his head.

"Grab a stool and have a drink," said Teddy. "I'm making

a batch of Margaritas and the pretty ladies drink free and by free, I mean on Kirby's tab."

"How can a girl say no to that," said Andi as she came in. She had changed from the little black number she had worn at the opening night party to a pair of denim cut-offs, a men's white dress shirt that only added to her femininity, and a large white purse slung over her shoulder. "Henry's a big boy, so I guess I could continue my search later."

"You don't know where Henry is?" asked Molly.

"He's probably off talking business," said Andi. "He's not finished one show before he's on the phone hustling for another one. This is a nice little set-up."

"Thank you," said Teddy.

"Oh," said Kirby, "I'm being an idiot. Teddy Ricci owns Trader Ted's online store, and he's our host for this evening. Teddy, this is Andi–"

"Andrea Stallworth," said Teddy, "the model." Then he said to Kirby in his own defence: "My wife's a buyer for a clothing store chain. Our house is divided equally between comics and issues of Vogue."

"It's Hack now," said Andi, "but thanks for remembering an old war horse like me."

"It wasn't that long ago," said Teddy, passing her a newly made Margarita.

"It's a lifetime and a half in the modelling business," added Andi as she tasted her Margarita, "this is delicious."

"By the way," Andi asked Kirby, "where's your big friend?"

"Gustav's a big believer in a good night's sleep," said Kirby, "and it is," he checked his watch, "past one thirty in the morning."

"I should just call Henry," said Andi, opening her capacious purse.

While Andi searched her bag, Molly leaned over to Kirby.

"Kirby?" she asked.

"Yes," he said.

"I want to tell you something," said Molly, "something

that I can only say because I got a belly full of Mai Tai."

"What is it?"

"Hello," said Bruce Haring's voice from outside the door. "Is anyone in there?"

"Is that Bruce?" asked Molly.

"Come on in," said Teddy.

"Looks like you've got a little party going on here," said Bruce as he came in.

"Can we get you a Margarita stranger?" asked Teddy.

"No, thank you anyway," answered Bruce, "I'm still on the job so to speak."

"Teddy," said Kirby, "this is Bruce Haring, he's Erica's assistant."

"Nice to meet you," said Teddy.

"What's wrong?" asked Molly.

"Found it," announced Andi, "oh, sorry. Now, can I get this damn thing to work?"

"It's Erica," said Bruce. "She's not in her room and she's got a wake-up call in five hours."

"I could call her?" asked Andi holding up her iPhone.

"I've got her phone right here," said Bruce, pulling another iPhone out of his elegantly tailored jacket.

"Well," said Andi, "I'm going to call my husband, maybe he's... Shit."

"What?" asked Kirby.

"I must be tired," said Andi, "I just dialled my own home. It's unlikely for anyone to be there now." Andi's fingers danced across the iPhone's touchscreen.

A blood curdling scream sliced through the relaxed swaying melodies of Don Ho. The few remaining Luau Room customers all sat up straight. Their ears pricked up to make sure that they really heard what just happened.

"What was that?" asked Kirby.

"It sounded like Erica," said Bruce. "Erica!"

"Where did it come from?" asked Teddy as everyone stepped out of the makeshift Luau Room and onto the convention floor.

"Over there," said Molly, pointing to Artist's Alley.

"No," said a penciller from Marvel, pointing to Room A, the open entrance still draped with material from The Vengeance Sisters movie, "it came from over there."

"Don't be stupid," said an inker from DC, "the scream was over by the main entrance."

"Where did it come from Kirby?" asked Molly, trusting her old friend's legendary sense of hearing.

"I don't know," said Kirby, and he didn't. He really couldn't place where it came from. In fact, it seemed to come from everywhere. "There must be some kind of weird echo in this hall or something."

"What do we do?" asked Bruce.

Kirby took out his cell phone and pointed at the inker and the penciller. "You two go to the main door and get the security guard. I'll call Gustav."

"Why Gustav?" asked Bruce as the two artists ran to the main door.

"It's just good to have him around when there's trouble," said Kirby as he hit the speed dial. "Hello, Gustav, could you come down to the convention floor. Something's happened." Kirby hung up. "He'll be here in five minutes. Okay, we need to look around and to do that we have to split up. I suggest we stay in groups. Teddy and Keith, could you help Bruce and Andi look, you know the layout pretty well?"

"Sure," said Teddy.

"Molly," said Kirby, "I'd like you to stick with me. We're going to get hotel security."

"You got it captain," said Molly.

"Okay," said Kirby, "wait for the guard from the main door before you start looking around."

"Okay," said Bruce.

"Let's go."

"Mitch?" asked Kirby, as he opened the door into the hotel. "There you are."

"Yes," said Mitch, wearing his homemade Hawaiian shirt and a stupid grin on his face, "I'm here, when I'm supposed to be in there, but this guy doesn't believe my VIP all access pass."

The security guard, a big bear of a man, turned to look over Kirby. "Is he with you sir?"

"Yes," said Kirby, "but we need both of you in here."

"What for?" asked the security guard.

"Someone screamed," said Kirby, "but we can't find them."

"It sounded like Erica," added Molly.

"Damn," said Mitch, "I leave you people alone for a little while and it all goes to hell."

"Get in here, you can help with the search," ordered Kirby.

The elevator door in the lobby chimed and Gustav came out. He had left his usual black suit jacket back at the suite, meaning his shoulder holster and pistol were out in the open.

"Holy shit," said Mitch, "the big guy's packing heat."

"I can't let you go in there with that," said the security guard.

Gustav pulled a card holder out of his pocket and showed a card inside to the guard.

"Oh," said the security guard, "sorry, come on in."

"What did he show him?" asked Mitch.

"It doesn't matter," said Kirby. "Get in here."


"Erica!" cried out Bruce, his voice echoing across the vast expanse of the otherwise dead and silent convention hall.

"She's not in here," said Mitch, pulling his head out of the Dark Horse Comics booth.

"Not here," said Molly from the Image Comics booth.

"Erica!" echoed again from across the hall, this time it was Andi Hack.

Kirby didn't say anything. He needed to concentrate on what he had heard, he needed to understand what had happened to figure out where it had come from. Something wasn't adding up.

"The concierge checked her suite again," said the security guard as he clipped his walkie-talkie back to his vest. "There's no sign of her in there."

"We heard her in here," said Molly.

"What about Room B?" asked Kirby.

"What do you mean?" asked the guard.

"The reason we all disagree on where the scream came from," said Kirby, "is that it came from all over."

"Now you're talking in riddles," said Mitch.

"Where's the centre of the public address system?" asked Kirby as he charged toward the door to Room B. "Where do they make all the announcements?"

"From the DJ booth in Room B," said Molly.

Kirby tried the door. It jiggled slightly, but wouldn't open. It was locked tight.

"Do you have a key?"

The security guard took a ring of keys off his belt and unlocked the door.

"Erica!" cried out Kirby as he charged in.

"Erica?" asked Kirby as stony silence greeted him.

"Maybe she left," said Mitch pointing to the side door. It was ajar, a crushed soda can propping it open. Gustav approached the door, opened it and looked into the hall on the other side. He shrugged, there was no sign of anyone in there.

"She's not in here," said Molly. "Maybe she saw a mouse and ran down the hallway."

"I don't know," said Kirby. "It doesn't make any sense at all."

"There's a microphone on somewhere," said the security guard. "I can hear us talking outside."

"Excuse me," said a voice from the main door. It was Henry Hack, still in the black blazer, jeans and t-shirt he had been wearing at the party. "What's going on? My wife called me and she is near hysterical."

"We heard Erica scream," explained Kirby, "I thought it came from here, but there's no sign of her."

"I'm sure it's nothing," said Mitch. "It's got to be."

"I hope you're right," said Kirby.

"I sent Andi back up to the suite to see if she's come back," added Henry. "Why is everything on? Did any of you touch anything?"

"No," answered Kirby, "everything was like this when we got here."

Henry reached into his jacket pocket for the small tablet that he used as his remote control. The monitors suddenly went dark, and the electric hum of the dormant speakers disappeared.

"Now what do we do?" asked Mitch.

"Not much we can do," said Kirby. "She's not here, she's not anywhere. I think we should let hotel security check the rest of the building."

"Since we're all here and have to wait," said Mitch, "why don't we have a Freezie Pop?"

"What do you mean?" asked Kirby.

"Your friend asked if he could store some those things in my dry ice container," answered Hack. "Some sort of quick freeze."

"Sure," said Kirby, "might as well. Do you have any grape?"

"Grape coming up," said Mitch as he made his away to the back of the platform. "Any other orders?"

The others, except Gustav, asked for different flavours, and Mitch tried to open the freezer.

"Did you lock this?" asked Mitch.

Hack and Kirby went over to the deep freeze.

"I didn't lock it," said Hack, then he tried the lid. "It's stuck."

"Gustav," asked Kirby, "could you please give us a hand?"

Gustav nodded and one of his big hands gripped the corner of the lid, and with one heave wrenched it open. Pale mist poured out of the deep freeze and onto the floor.

"Oh hell!" screamed Mitch.

"Oh my God," gasped Hack.

Kirby looked into the deep freeze to see a pale delicate hand poking out of the mist.

"Erica!"

# VOLUME TWO

# THE DORK KNIGHT

ISSUE #8
THE LUNCH TRICK

Even though the city had banned smoking in all public buildings, police headquarters included, Detective Sergeant Elizabeth Darling swore she could still smell burnt tobacco. She suspected it hid beneath the flat white and grey paint which lined the walls, possibly nestled alongside the asbestos she was certain still lurked somewhere in the building's structure, waiting in ambush for her.

"I think we've left them stewing for long enough," grumbled Inspector Brian Spasky as he forced himself up from his chair. The chair's metal body let out a small groan of what Darling thought had to be relief.

"I'm not sure why we had to leave them stewing," said Darling, which was a lie, she was sure why. Spasky, her once illustrious boss, had to step out for a bit to 'check some files,' when she knew he was perfectly capable of looking up any files on his desktop. He had snuck out for a shot of something nasty at the tavern across the street, and Darling deduced that because he returned from the 'File Room' reeking of at least three different brands of breath mints.

"They're rich," said Spasky, "they're famous in their own weird little worlds, and they're foreign."

"Even the Americans?" asked Darling as she rubbed a squirt of sharp smelling sanitizer into her hands.

"Especially the Americans," grumbled Spasky. He then sighed, and went into his 'mentor mode' trying to teach the poor dim little policewoman something about detective work. "These people come to Canada and they think we're going to get on our knees to kiss their asses. We have to keep them off balance."

"What for?" asked Darling, biting back the temptation to make a comment about Spasky's own balance. "I thought you said this whole thing was probably an accident." In fact, during their time at the convention centre's Room B the words 'dumb bitch' and 'fallen on her ass' popped up several times.

"We might have a case of criminal negligence," said Spasky. "So I won't say no to a confession."

"Then who do we talk to first?" asked Darling.

"The limeys first," said Spasky as he put on his grey jacket and bulled his way down the hallway to the interrogation room.

"The Chief called while you were in the file room, he wants us to wrap this up before it gets all over the press," added Darling. That was true, almost a dozen world leaders were coming to Toronto in less than a week for a summit meeting, and word came from on high that when the summit started it was going to be all hands on a clear deck, ready for the oncoming security shitstorm.

"Really," said Spasky with an expression somewhere between a smile and a snarl, "I thought you'd have heard that straight from your Uncle Larry." He loved to bring up that Darling's maternal uncle was a Deputy Chief in charge of personnel, and imply that her advancement to Detective Sergeant by her thirtieth birthday had more to do with her relatives than her work. If anything Uncle Larry was more of a hindrance, forcing her to meet a higher standard, not just out of a desire to avoid playing favourites, but to see if she could measure up to the work done by the other members of her family, her father included.

However, even though Spasky was a Neanderthal, who treated her with all the warmth he'd show one of the many stains on his tie, the one redeeming quality he had was that he never pronounced her name as if he were some kind of campy reject from the British theatre. The cops who did that, and they were legion, always made her wish she could use her taser on them, just once.

"I thought I told you to keep everyone apart," growled Spasky as he looked in the window for Interrogation Room One. Inside the pale grey room sat Henry Hack and his wife Andi, they clung to each other like wet laundry. Darling didn't know who Henry Hack was, though the initial interview said he was some sort of celebrity DJ, but she did recognize the wife. Andrea Hack used to stare down from a billboard across from her apartment, demanding that her brand of lipstick was just what she needed for that nagging self-esteem problem. Darling never bought that lipstick.

"We were going to do that," said the uniformed officer, "but MacDougal needed Room Five for a drugs case, and these two raised holy hell when we tried to separate them."

"Have they talked about the case?" said Darling. The uniformed cop shook his head.

"They haven't talked about anything really. She cried a lot."

"We might as well try to make something out of this pig's arse-hole," grumbled Spasky as he went in.

"Are you in charge?" asked Henry Hack. Spasky nodded.

"I'm Inspector Brian Spasky," answered the detective as he took his seat across from them, "and this is my partner Sergeant Darling." Darling stood in the corner and crossed her arms. "We're recording this interview. Is that a problem?"

Henry and Andi Hack shook their heads. Darling noted that both their faces were wet from tears, and Andi kept a tissue balled up in her hand.

"What was your relationship with the victim?" asked Spasky.

Andi Hack blew her nose, while her husband rubbed his eyes.

"She was a friend," said Henry.

"She was my best friend," added Andi.

"Do you know why she was in Room B?" asked Darling from the corner.

Both shook their heads.

"The party was over," said Andi. "In fact, it had been over for at least an hour."

"And you were at something called the 'Luau Room' when you heard her fall?" asked Spasky, checking the notes made by the first officer at the scene, a thorough young cop named Chang.

"Yes."

"What is the Luau Room?" asked Spasky.

"It was a little after hours get-together," added Andi, "looked like comic book people mostly. I only stumbled on it when I was looking for Henry."

"Were you at this Luau Room Mr. Hack?" asked Darling.

Hack shook his head. "I had a call from a prospective client for a corporate gig, and I went someplace quiet to talk."

"Where was this quiet place?" asked Darling.

"Out behind the convention centre," answered Hack. "Out by the garbage bins. It was a complete tosser anyway."

"What do you mean?" asked Spasky.

"I couldn't get a word in edgewise," answered Hack. "The call kept cutting in and out. The reception turned to bollocks and it was mostly static."

"But you got the call from your wife?" asked Darling.

"After I gave up trying to talk to this client," said Hack, "the call from my wife did get through."

"How do you explain this erratic phone behaviour?" asked Spasky. "The reception's pretty good in that area."

"The call was long distance from Australia," answered Hack with a shrug, "that's the other side of the world. They must have been having bad weather, a bad connection, or something like that."

"Can we get this client's name?" asked Darling.

"That's it," said Hack, "I didn't get any one person's name. Just a text message to call a certain number belonging to some company called Bascomb Holdings in Australia, but all I got was an ear-load of static. I can give you the number, if it'll be any help."

"Let's get back to the case at hand," said Spasky. "I'd like to talk about this big freezer you keep in Room B."

"I use dry ice for my light and sound show," said Hack.

"Did you leave the freezer open after the show?" asked Spasky.

Hack shook his head. "No," he said, "I closed it tight, because if I didn't the freezer wouldn't work right, dry ice would evaporate, and I'd be screwed."

"So you closed it?" asked Spasky.

"Yes," restated Hack. "I had to. Would you like to ask that again? You can just loop the tape back for the answer, because it would still be the same. The freezer was closed, because it had to be closed."

"What about these Freezie Pops?" asked Spasky.

"We put those in before the party," answered Hack, "then we closed the lid, because you have to close the lid."

"Do you know any reason why Erica Cross would go back to Room B?" asked Darling, aiming it at Andi Hack who had been sitting quietly while her husband and Spasky talked.

Andi shook her head. "I don't know why. I'm not even sure how she got in. The room was supposed to be locked."

"Did you lock the doors?" asked Spasky.

"I have a key to the main doors, but the convention security was supposed to lock everything up," said Hack. "However, it looks like they missed something because someone propped open the emergency exit."

"We're going to talk to them," said Spasky. The older cop paused, scratched his thick moustache, and asked: "What do you know about Kirby Baxter and this bodyguard of his?"

"Your name is Gustav?" asked Darling.

The big man with the bald head and the bull-thick neck nodded. His hands, which reminded Darling of snow shovels, rested flat on the little white table, making it look even tinier. It was a mistake to put him in Room Three, the smallest of the interrogation rooms, because he pretty much filled it just by sitting there.

"Is that a first name or a last name?" asked Spasky, he wanted to know the difference, because it was the only name on his European Union passport.

Gustav shrugged.

"Okay, we can settle all that later," said Spasky. "According to Mr. Baxter's initial statement you've been working for him as a bodyguard and driver for a little more than a year and a half. Is that correct?"

Gustav nodded.

"You do understand English?" asked Spasky.

Gustav nodded.

"Man of few words?" asked Darling.

Gustav nodded again.

There was a knock on the door.

"You do know that you are not allowed to carry a firearm in Canada?" asked Spasky.

Gustav shook his head.

"You think you are allowed?" asked Darling.

There was a knock on the door. Darling opened it and a detective named Larson poked his head in.

"Hi," said Larson, "sorry to interrupt but that card you found, the one with all the symbols and numbers on it, it's legit."

"What do they mean?" asked Spasky.

"He really is allowed to carry a gun in Canada," said Larson poking in a manila folder. "You really should read this file, because I'm not sure if we're even allowed to question him."

Spasky looked at the printout Larson passed to him.

"I don't believe it." He passed it to Darling, who didn't believe it either, but she didn't make as big a deal about it.

"Is this for real?"

Larson nodded and Gustav shrugged.

"Are you still willing to talk to us?" asked Darling. Gustav nodded. According to the contents of this new file, both he and Baxter could just walk out if they felt like it, and there would be nothing the cops could do about it.

"Are you willing to tell us what you know about Molly Garret?" asked Spasky.

Darling took the seat this time and Spasky stood in the corner. Darling put her laptop on the table.

"Are you awake?" asked Darling, because the woman named Molly Garret had her head buried in her arms on the table of Room Two.

"Yes," moaned Garret. "I'm not sure if I'll ever sleep again."

She slowly lifted her head from the table and rested it on her hands.

"You don't look too well," said Darling.

"I don't feel too well," answered Molly, her brown hair a disheveled mess and her big brown eyes bloodshot. "I never saw a dead body before, plus, I think those tropical drinks I had are coming back to haunt me."

"Are you able to answer a few questions?"

Molly nodded.

"You're a comic book writer," asked Spasky.

"Yes," answered Molly.

"And this Baxter fellow is a comic book artist?" asked Spasky.

Molly nodded.

"He writes his own stuff too," said Molly. "He's actually pretty good at it."

"Are you two close?" asked Darling.

Molly nodded. "We're pretty good friends. We even worked on The Vengeance Sisters together for one of those big crossover events. We're very good friends."

"Are you sure it's not more than that?" asked Spasky from the corner.

"What?" asked Molly.

Darling popped open her laptop, revealing the picture of

Erica Cross kissing Kirby Baxter.

"Are you sure this didn't make you jealous?" asked Darling.

"I really don't want to laugh right now," said Molly, "because that poor girl is dead, and I think I'm going to be sick."

"But otherwise you'd laugh at this picture?" asked Spasky.

"I was there when it happened," answered Molly, "despite what the picture says, it was a totally innocent kiss on the cheek. Poor Erica got into a spat with one of her co-stars, the one from that TV show, and it got embarrassing. Kirby did her a favour by doing some of his old magic tricks to distract everyone."

"Do you think Kirby may have misunderstood this gesture?" asked Darling.

Molly shook her head. "He was more embarrassed than anything. Deep down he's a very shy guy."

"What do you know about his time in Europe?" asked Spasky, picking up the manila folder he got just ten minutes earlier.

"Not much," answered Molly. "He got involved in a criminal case over there. He doesn't like to talk about it, but from what I gather it got a little hairy for him."

"Just one?" asked Darling.

"As far as I know," said Molly, "it's not like he's on Murder She Wrote, finding dead bodies everywhere he goes."

Darling looked over at Spasky, it was obvious that this girl didn't know the whole story.

"You were with Kirby Baxter when you heard the scream?" asked Spasky.

"There was me, Kirby, Andi Hack, Teddy Ricci and half a dozen other people, most of them in the comics business."

"You heard the scream and you went looking for Erica?" asked Darling.

"Yes," said Molly. "We first went to get one of the security guards and ran into Mitch at the door to the hotel, and Kirby called Gustav to come down to help."

"Tell us what you know about your friend Mitch," said Spasky, opening the manila folder and seeing that it told him a lot more than what Gustav told him.

"My full name is Marvin Mitchell Mandelbaum," answered the man in the absolutely bizarre Hawaiian shirt, "but everyone calls me Mitch, and my pen name is 3M."

"You're friends with Kirby Baxter and the victim?" asked Spasky, sitting at the table at Room Four with Darling standing by the door this time, holding the manila folder.

"I'm friends with Kirby," explained Mitch, "we only just met Erica Cross," he checked his watch, "literally the day before yesterday. So we weren't exactly friends with the victim. In fact, I've probably clocked more time talking with you guys than I did talking to her."

"But you know Baxter well?" asked Spasky.

"We started out together at Atlantic Comics," answered Mitch. "We were part of the last group hired by Smiling Sam Ash before he retired."

"And you're something called a 'colourist?'" asked Spasky, looking at his notes.

Mitch nodded. "You have no idea what that is, do you?"

"I'm not exactly hip to your lingo," said Spasky.

"It's a common problem," replied Mitch. "Not many people can do the sort of quality work that Kirby can do all by himself as fast as Kirby. That's why the industry traditionally divides the labor when we're making comic books. First there's a penciller who sketches in all the pictures and layout in pencil. The penciller then passes the pencil artwork on to someone called an inker, who traces over the pencil art with ink, and fills in the shadows, and works out the finer details. Then they pass over the inked artwork to me."

"And you fill in all the colours?" asked Darling.

"I don't just fill in the colours," answered Mitch. "I believe that it's my job to make sure everything looks its best."

"So all you do is colour things in with crayons or something?" asked Spasky.

"I haven't used crayons since I was four years old," answered Mitch. "It's all done on computer now, and it's not the only thing I do. I'm trained as a painter, so when someone needs some extra fancy hand-painted cover artwork for their book, they call me, and I whip something up for them."

"And you worked with Baxter on the Shadowknight book before he won the lottery?" asked Darling.

"Among others," answered Mitch.

"So you worked with Baxter," said Spasky, "and you are friends with Baxter?"

"Yes."

"Did you know about his work with Interpol in Europe?" asked Darling.

"Interpol?" asked Mitch.

"Yes," said Spasky, "Kirby Baxter worked with Interpol."

"Pull the other one," said Mitch, "it'll tell you that I'm really Inspector Harry Balls of Scotland Yard operating deep undercover."


"We're not sure why you played coy with us," declared Spasky. They had been talking for over half an hour. Carefully going over every detail of what was now the night before. Elizabeth Darling knew that the sun was rising outside, but they couldn't see it since the interrogation room didn't have any windows.

"Coy about what?" asked Baxter. Darling found him hard to read. He looked upset, tired and sad, but most of all, he looked frustrated, like something or someone threw a wrench in his life that went beyond the simple inconvenience of talking to the police.

"Your police background," said Darling.

"I don't have a 'police background,'" declared Baxter. "I have been involved in certain situations in Europe that have involved the police, but they were just unpleasant coincidences, and I tried to help where I could."

"Interpol has you down as something called a 'special investigative consultant,'" read Spasky from the file folder, "can you tell me what that means?"

"It's an honorary title," explained Baxter. "After the incident in London the powers that be at Interpol gave me and Gustav honorary badges to go with the honours we got in Lichtenstein."

"What exactly happened in London?" asked Darling. "The Lichtenstein incident is laid out pretty clearly, but the file is all vague about what happened in London."

"That's because most of it is classified," explained Baxter.

"Did you know that these papers from Lichtenstein and Interpol give you and Gustav a form of diplomatic immunity?" asked Darling, fascinated by the extremes these important people went to for this unremarkable looking person.

"After Lichtenstein, London and the other business, the people at Interpol thought I needed an official armed bodyguard, and since I already had Gustav working for me, and he used to be a cop in the Czech Republic, it was just a matter of paperwork."

"You and this Gustav fellow met during the Lichtenstein incident," asked Spasky. "What happened over there that made him so loyal to you?"

"The woman who was murdered in Lichtenstein was his adopted sister," said Baxter. "When I uncovered the killer's identity he was very grateful for my help, and he's been working for me ever since."

"He doesn't talk much," stated Spasky.

Baxter shrugged. "People say that about him but I don't think so, he can be very chatty when the mood hits him."

"How exactly did you help those police departments in Europe?" asked Darling. "They speak very highly of you."

"I notice things," answered Baxter. "Little things mostly, that everyone else ignores, I then put them all together and they form a picture of the situation in my mind."

"Really?" asked Spasky, unable to hide his cynicism.

"You're divorced," said Baxter, "at least twice. The second split hurt you a lot, and deep down you wish she would come back to you. You drink too much, a habit that cost you your status as the police department's golden boy. You waver between wallowing in self-pity over your inability to get promoted, and periods where you make pledges to yourself to straighten up and get back into shape, but they never last."

"Whoa," said Darling.

"How in the hell did you know that?" asked Spasky. "Did you read my shrink's file or something?"

"I read you," answered Baxter. "Your shirt is wrinkled, and its lime green colour doesn't match your blue jacket, and the jacket in question is old and a little worn around the edges. There are also several grease stains on your burgundy tie, and neither the grease stains nor the tie match the rest of your outfit. There's no way a wife would allow her husband to go out in public like that. But you are still wearing a wedding ring and, compared to your watch, it's the only thing you polish on a regular basis. You're not a widower, because there's no picture of her on your desk. That tells me that she left you in a bit of an emotional lurch. Your desk also has a stack of pamphlets for gym memberships, but they have a thin layer of dust on them. There are also some forms for the promotion exams next to a framed photo of a much younger you, in uniform, getting a medal, both of which also have dust on them."

"You saw all that just walking past my desk?"

"I told you that I notice little things," answered Baxter, "and these little things form a picture for me. How accurate was I?"

Spasky just crossed his arms.

"That is impressive," said Darling. "What's your picture of me?"

"Are you sure?" asked Baxter. "As you can see people can find this very unsettling."

"I have a thick skin."

Baxter shrugged.

"Your father was a high ranking member of the police department," answered Baxter. "He is probably since retired. You are ambitious and determined to succeed on your own merits, and you work very hard on your job, at the expense of just about everything else in your life. You are also not interested in a relationship with another cop, and you are a bit germ-phobic. Your parents are divorced, probably because your mother had an affair, and you resent her because of it."

Darling froze; Spasky had to choke back a laugh.

"How the hell?"

"All rather obvious," said Baxter. "Your clothes are very simple and practical, you're not wearing any make-up and your hair is in a ponytail and judging by your roots, and split ends, it hasn't seen the inside of a salon in a very long time. It's obvious that you are only interested in hunting criminals while on the job and don't have time for a life outside of the job. You're basically a cliché."

"What about the germ phobia?"

"Your hands smell of sanitizer. The same brand you keep on your desk, and it was your desk that told me the rest of the story. You keep a stack of study guides for the promotion exams next to your computer and, judging from the dog-eared pages and wrinkled spines, you read them frequently. You have no pictures of friends, boyfriends or girlfriends on your desk, just two separate pictures of you posing with your parents at your police academy graduation. Your father is wearing a uniform with a lot of gold braid and, while I'm not that familiar with Toronto police ranks, I don't think he was a humble patrolman. In that photo both of you are smiling very widely. You have a separate photograph with your mother. It's the same happy event, but your body language is tense and neither of you is smiling, that shows some emotional distance, if not outright resentment. What can separate a mother and daughter like that in the high stress world of a policeman's family? Usually it is the discovery of infidelity."

"Damn," said Spasky.

"Very interesting trick," said Darling, her hand was pressed flat against the table to keep it from trembling, or forming a fist.

"I try not to do it to people," said Baxter, "but I really can't avoid it."

"Well," explained Darling, "now I understand why Interpol thinks you are so useful."

"It doesn't really matter what Interpol may think," replied Baxter, "it doesn't make me any more involved in this mess than I have to be."

"Okay," said Spasky, "forget Interpol, it's not like this is something they'd be interested in anyway."

"How?" asked Baxter.

"It looks like this Cross woman," continued Spasky, "snuck back into this Room B, probably a little drunk, went up to the platform, fell into the freezer, screaming before the lid snapped shut, and died from either freezing to death or carbon monoxide poisoning."

"You really think this was an accident?" Baxter's eyes focused sharply on the two cops, looking at them like a teacher confronting two particularly stupid pupils.

Darling nodded.

"Everything is pointing to an accident."

"Did you test her blood for cyanide?"

"Why should we test her for cyanide?" asked Spasky.

"Because someone murdered her with cyanide," declared Kirby, "then put her in the freezer with the dry ice. She was already dead when she went in."

"And how do you know this?" asked Spasky. "Are the little things drawing you a picture in your head?"

"I smelled bitter almonds when I tried CPR," stated Baxter, a look of stern determination on his face. "It's all a bit Agatha Christie, but I do believe that it's a clear sign of cyanide poisoning."

"Cyanide is very tricky to smell," explained Darling, "despite what they say on TV."

"I have a very good sense of smell," declared Baxter.

"Really," asked Spasky, "you expect us to waste the coroner's time running extra tests because you believe that you have a good sense of smell?" Baxter nodded.

"Just how good is your sense of smell?" asked Darling, figuring that this fool was thinking too much of himself and had finally painted himself into a corner.

Baxter just took a deep breath through his nose and said: "Your last meal was one of those faux Thai chicken and salad deals. It was a little heavy on the garlic. Afterward you splurged on possibly a piece of chocolate cake, but more likely a chocolate cupcake."

Darling's hand shot to her mouth. Spasky laughed.

"Your last meal was pepperoni pizza," added Baxter, making Spasky pause, "and you followed that up with a shot of...hmmm...tequila."

"Whoah," muttered Spasky.

"It is that good," said Darling.

ISSUE #9
SCENES FROM A FLOOR

Kirby stared at the narrow blade of sunlight that snuck between the heavy curtains of his bedroom. It stabbed at his eyes, but he didn't dare close them, because closing them stung even worse. Whenever he closed his eyes he saw Erica's face, eyes wide, staring into nothingness, her pale skin cold as marble.

Kirby rolled over and stared at the blade of sunlight reflecting on the white bathroom door. He had attempted sleep, but reality interfered with his dreams and kept slapping him awake. He and the others had left the police station shortly after dawn. The cops took them back to their hotel in an unmarked minivan, no one felt like talking. Molly had her head on Kirby's shoulder through the whole ride, and he had his arm around her shoulders, feeling her body tense every time their ride hit a pothole or a bump.

The group split up and headed straight to their bedrooms as soon as they arrived. No one made any plans for the dawning day, no one said anything at all. Kirby hoped they were sleeping, but doubted it. He and Gustav had some experience in this sort of thing while they were in Europe, but to Mitch and Molly this was a completely new experience, and if they felt anything like he did his first time, they were naturally horrified.

Kirby sat up and rubbed his face. Even though this room was bigger than the New York apartment where he spent five comfortable years, it now seemed to be too damn small to contain his anxiety. He got up and grabbed his bathrobe. It was a heavy dark blue terry cloth behemoth that he bought in a moment of splurging at Harrods in London. He opened the curtains, slid open the glass door and stepped out onto the balcony. The crowds were still milling around on the street below. He wondered if they were talking about what happened just ten hours earlier. They probably were, since the story of Erica's death was probably all over the internet, if not the mainstream news, by now.

Kirby remembered what the detective named Spasky said to him as he left the police station to rejoin his friends. The fat cop warned him that it didn't matter what happened in Europe, or what the cops over there called him, Kirby was not to get any more involved with this case in any form whatsoever. Spasky was quite adamant about it, and Kirby could see the veins in his head flexing through the layer of fat.

Kirby agreed, he knew where this sort of meddling could lead, and it was never anyplace good. He didn't want that kind of confusion, the fear, and the stress in his life again.

Still...

Erica's face stared at him from the mist of that deep freeze. He was seeing a look of pleading on her face that he knew wasn't there in reality, but it was there in his mind.

Kirby leaned on the balcony railing and looked over the city one more time. It wasn't his city, it wasn't his country. Spasky was right, despite his experience in Europe, despite whatever silly-ass title the European cops gave him, he was still just an amateur, a meddler, who had no business getting any more involved than he already was.

Kirby went back into his bedroom, grabbed his clothes and headed for the bathroom. He did it quietly, not wanting to wake anyone lucky enough to sleep. He didn't want to do it, but he was going to have to piss Inspector Spasky off, and he felt that he had better do it alone, because, unlike the others, he had no choice in the matter.

She was dead.

The bitch was dead.

He should have left, he should have gone far from this place. He got what he wanted. He got even more than he wanted.

But what he should have done and what he wanted to do were two completely different things.

It burned him to have to pay to get into the convention centre. Security was so lax before the murder that he was able to find several easy ways to sneak into the place. But now instead of the minimum wage yahoos in yellow windbreakers, there were real Toronto cops, in real uniforms, with real bulletproof vests and carrying real guns. These cops meant business, and they didn't let anyone just sneak in, let alone get anywhere near the scene of the bitch's death.

He was worried that he'd stand out because he wasn't dressed like some kind of cartoon retard, but the cops weren't paying attention to the people beyond the occasional cute girl dressed in an outfit that was either tight, skimpy, or both. They still didn't let anyone get close to the room where Erica Cross died, and the yellow tape sealing the doors to Room B like a Christmas present made sneaking in unnoticed impossible. That didn't stop a crowd of rubberneckers from clustering around those big double doors in the vain hope that a member of the spaz league might actually develop X-ray vision and see past solid matter to glimpse something worthwhile. Most just milled around for a bit and asked the cops some stupid questions, then they would wander off and some other fresh geek would take their place. The aforementioned cute chicks in the outfits might get a smile, or a request for a phone number, but no answers as to what exactly happened there during the night.

The ones with internet access could get some of the story, the comic book fan and news sites were already all over it. He had visited some of those websites for the first time to see what they knew. It wasn't much. All they knew was that

Erica Cross was dead, the cops weren't talking, and there was nothing about any suspects, who found the body, or if the powers-that-be thought it was foul play or an accident. The regular media was slow to pick up the story, with only a couple of local reporters hovering around police headquarters waiting for a statement, but that was going to change soon. The Drudge, Breitbart and Huffington websites had picked up the story. That meant that in a matter of hours the big American and international media outlets were going to notice that something big happened at OmniCon. Of course they'd have to have someone do what he did and find out what OmniCon was and where it was located, then, maybe they'd be able to spare someone to send into this unknown and unknowable territory.

He scanned the crowd and caught a face he sort of knew at the door. It was that skinny geek, the one TMZ identified as some sort of rich bastard, the one Erica Cross kissed Thursday night, the one called Baxter. Baxter was dressed in a dark blue t-shirt with some sort of bullshit superhero logo on the front, blue jeans and some sort of light khaki jacket that looked like it came out of an army surplus store.

He stepped back, nestled himself between a display from a video game company and watched Baxter cross the floor in front of him. The geek's hair was still wet from the shower, and he hadn't shaved. He looked like he hadn't slept.

Those cops can take up a lot of time.

He watched Baxter walk between the displays, pause and look at the ever-shifting crowd in front of Room B, then turn toward the booths for the comic book companies. He left his hiding place and turned for the main entrance. He wasn't sure if Baxter knew who he was, or if he ever saw him where he wasn't supposed to be, but he didn't want to take that chance.

"So it's just like the airport?" asked the recent graduate of the Ontario College of Art, her portfolio under one arm clad in a long fishnet and lace glove. The recent graduate's style was a little old school Goth meets Steampunk for Kevin's tastes, pale with lots of make-up and artificially ink-black hair, but she was a good enough distraction for this weird-ass morning. Cops were all over the convention centre, there was talk about someone dying in Room B the night before, Madden was keeping his distance and Ashmore was acting odd.

"Yes," answered Kevin LaGuardia, managing to simultaneously take her portfolio, look her in the eye and check out the cleavage struggling for freedom against her black lace bustier. Truly a marvellous achievement in the art of eye-hand coordination. "But we're not related."

"I loved your work drawing Answer Man," said the recent graduate, revealing her long memory while her smile revealed teeth that just barely beat her complexion in the whiteness department. "You really captured the essence of that character."

"Thanks," said LaGuardia as he opened the portfolio on the table that lay to the side of the Atlantic Comics booth. Normally, he had a set time for looking at the portfolios of aspiring artists, but he made an exception for the recent graduate. Sure, he had more interest in the contents of her bustier than the contents of her portfolio, but he was an editor, she was an artist and she remembered those halcyon days, when she had to have been in junior high, and he was the working artist that she now wanted to be.

The work itself was technically competent; the style was strictly imitation anime/manga with a dash of emo as big eyed characters with wild hair emoted their angst dramatically in the face of what looked like elaborate vampire, reptile and cyborg hybrids. One elf-type creature sort of reminded him of Molly Garret. The posing was a little melodramatic, but this was a business built on melodrama.

"This is very promising," said LaGuardia as he flipped to a page showing two long limbed, androgynous humanoids in skin tight armour, kissing atop the ruins of some battle robots. "Very promising indeed. You really should leave me your email, because you never know when we might have some work for you."

"Really?" asked the recent graduate, the hope in her heart making her chest heave in a way that put hope in LaGuardia's heart. "I'll write it down for you."

"That's great," said LaGuardia, thinking this might be promising, and not only artistically. Then he managed to tear his eyes away from her cleavage for a second but that was just long enough to ruin his morning.

"Shit."

"What?" asked the recent graduate.

"Just write down your email," said LaGuardia.

The recent graduate looked over her shoulder.

"Isn't that Kirby Baxter?" she asked.

"Yes," said LaGuardia as he nudged her away from the table. "I'll have to see you later."

"Hello," said Kirby.

"Hi," said LaGuardia, trying to sound casual. "You don't look so hot." In fact, he looked like a drowned rat with his wet hair, dark circles under his eyes and a jaw line dotted with patches of stubble. He had that crazy bag he always took to cons slung over his shoulder.

"I spent the night with the police," answered Kirby.

"Really?" asked the recent graduate.

LaGuardia turned to the recent graduate. "Are you still here?"

The recent graduate gave LaGuardia a slip of paper, then slipped away, but not before saying: "I really liked your work," to Kirby before she left.

"So you were involved in all that business last night?"

"I guess you heard what happened," said Kirby.

LaGuardia nodded. "Yeah," he said, "I heard there was some sort of an accident or something, and someone died."

"Or something," said Kirby, and LaGuardia could see that he wanted to say more but couldn't. Baxter than looked around to see if anyone was listening in on them, and then

139

he said: "I need to talk to you about something."

"About what?" asked LaGuardia.

"Business," said Kirby. "What's going on with Atlantic Comics?"

LaGuardia shook his head.

"I'm just an artist posing as an editor," answered LaGuardia. "All the business decisions are handled by Ashmore."

"But the company does have a lot of valuable assets?" asked Kirby.

"Like original art?" asked LaGuardia, hoping to all that was holy that he wasn't talking about original artwork.

"That could be part of it," said Kirby, "but I'm talking about all the attention the movies are bringing to the company."

"There are a lot of comic book movies coming out these days," said LaGuardia, not sure where this was going, "I'm sure Atlantic's overdue for some of that movie money."

"But you don't know any details?" asked Kirby.

"That's Ashmore's department," said LaGuardia, wondering what the hell this guy was talking about. "Why are you so curious?"

"I'm just trying to figure some stuff out," said Kirby, "it's good seeing you. We missed you at the Luau Room last night."

"Oh," said LaGuardia, "I was really tired yesterday; I hit the sack as soon as I could. I must be getting old."

"Aren't we all, if we're lucky," said Kirby. "I'll talk to you later."

LaGuardia watched Kirby Baxter saunter off into the crowd. He then pulled out his cell phone and hit speed dial.

"Madden," said LaGuardia, "check your damn voicemail, I think we have a really big problem that you really have to take care of quick."

"Hey Teddy," said Kirby as he came to Ricci's booth. Teddy Ricci and Keith the regional manager were trying to keep business going as normal. The spinner racks and shelves were all still outside Ricci's cubicle, forcing the men and customers to bob and weave to get around them.

"They let you out," said Teddy.

"Yeah," replied Kirby, "mind if I borrow your laptop for a second? I left mine in my room."

"Mi casa su casa," said Teddy, "follow me."

Kirby followed Teddy through the chains of linked bamboo into what was the Luau Room the night before. It was sort of halfway between its daylight identity as a temporary shop, and its secret identity as a nocturnal drinking spot.

"We barely had any time to get things back to normal," said Teddy. "How long did the cops keep you?"

"I got out about four hours ago," answered Kirby.

"Sheesh, I wonder what they'd do with a suspect?"

"I'd rather not know."

"There won't be any Luau Room tonight," added Teddy as he took his laptop out of his bag. "It just doesn't seem right."

"That's understandable," said Kirby. "Maybe some of us can get together at my suite some time. Just a few of us talking about better times."

"That's a great idea." Teddy booted up his computer, and clicked on his browser. "There you go, the world is at your fingertips though the WiFi here is a little pokey. What do you need?"

"Do you know who Jackie Paine is?"

"You don't?"

"I think that's obvious," said Kirby, "I've never really given much thought to Hollywood."

"I have her old site and her new site bookmarked," said Teddy clicking the link. "There you go."

"Thanks."

"I got to get back to the front," said Teddy, "let me know when you're done."

Kirby put the laptop on the improvised bar and pulled up

a stool. Jackie Paine's top story of the day was the death of Erica Cross, and how Sandra Doyle was now campaigning to replace her freshly deceased co-star. So far the site only had the bare bones of the story, but it promised more info later. The bottom of the piece had links to related stories. Kirby clicked each one into another tab and started reading them, starting from the earliest to the most recent.

The other stories were basically built on the same basic themes:

1. Unhappy investors, creditors and more than a few litigators had MaxCo Films under siege. It was also a possibility that MaxCo may not have enough money to complete The Vengeance Sisters movie.

2. Molly's story about MaxCo screwing Atlantic Comics by rushing into production with The Vengeance Sisters was true.

3. Jackie Paine was really, really fond of saying: TOLDYA! in big bold letters whenever she was proven right.

4. The producers of Sandra Doyle's TV show had just fired her for physically assaulting a co-star, the final nail in a coffin made from years of bad on-set behaviour.

So that's why she showed up a week early, thought Kirby, and it also said a lot about her behaviour around Erica at the publicist's Thursday night party. Kirby only caught a glimpse of her at the beginning of the opening night bash, and then no more, did she leave early, if so, where did she go?

Kirby made mental notes of everything. He wasn't sure if Spasky would be interested in this information. He was sure that he wouldn't react well to Kirby's meddling, but he thought that Darling might be a bit more open-minded. She seemed more impressed than annoyed by Interpol's file on him.

Besides, he wasn't meddling; he was just looking up some publicly available information. What was the harm in that?

"Things have become a little complicated," said Karl Weatherby into his cell phone. "It's good to know that you're aware of my situation, but someone is dead." Having been questioned by the police, his boss Max Cooperman, had popped open the suite's minibar and retired to his room with a handful of overpriced liquor bottles, potato chip bags and candy bars. Weatherby had seen such moods before, but only in situations where his status as a Hollywood player wasn't enough to buy him a pass for one of his epic temper tantrums. The time Cooperman spent in the jaws of his personal black dog never lasted more than a few hours, and then he started broadcasting his rage outward again.

That bought Weatherby a little time to handle some of his more extracurricular duties.

"You want to know where he was after the party?" asked Weatherby. "As far as I know he was in his room either asleep or watching pay-per-view porn... Yes, that's all I know, I'm his assistant, not his babysitter, I can't be by his side twenty-four seven... What? Sure, it probably has something, but I'm not going to risk my ass at this stage to get it... We have to stick with the plan and act like this whole stinking business never happened... Damn, why am I the one who has to tell you how to run a goddamn railroad? ... Okay, we're agreed. I got to go."

Weatherby clicked off and sat down on the plush lounge chair and took a little time to study the lobby's inlaid marble floor, ignoring the conventioneers mingling with the hotel guests and staff. An elegantly sculpted foot appeared on the floor in front of him, clad in an extremely expensive red Prada shoe.

Weatherby tilted his head and his eyes ran up an equally elegantly sculpted leg, then a very short, very black skirt, a tight electric pink t-shirt, baring just enough belly and promising just enough cleavage, and finally a coldly beautiful face framed in blonde locks. Sunglasses hid her eyes, but he knew she was staring right at him, he could feel them drilling right through him like a pair of sharpened icicles.

"Hello Miss Doyle," said Weatherby, not bothering to fake a smile. He didn't let her beauty confuse him the way it did others, he was immunized by cold hard experience with her type, who felt entitled to their entitlements just for showing up looking pretty and not for their talent or work ethic. "What can I do for you?"

"I need to see Cooperman," said Sandra Doyle with a flip of her hair. "There's a way we can save The Vengeance Sisters."

"I know where you're going," said Weatherby as he sat back in the chair. "I've been taking messages from your agent all morning telling me that the show must go on."

"That's one way to put it," said Sandra, "I need to see Cooperman."

"Let me guess," theorized Weatherby, "you think you can take Erica Cross' part?"

"Like you said, the show must get going," said Sandra. "The redhead is dead, but we shouldn't let that stop this movie from getting made. You've already scheduled everything to shoot around my old part for the first week, so why don't we just stick with that plan and find someone to take over that part. It's so simple there's no reason why we can't do it."

Weatherby took a deep breath and caught a whiff of her perfume. Like her it appeared sweet at first, but grew harsher with time. While part of him wanted to laugh in her face, his recent telephone conversation put some crazy ideas in his head that kept him from doing that. He had told his 'friend' that they should act as if nothing had happened, and let everything take its course. Here was an opportunity to get their original plan back on course.

"All right," said Weatherby, "I'll talk to him. I think he might go for it." In fact, he knew that Cooperman was going to go for it, he had no other choice.

"That's all I ask," she said, trying to be coy, but there was just a hint of demand in her voice, then she turned and sashayed away. Weatherby took a second to enjoy her exit on a visual as opposed to an intellectual level, then started going through his notes.

"You're Karl Weatherby?" asked a voice behind him.

Weatherby looked over his shoulder and saw Kirby Baxter standing by his seat, looking a little worse for wear. In fact, he looked like he could use a good night's sleep, or some sort of chemical simulation of one.

"Right," said Weatherby, "and you're Kirby Baxter."

"Did I just hear that Sandra Doyle was getting Erica Cross' part?"

"Were you eavesdropping?"

"Unintentional," answered Baxter, "these big ears tend to hear everything. If they were any bigger, I'd be getting satellite signals from China. If I don't deliberately tune things out I end up hearing things like that couple behind you arguing about getting a divorce."

Weatherby turned his head to see a middle-aged couple pointing fingers at each other while their mouths moved, but the most he could make out were the occasional hiss and gasp.

"She's accusing him of sleeping with her sister," continued Baxter, "he's accusing her of running around with his law partner. I think his name is Edgar, or Igor, but it's most likely Edgar."

"That's incredible."

"It's more of an annoyance than anything," said Baxter. "My sense of smell is even stronger; in fact, someone in this room is using way too much cologne."

"I was thinking that too," said Weatherby. "Well, since there are no secrets from you, I have to say that we are only considering the option of giving Sandra the part, because there is a lot of money and jobs relying on this movie getting started."

"Yeah," said Baxter, seeming a little out of sorts. "I really need to get some sleep, those cops kept me up all night. That's why I can't really think straight."

"They came to us after they were done with you," added Weatherby. "That was after dawn."

"Listen," said Baxter, "I'd like to talk to you later. I need some information on your movie."

"Why?" asked Weatherby, wondering where this was going.

"I just have some questions that need answering," said Baxter, "but I can't do anything coherently until after I get some sleep. I'll see you later."

"Sure," said Weatherby. Then Baxter headed for the elevators.

Weatherby hit redial. "Yeah, it's Karl here," he said, "I think I got rid of one complication and replaced it with another."

Kirby had the elevator to himself, so he slumped against the back wall and stopped trying to hold up the immense weight of his eyelids. The shower had given him a bit of a wake-up, but the effect was short-lived as the need for sleep came back to smack him hard across the head. It was a mistake to go sleepwalking around the convention, asking stupid questions and not knowing what the hell to do with the answers. A little imp in the back of his sleep-deprived head second guessed his idea about telling the police about what he found on the internet, telling Kirby that it was just pointless Hollywood gossip, and suspicions based on personal dislikes. It couldn't possibly be usable evidence.

The elevator chimed and Kirby forced his eyes open. It had arrived at the Excelsior floor and the door slid open. A thumping sound was coming from down the hall.

"Erica!" yelled a man's voice, between thumps. "I know you're in there! Come on!"

Kirby stepped out of the elevator and looked down the hall. A man was in front of the door of Erica Cross' suite, banging on the door. He was tall, with a muscular build clearly visible through the extremely tight Ed Hardy imitation t-shirt, a forest of dye-blond spikes on his head and a spray-on tan making him look like a slightly smaller, and orange, version of the Incredible Hulk.

"Excuse me?" asked Kirby. "Who are you?"

"Who am I?" asked the man, as if it was Kirby making the disturbance. "Who the fuck are you?"

"I think I asked first."

The man paused and looked Kirby over.

"I know who you are," snarled the man, as he approached, the classic swagger of the lifelong semi-professional bully in his walk.

"That's great," said Kirby, "you got your question answered, now answer mine."

"You're the shit-bird who fucked Erica on TMZ!" barked the man.

"I think you misunderstood the situ—"

"I ought to pound the shit out of you," growled the man coming closer to Kirby.

"Now I know for certain that you don't know what's really going on," said Kirby, not moving an inch.

"Where's Erica?" demanded the man, drawing even closer and clenching a beefy fist.

"You need to calm down before you get hurt," said Kirby.

"What's a skinny little shit-bird like you going to do to me?" asked the man.

"Me?" asked Kirby, standing his ground. "Nothing, but the very large man behind you will definitely do something."

"Do you think I'm stupid?" asked the man raising his fist. "Did you think I'd fall for that old 'look behind you' trick?"

"No," said Kirby, "in fact, right now I'm kind of hoping you don't fall for it."

The man pulled his beefy arm back to punch Kirby, who still didn't move, then the man found his arm locked into some sort of vice.

"What the fu—"

The man hit the wall first, hard enough to make the bronze plaque pointing to the ice machine rattle on its bolts, and Kirby felt the wind rushing out of the man as he seemed to almost completely flatten. Gustav then peeled the man off the wall and threw him to the floor like a sack of wet laundry and pinned him down hard.

"Gustav," said Kirby, "as usual, your timing is impeccable. I guess you were out looking for me."

Gustav nodded as he pressed the man's face into the carpet, and placed his knee on the man's spine, pinning him totally to the floor.

"It's a good thing you found me when you did."

The man let out a muffled squeal.

"Let's see who this guy is," said Kirby.

Gustav pulled an American passport of the man's back pocket and passed it to Kirby.

"Charles Leonard Healey," read Kirby. "Well, Mr. Healey, here's a little lesson for you, if a guy my size doesn't back down when a guy your size is threatening them, it's because there really is a large man behind you."

The door to the Royal Suite opened and Molly poked out her head.

"What's going on?" she asked. "I heard a thump and...oh, that must have been him."

"This guy was trying to get into Erica's suite," said Kirby, "call hotel security and the police. Gustav has things under control."

Hotel security had conveniently arranged for a spot by one of the hotel's back doors to be available for the police to pick up Healey who sat sullenly on a folding chair, his hands bound with plastic zip ties. A hotel security guard stood on each side of him, while Gustav stood in front, his arms crossed, his eyes burning holes between the frosted spikes on the top of Healey's head.

Kirby asked Healey if he knew what was going on, but all he got was a major case of stink-eye. He refrained from telling him that Erica was dead, he wanted the police to tell him, and hoped that he could watch, in order to gauge his reaction. The rush of adrenaline had beaten back the tide of sleep, but he didn't know for how long, and he wanted to get the most out of it.

Someone rapped on the steel door leading to the alley.

One of the hotel security guards opened it, and a uniformed Toronto city police officer stuck his head in.

"Is this the guy?" asked the police officer pointing to Healey.

The hotel security guy nodded and opened the door all the way to let the police officers in.

"You must be Baxter," said one policeman as he and his partner pulled Healey to his feet.

Kirby nodded.

"The powers that be want you to come to police headquarters to make a statement," said the policeman.

"Sure," said Kirby, following them into the alley behind the hotel, "should we come with you, or can my driver take me?"

"I think it would be better if you drove yourself," said the policeman, shoving the silent Healey into the back of the police car. "We're a bit shorthanded at the moment."

Kirby looked over to Gustav who nodded and immediately headed to the hotel's parking garage. Kirby then watched the police car glide down the alley, Healey glaring at him through the back window.

The steel door closed with a thud behind him, and Kirby realized that he was alone in the alley.

He kicked a crushed pop can across the alley and watched it bounce against a nearby brick wall. He ran all the information he had gathered this morning in his mind, and again reconsidered whether or not he could or should bring it up with the detectives. He had been flip-flopping on the issue all morning like a meth-smoking fish caught on a dock. Kirby finally decided that he should tell them what he knew. What harm could it do, it was only information?

A vehicle appeared at the end of the alley. It wasn't Gustav and the rented Mercedes, it was an SUV, an Escalade to be exact, and it just sat there for a second, its engine running. Then the engine revved, and the big machine came charging down the narrow alley. One of the side mounted mirrors snapped off against a metal pipe and flew spinning away from the vehicle.

Kirby realized that it was heading straight for him. He looked for a way out in the few seconds he had left, saw one, and went for it. Kirby leaped on top of a massive green trash bin with an agility he had no idea he had, then he leaped again.

Kirby heard the scream of twisting metal below him as he grabbed onto the ladder of a fire escape and pulled up his legs. The garbage bin popped open, unleashing a wave of odours that made Kirby's stomach clench, and he tightened his grip on the ladder. His long legs swung wildly in the air and his foot hit the roof the SUV. Then he lost his grip and hit the roof hard, the air shooting out of his lungs. Kirby heard a car door open, then footsteps. He pulled himself up and saw only a shape dashing around a corner. Some kind of an alarm was chiming from the SUV, and Kirby turned to see the Mercedes appear at the mouth of the alley.

"Timing's a little off this time," moaned Kirby to himself.

ISSUE #10
OFFICER DOWN

"It looks like you're going to live," said Dr. Gupta as he returned to the examining room carrying a clipboard.

"That's good news," said Kirby before turning to Gustav who stood in the corner like the spectre of death itself, "you see, I'm going to be fine."

"You have some bruises," added the doctor, "but no broken bones, no concussion and no internal injuries."

"So I can go?" asked Kirby.

"Yes," said Dr. Gupta, "your friends are here to collect you."

The door opened as if on cue and Mitch stuck his head in.

"Are you decent?" asked Mitch.

"Never," answered Kirby.

The door then swung wide open and Molly pushed Mitch aside and charged in like a tiny angry bull.

"You idiot!" she bellowed loud enough to wake a coma patient two floors up.

"I'll leave you and your friends alone," said Dr. Gupta heading for the door, "don't take too long, because we need the room, unless she hurts you, then just scream for help and you can stay."

"I should kick your ass into next week," said Molly, "for being so bloody stupid!"

"Please," said Kirby delicately pulling on his jacket, "I'm still sore, and I had to listen to Gustav chew me out all the way over here for not going with him to get the car."

"Well," said Molly giving him a surprisingly strong hug for such a tiny person, "at least somebody told you that were being stupid."

"I'm amazed you were able to jump onto a fire escape like an eighties action movie star," added Mitch.

"Too bad I needed both hands to grab that thing," said Kirby as he slid off the examination table, "or I'd have done my two guns blazing back-flip."

"I know this isn't the first time you've been involved in something like this," said Molly.

"Or the second," said Mitch.

"But you can't go sticking your nose in other people's business," continued Molly. "Especially when we're talking about a murder case, this is not a coincidence."

"Hear, hear," said a voice from the door.

Everyone turned to see Inspector Spasky, his arms crossed and his face sterner and redder than usual.

"Follow me Baxter," ordered Spasky. "We need to talk."

"What's your problem?" asked Spasky as Kirby followed him into an office where Sergeant Darling was waiting. Gustav followed close by.

"Someone did try to kill me," said Kirby, "that might be a problem."

"I don't care what Interpol says about you," growled Spasky, his face turning a bright pink. "I don't care if some cops over there think you're the goddamn reincarnation of Sherlock Holmes—"

"I'm no Sherlock Holmes," said Kirby, "I just helped them where I could."

"But that doesn't give you some sort of license to butt into a criminal investigation!"

"I wasn't butting in," said Kirby.

"You had to be butting in!" barked Spasky. "Someone's put you on their shit list and tried to grind you into a stain in the alley! You don't have to be a goddamn master detective to figure out that you did something to set them off!"

"Okay," said Kirby, "I asked some people some questions—"

"JUST SHUT THE HELL UP AND LISTEN!" screamed Spasky, his face now lobster red. "This is a murder investigation! Not one of your goddamn funny page stories!"

"I do comic books," said Kirby, "comic strips are a related but different—"

"This is Toronto! This is a Toronto Police Department investigation! It's not Europe where it looks like they let any asshole swan into a crime scene and start disturbing the shit! This is not Luxembourg!"

"I think you mean Lichtenstein."

"SHUT IT!" The framed degrees on the wall rattled from the violence of the detective's bellow, and the coma patient two floors up collapsed back into his coma out of sheer terror. Gustav stepped forward, but Kirby put his hand out to stop him.

"A woman has been murdered," continued Spasky, in a slightly lower roar, "you were almost murdered yourself! I do not want another body on my patch! Especially some beanpole idiot Ichabod Crane Sherlock fucking wannabe..."

Spasky stopped. His words and his rage trailed off into nothingness, his eyes, already bugged out and bloodshot, suddenly shot upward.

"Oh hell," said Kirby, and he and Gustav leaped to catch Spasky whose entire body shuddered and collapsed.

"What the—?" Darling sprung from her seat to catch her crumbling partner.

"Get the doctor," said Kirby, "I think he's having a heart attack!"

"He's stable," said Dr. Gupta.

Darling slumped against the wall, surprised that she was actually relieved to hear that the growling heap of a man was going to live.

"Is he conscious?" asked Darling.

"We sedated him," answered Gupta. "He won't be awake

for several hours. Was his family notified?"

Darling nodded. Right after notifying headquarters she had called Lucinda, A.K.A. Ex-Wife #2, and Lucinda had volunteered to call the other members of what Spasky called his Personal Coven. "They're on their way."

"Good," said Dr. Gupta.

"I have to talk to someone," said Darling, thinking it was good that Spasky was unconscious, because if he knew what she was thinking he'd have another heart attack while strangling her. "I'll check back in a bit."

Darling walked slowly down the hall. Part of her sort of hoped that he'd have returned to the hotel by now, even though she had asked him to stay. Sure, she could have tracked him down, but him leaving early would give her the time she needed to change her mind.

Darling turned a corner into the cafeteria.

Damn it, he was still here with his friends.

Kirby Baxter, the big man Gustav, and the two named Mitch and Molly were at a corner table by the window, talking in hushed tones.

"Mr. Baxter," asked Darling, "can we talk?"

"How is Inspector Spasky?" asked Kirby.

"He's going to live," she answered, "but I really need to talk to you."

"Would you like a seat," asked Baxter, "or do you need this to be private?"

"I don't think there are any secrets between all of you," said Darling pulling up a chair, "so I'll get to the point. You probably heard that this city will be hosting a summit of world leaders next week."

Baxter nodded.

"All the work setting up the security for the summit," continued Darling, "and our gang crackdown operations, have left the police department short-staffed in the field of criminal investigations."

"What are you getting at?" asked Baxter, knowing where she was going, but hoping against hope that she wasn't taking him with her.

"Mr. Baxter," said Darling, "did you ever read the fine print when your friend at Interpol gave you that card saying you were a special consultant?"

"No," said Baxter, "at the time I thought it was just a formality for Gustav to carry a gun when we travel, but right now I'm feeling that I should have."

"The fine print," said Darling, "says that to maintain your special status you must be available to aid and assist in criminal investigations in any way, upon the request of the investigating officer."

"Oh," said Baxter.

"With Spasky out of commission for the foreseeable future," continued Darling, "and our department's resources stretched too far, I'm now the investigating officer."

"And you're requesting my aid and assistance?" asked Baxter.

"You're drafting Kirby?" asked Molly. "No way, he's already been almost flattened. I'm trying to get him to go home tonight."

"Molly," said Baxter, "I think they must really need my help."

"But there's a killer gunning for you," declared Molly.

"But I have Gustav and the police watching my back," said Baxter, "and I'll be a lot more careful from now on."

Molly's hand shot across the table and clasped Baxter's hand.

"I'm worried about you," said Molly.

"I'm worried too," said Baxter patting her hand, "but this isn't the first time I've been involved in this sort of situation, and you know it. Besides I've learned a few lessons today that should really help."

"Like what?" asked Molly.

"Never get caught alone," explained Baxter, "and when a Scotland Yard Superintendent tells you a title is honorary, he's just setting you up."

ISSUE #11
ALIBI BYE BIRDIE

The first thing Healey did when Kirby Baxter and Sergeant Darling came into the interrogation room was to stop adjusting his spiky hair with his free hand. The second thing Healey did was look at Kirby and say: "What the hell is he doing here?"

"He's a special consultant on this investigation," declared Darling without any emotion, as Gustav came in to stand in the corner behind Healey. His looming presence caused Healey to shift uncomfortably in his seat.

"Listen," said Healey trying to point with his right hand, but unable to because it was handcuffed to the white metal table, "I've been waiting here for hours because of these bullshit charges! I don't care if this guy's some kind of cop, or the goddamn president of this stupid country, I demand my rights as an American citizen."

"Too bad you're in Canada," declared Darling as she took her seat across from Healey. Kirby sat next to her, leaving him a clear path to the door, an arrangement specifically ordered by Molly, in case Healey somehow got out of his handcuffs. "An attorney can be arranged for you, but we'd like to ask you some questions first."

Healey looked over his shoulder at Gustav looming over him like the spectre of doom, and slumped in his seat.

"Sure."

"Your name is Charles Leonard Healey?" asked Darling.

"Yes," answered Healey, "but everyone calls me Chaz.

What is this about? Because I didn't lay a finger on this consultant asshole of yours. Besides, if I did I've got good cause, because he was boning my girlfriend."

"You based this theory on the picture on the internet?" asked Darling.

"That," said Chaz with a shrug, "and other things."

"What other things?" asked Darling. The questions and the order she asked them had been carefully prepared before they went in. Kirby knew that information was power, and that they needed to control that information when it came to finding out Chaz Healey's involvement in the case.

"We went out like five times," said Chaz, tapping a finger on the table, "and I got nothing for my effort."

"What do you mean?" asked Darling.

"Come on," said Chaz, leaning back in the chair, scratching his pencil thin jawline beard, and puffing up his chest like a pigeon, "you know what I mean. Sex, you know s-e-x. A girl like that doesn't turn down a piece of prime real estate like this unless she's getting something from somewhere else."

"So you're saying that she wasn't having sexual relations with you?" asked Darling.

"Yeah," snapped Chaz as if Darling was stupid for even thinking of that question. "It had to be because she was putting out for someone richer like this dick-weed here."

Gustav shifted position; Chaz heard the movement and his body language retreated from cocky to worried for his safety.

"So this made you feel jealous?" asked Darling, giving him enough rope.

"Sure," answered Chaz. "I'm a man, and a man doesn't let some bitch run rings around him like he was an asshole."

"Does a real man do something about it when they see their girlfriend kissing someone else on the internet?"

"Listen," said Chaz, "what kind of crazy Canadian investigation lets the guy I am allegedly accused of trying to punch and his pet gorilla sit in on the questioning? I mean come the fuck on here people. You've got the making of one hell of a lawsuit for wrongful arrest."

"It's a murder investigation," said Kirby, choking back the urge to leap across the table and slap Chaz Healey across his face, knowing that not even Gustav could knock any sense into that thick skull.

Chaz froze, his eyes widened for a second and he just stared at Kirby, looking for signs of lying and finding none.

"Who got murdered?" asked Chaz, his finger beating an anxious tattoo on the table. "Because you're sitting right in front of me."

"Erica Cross was murdered," said Darling.

"This is bullshit!" yelled Chaz trying to leap to his feet, but all he could manage was a hunch with his right hand cuffed to the table. Gustav put a large hand on Chaz's shoulder, and gently guided him back to his chair while exerting just enough pressure to tell Healey that he could seriously hurt him if he wanted to. "It's just bullshit. You're making this up. Aren't you?"

"Where were you last night?" asked Darling.

"You don't think I did it?" asked Chaz.

"We checked you out," said Darling, "you arrived in Toronto late on Thursday night and checked into a downtown hotel. But we don't know what you did during Friday, and Friday night."

"I'd like to say for the record thing that I came just to talk Erica into getting back with me," said Chaz. "I didn't want to hurt her. I used to get the best tables when I went out with Erica, and you could forget about waiting in line at the club when she was on your arm."

"Let's get back on topic," said Darling. "What did you do on Friday?"

"I worked out on Friday morning," said Chaz, his lower lip trembling. "I got a friend who works at a gym in town; we ended up hanging out at the hotel pool."

"What about Friday night?" asked Darling.

Chaz shrugged and rubbed his face with his free hand.

"I saw that picture on the web Friday afternoon," said Chaz. "It got me all pissed off. I mean she's all 'saving herself for that special moment' bullshit with me, but is slobbering all over this rich spaz. No offence."

"None taken," said Kirby, cold.

"So what did you do?"

"My friend knew some girls," said Chaz. "We went to a couple of clubs, got plastered, and I woke up this morning at her place."

"And what is her name?"

Chaz shrugged: "Lindsay something. I got her number, she lives in a condo somewhere on Queen Street...or something."

"I have some questions," said Kirby.

"You do?" asked Darling.

"Yes," said Kirby.

"Ask away," declared Chaz.

"What's the capitol of Florida?"

"Miami."

"Who made your shirt?"

"Ed Hardy."

"How many states are in the USA?"

"Fifty-two."

"Did you kill Erica Cross?"

"No."

Kirby leaned over to whisper in Darling's ear.

"He's a douchebag and an idiot," whispered Kirby, "but he's not our murderer."

"Okay," said Darling as they left the interrogation room and went into the observation room, "first you insisted that this is murder, and now you're saying that our top suspect is innocent."

"I still think it's murder," said Kirby as Gustav silently closed the door behind them.

"Then why are you in such a rush to clear our only suspect?"

"You have to hear me out," said Kirby. "If you're going to draft me to be your consultant, you must let me consult a little."

"All right," said Darling, "then consult."

Kirby turned and studied the monitor showing the interrogation room. Chaz Healey fidgeted in his chair like a chained bull calf, unable to do the stomping around he wanted to.

"Okay," said Kirby, "my first point is that Erica Cross was poisoned."

"The toxicology tests haven't been finished yet," said Darling.

"But all the evidence tells you that I'm probably right," said Kirby, not needing to study her minute expressions to find out he was right about that. "So let's just assume that she was poisoned."

"All right," said Darling, taking a seat in a hard plastic chair. "I will assume along with you, even though my mother taught me that it will only make an ass out of you and me."

"Look at him," said Kirby, "I'll bet that when the Los Angeles Police Department gets back to you, they'll say that he's got a record for stuff like public intoxication, drunk driving and most likely the occasional bar fight. Test his blood and you'll probably get positives for marijuana, ecstasy and steroids."

"Even I can guess that."

"Does he look like the kind of person that is smart enough to poison someone?" asked Kirby. "No. Everything about him, from the way he talks to his body language screams that he's the sort of guy who punches smaller people in the face and runs away before they can punch back. He's not the type to put together an elaborate plot to poison someone and toss their body in a freezer full of dry ice to try to make it look like accidental asphyxiation."

"Go on," said Darling, folding her arms and looking straight at him, and through him. He knew that look, he had seen it before from cops. It screamed 'Amaze me nerd-boy,'

160

and it required Kirby to do some explaining.

"What do you know about micro-expressions?" asked Kirby.

"Not much," said Darling. "We're supposed to take a course about them next month."

"Well," said Kirby, perching himself on the corner of a metal table, "before scientists called them micro-expressions, my grandfather, and other people in his profession called them 'tells.'"

"What was his profession?"

"He was a magician," explained Kirby, "and he'd do a mind reading act as part of his show. He did the 'mind reading' just by reading people's micro-expressions."

"And he taught you how to do it?"

Kirby nodded: "You might find it hard to believe, but I was a shy and awkward kid, and he thought it could help."

"Really?" Irony dripped from her statement like paint from a brush, thick and obvious.

"My grandfather taught me to read micro-expressions so that I'd be more confident talking to people," continued Kirby.

"Remind me to never play poker with you," said Darling.

"That's a good idea," said Kirby, "because he also taught me to count cards and trick out the shuffle, but that's all a distraction."

"Then let's get back to the point."

"Right," said Kirby. "Look at Charles 'Chaz' Healey. The only micro-expressions I caught from him were hatred for me, contempt for you and pants-wetting fear of Gustav. Otherwise he's literally a blank slate. I asked him all those questions, which he answered wrong, as fast as I could to throw off his guard, and then I hit him with the big one. There were no hesitations, tics or twitches that are the signs of deception. He's an open book, and that book is titled: This Man Is An Idiot Douchebag, But He's Not A Killer."

"I can see your point, but," said Darling rising from her seat, walking to the monitor and studying Healey for herself,

"I'll have to disagree with you on one point."

"About what?"

"I don't think this guy is smart enough to run away after punching someone," said Darling. "All right, we'll check his alibi, and if it checks out we'll hold him on disturbing the peace, unless you wanted him charged with assault?"

"That sounds good enough," said Kirby. "We just have to keep him out of the way while we look into the others."

"Okay," said Karl Weatherby, "I'll admit that the car was ours—"

"But it's a rental," declared Cooperman pointing a thick finger across the table.

"That is to say," declared Cooperman's lawyer, a man named Thurston, who looked to Kirby like some form of evolved Chihuahua with male pattern baldness, "that my client does not own the car, nor is he liable for any civil or criminal action if someone else uses it, without my client's permission, to do something illegal or dangerous."

"So someone else was using your vehicle?" asked Darling. Kirby watched both men closely, looking for the slightest sign of guilt. So far he was getting a lot of facial static illustrating annoyance, contempt and disdain.

"Somebody else had to be using our vehicle," boomed Cooperman, earning a please shut the hell up look from his lawyer.

"What my client is saying," said Thurston, "is that during the alleged incident with Mr. Baxter, he, and his associate Mr. Weatherby, were in a press conference attended by over twenty entertainment reporters."

"Why were you having a press conference?" asked Darling.

Cooperman looked over to his lawyer and Thurston nodded.

"We were announcing that Sandra Doyle was taking over Erica Cross's role in The Vengeance Sisters movie," announced Cooperman, puffing up his chest. "I know what you're thinking, that it sounds pretty cold to be replacing the star literally the day after she died."

"It does sound cold," said Kirby, hoping to poke a reaction out of him. "In fact it sounds like a pretty nasty thing to do."

"Are you trying to provoke my client?" asked Thurston.

"Well," replied Cooperman, "it goes to show just how little you know about the movie business."

"Then teach me," said Kirby, playing with the fat man's ego.

Cooperman puffed up his chest a little bit more, and his tone shifted from contemptuous to professorial, well, more like a contemptuous professor, but it was still a shift. His lawyer was about to object but Cooperman waved it away and Thurston sat back, figuring the billable hours would be the same whether his client hung himself or not. "A lot of jobs are depending on this movie getting made. People with families have to work those jobs or they can't pay their bills or handle their other piddly shit. If there's a way we can get this film made, and save their jobs, then we have to do whatever it takes. Even if it seems a tad cold or nasty to you people."

"Point taken," said Kirby.

"Fucking right," said Cooperman. "And I'm still not sure why you're even here."

"We explained that already," replied Darling.

"Still seems screwy to me," said Cooperman.

"How do you think this unidentified someone else could have taken control of your vehicle?" asked Darling, her voice a monotone.

"I think I can answer that one," said Weatherby. "We were in a meeting in Mr. Cooperman's suite with the people from Atlantic Comics before the press conference—"

"We were giving them the heads up about the recasting," explained Cooperman.

"After that meeting I realized I didn't know where the extra valet parker key was," continued Weatherby, "I couldn't remember if I had left it in the suite, or in the car, but I'm sure that you have the answer to that already."

"No shit Sherlock," growled Cooperman.

Kirby leaned forward.

"Do you know anyone in Quebec?" he asked.

Cooperman shrugged. "I produced a couple of pictures in Montreal," he answered, "I know some movie people there but not many. Why do you ask?"

"Just curious," said Kirby. "I think we're done here. Thank you for your time."

"Why are you here?" asked Sergeant Darling as she came into the conference room.

Molly Garret's big brown eyes popped up over her laptop. "Oh," she said, "Kirby called and asked me to bring him his drawing gear."

"I know I should have asked you first," said Kirby Baxter, not looking up from his oversized sketch pad, "but you were busy with checking alibis and I didn't see any harm in her coming to the station."

"We do have a sketch artist on the department payroll," said Darling. She expected to see Gustav, standing silently in the corner and watching the door, but not Molly, who she expected to be back at their hotel.

"I'm not that good at describing people verbally." Kirby changed pencils and continued drawing, "However, I'm pretty good at drawing them."

"Who are you drawing?" asked Darling.

"Remember when I asked Cooperman about knowing anyone in Quebec?" he asked.

"Sure," said Darling, "was that one of your little test questions to see if he's lying about anything?"

"It was sort of a test," said Kirby, "because he definitely lied to us about it."

"Really," asked Darling, "do you have any proof?"

"If you can identify the face I'm drawing," replied Kirby, "you will. What's the word on the alibis?"

"Chaz Healey's alibi checked out," answered Darling. "He spent the night of the murder passed out drunk on the couch of a woman with the stage name of 'Lindsay Hohan.' She's a stripper and her real name is Enid Cosgrove. As for Cooperman and Weatherby, they were both on the phone with different people in Los Angeles during the murder, and they were holding a press conference when someone tried to run you over with their truck."

"Alibis are all well and good," said Baxter, "but don't you think it's in the realm of possibility that they may have hired someone to do everything for them?"

"That's definitely within the realm," said Darling, "could you please explain what you're holding out on me?"

"I'm not holding out anything on you," said Baxter as he continued drawing, "I just didn't mention something that didn't make sense to me at the time."

"But it makes sense now?"

"Not completely," said Baxter, "which is why I need you and your resources."

"Does he always talk around the point like this?" Darling asked Molly.

"Sometimes," said Molly.

"Okay," said Baxter, putting a few carefully chosen strokes of pencil on the paper, "I'll get to the point. On the morning of the murder I was in the washroom and overheard Cooperman talking to a man with a French accent, or, to be more specific, a French Canadian from Quebec kind of accent. They talked about Cooperman paying him for something, and how it had to happen on Tuesday. Cooperman left, and I got a glimpse of the man before he left."

"Now you're drawing him from memory?" asked Darling.

"He's got a pretty freaky memory," said Molly.

"He's got a lot that's pretty freaky," added Darling.

"Did he do that trick where he told you what you had to eat?" asked Molly.

Darling nodded.

"That is as freaky as his bag of tricks can get."

"In some circles," said Baxter, still drawing, "it's considered rude to talk about someone while they're in the room."

"I'm just trying to help the police with their enquiries," answered Molly.

"Are you almost done?" asked Darling.

"Yes." Baxter turned the sketchpad over to show his handiwork to Darling, "this is the man I saw talking to Cooperman."

Darling was impressed, the level of detail was incredible, every remaining hair was carefully rendered, as well as every wrinkle and fold of skin. It was a round head on a thick neck, the nose was bulbous, the eyes watery with bags beneath them, and old acne scars dotted the man's stubbly cheeks. The man's hair was curly, but receding fast from a high forehead. A small scar lay beneath the man's left eye.

"It was tricky to do because I only saw his reflection in a mirror," said Baxter as he carefully tore the page from the sketchpad. "So I had to do a quick first draft, mapping out the main details, then use that as a model with everything flipped over."

"That face looks like it has a criminal record," said Darling as she took the page and studied it closely. "I'll call the Quebec Provincial Police, I'm sure there's someone there who knows this face."

"Are we going to bring in Sandra Doyle for questioning?" asked Baxter as he packed his art supplies back into his case and passed the case to Gustav.

"Gee," said Molly, "he's all eager to question the hot blonde actress."

"Very funny," said Baxter, "I'm also eager to talk to Ashmore."

"This is about him wanting to stop the movie from being made?"

"Ashmore's always had a tendency to overreact to everything," explained Baxter, "plus, he didn't attend the press conference."

"But he did attend the meeting before the press conference," added Darling.

"Where the spare key to the SUV disappeared," added Molly. "What?" she asked when Baxter and Darling turned to stare at her for stating the obvious, "In the writing game it's called 'exposition.'"

"It's a little obvious," said Baxter.

"Let's just get back on this case," said Darling.

"I think I'll head back to the hotel," said Molly, "and leave you two to bust this thing wide open."

"Yes," said Sandra Doyle, crossing a pair of epic length legs wrapped in a haiku length skirt, "I did arrive on Thursday. My schedule opened up and I could start work on the movie early."

"I understand you were fired off your television series Miss Doyle," said Kirby, keeping his tone even and his eyes from straying. They were in her suite at the Royal York Hotel, about eight blocks south of the Waterloo Hotel and convention centre.

"There were some creative differences," said Sandra, "between me and the show's producers. It was thought best that I take a hiatus from the series."

"According to the producer's twitter feed," said Sergeant Darling, "they're going to edit together something where your car explodes with you in it."

"That sounds like the beginning of a long hiatus," added Kirby.

"You can't believe everything you read," replied Sandra with a disdainful shake of her long blonde hair. "That's especially true of stuff on the internet."

"All right," said Darling. "I understand you had originally auditioned for the part that went to Erica Cross."

"A part that you have now," said Kirby.

"I see where you're going," said Sandra, studying her carefully lacquered nails in a failed effort to look nonchalant.

"You think I killed Erica?"

"Did you?" asked Kirby.

"I wouldn't risk chipping a nail on that slut," said Sandra.

"You can understand why we're concerned," said Kirby, "you were once banned from your own set for a week for assaulting a co-star."

"That was just a slap," said Sandra, "it was not assault, it was what she deserved for getting in my light. Besides the bitch got a big fat pay-off to go away, and she did."

"Yes she did," said Kirby, who had done his research on the way to Sandra's hotel, "all the way to an Emmy win and better ratings on another series."

Kirby caught a flash of anger dance across her perfectly sculpted face. If they weren't in the presence of a police detective with Gustav looming behind her like the spectre of death, she'd have been on Kirby like a pit bull and using those carefully lacquered nails to surgically remove his own less than perfect face. The flash lasted less than half a second, but he saw it, and she knew it.

"I know how these models work," she snarled. "They use their looks to get what they want."

"And you think that Erica Cross did that to get the lead part in the movie?" asked Darling.

"Those types of girls have to give head to get ahead," hissed Sandra, "it's obvious, just look at how hard she came onto you, when she found out how rich you are."

Kirby coughed into his hand to hide his own flash of anger from her cold blue eyes.

"Where were you at the time of Erica Cross' death?" asked Darling. "That was at one forty-five in the morning. You left the party early, and there's no evidence that you returned to this hotel that night, which means that we need to know where you were."

Sandra shrugged. "I guess you could say that I was doing charity work."

"Charity work?" asked Darling.

"I was making some nerd's life worth living from about

twelve thirty to around two o'clock in the morning."

"This was at the Waterloo?" asked Kirby.

"As you probably already know," said Sandra, "there had been an incident at the party the night before—"

"Erica Cross threw her drink in your face," said Darling, getting her own flash of anger from Sandra.

"Yes," answered Sandra, her voice low. "I didn't want a repeat of that incident, so I cut out of the second party early, before she could bitch out on me again, and went to the hotel bar, for a drink that wasn't all over my face. A bit after midnight this guy showed up and started sweet talking me like I was the most important woman in the world."

"Did you know him?" asked Darling.

Sandra shook her head and smiled. "Some rich guy, I think he had to be into computers or something...aren't they all? Anyway, he was short, had curly hair and was wearing some crazy looking shirt. He wasn't the best looking guy to hit on me, but he earned an A for effort and I gave him the gold star night of his life."

"Do you know his name?" asked Kirby, fearing the answer.

"His name was Harry Pairatestes," said Sandra, "I think he was Greek or Spanish or something like that. He had to be rich, he was staying in the biggest suite in the Waterloo."

"Oh hell," said Kirby, putting his hand over his face.

"What?" asked Sandra.

"Nothing," said Kirby rising from his seat and shaking Sandra's hand. "Thanks for your time."

"Finally," said Sandra. "I really must go see the hair and make-up people, for some reason they're insisting that my character remain a redhead. I say why mess with perfection."

Gustav closed the door behind them as they entered the hallway.

"Thanks for your time?" asked Darling.

"She has an alibi," said Kirby, "and I'm surprised we haven't heard all about it already."

"What do you mean?" asked Darling. "I had to keep from

laughing over that silly fake name she gave us. I thought you'd be all over it like a dog on a bone."

"I know who gave her that fake name," said Kirby. "We need to get back to the Waterloo. I have to ask Ashmore some questions."

"What does Ashmore have to do with Erica Cross' death?"

"A motive."

"What about her alibi?"

"I know her alibi."

"Who is it?"

"It's that little bastard Mitch."


"Hello Fred," said Kirby as he took a seat across from Ashmore. They were in one of the multi-purpose rooms that ringed the main convention floor. Characters and logos from DC Comics papered the walls. Kirby picked it himself; he wanted Ashmore surrounded by the symbols of a bigger and more successful company. There was no table, nothing for Ashmore to lean on.

"Should I have a lawyer here?" asked Ashmore.

"We're just confirming alibis," said Darling as she sat in the folding chair Gustav put out for her, "you don't think you need a lawyer for that, do you?"

"Really," said Ashmore, craning his long neck to watch Gustav take a position behind him. "So why are Kirby and his...um...friend here?"

"He's a consultant on this case," said Darling.

"No, really," said Ashmore with a nervous laugh, "why is he here?"

"He's a special consultant on this investigation," said Darling.

"I even got a fancy ID card and everything," said Kirby, showing the warrant card Interpol gave him.

"You must have had this printed by someone," said Ashmore as he leaned over to study the card.

"A lot can happen in two years," said Kirby, "especially

when you are trying to get a life outside of work."

"Yeah," said Ashmore, "but it's supposed to be a life drawing greeting cards. Not running around conning the cops into thinking that you're somehow Sherlock Baxter the boy detective."

"You can Google me after this interview," said Kirby.

"Sure," said Ashmore unable to contain the sarcasm and disbelief, "that means it must be true."

"I Googled you on the way over here," said Kirby. "Do you know what it told me?"

"What?" asked Ashmore.

"That everything people have been telling me since I left the company is true," said Kirby, "that all the top people are gone, sales are down and the company's losing money at a level not seen since the big crash of the nineteen nineties."

"We're not that bad," said Ashmore, shifting uncomfortably in his seat. "I will admit that the company's hit a bit of a rough patch, but we're going to survive bigger than ever."

"How can Atlantic Comics survive if the sale to Continental Pictures goes down the toilet?"

Ashmore's eyes widened for just a flash.

"What are you getting at?" asked Ashmore, trying and failing to appear calm.

"You signed a pretty crappy contract with Cooperman," said Kirby, "if they even start filming The Vengeance Sisters movie within the next week, his MaxCo will control the movie rights of all of Atlantic Comics' characters, especially its most popular and potentially profitable franchises, for another two years. I don't see Continental Pictures sitting around for two years waiting to make movies out of characters they're supposed to own, and I don't see Max Cooperman letting them do it without paying him off big time."

Ashmore crossed and uncrossed his legs.

"It must make you look pretty bad to your family," continued Kirby. "They owned Atlantic Comics for what, almost eighty years? Eighty years of fairly smooth operation, and now it looks like it's all going to crash and burn with a pot of gold just within reach. Because you screwed it up with your contract with Cooperman."

"There are ways around that contract," said Ashmore.

"Like killing the lead actress a few days before principal photography begins?" asked Kirby.

Ashmore's entire body stiffened, then he started to stand up. Gustav took a step forward but Kirby signalled him to stop.

"Unless I'm under arrest," said Ashmore as he rose, "I'm leaving."

"We still need to confirm your alibi," Darling declared, "because if we don't then we might have to put you under arrest for real."

Ashmore stopped in front of the door and slumped down his head.

"At one forty-five I was on the phone with my father," said Ashmore, "he was calling from Hawaii and spent half an hour carving me a new asshole over this MaxCo deal. Today, when someone tried to run over your precious little consultant, I was on the phone with my Uncle Leonard from New York. It was his turn to carve me yet another asshole, because my family doesn't think I have enough. If you ask them, they'll probably repeat everything they said to me verbatim. Are you happy now?"

"Sure," said Kirby, actually feeling a little guilty for pushing those buttons, but he wasn't going to show it to Ashmore. Kirby hid his own guilt because he knew Ashmore didn't feel even a little bit guilty for crushing his career and life over a petty fit of ego. "That's all, thank you for your time."

"So," said Darling as they stepped back onto the main convention floor. "We have suspects, but they all have alibis, and so far they all seem to be checking out."

"Ma'am," said a young uniformed patrolman as he

approached, followed by Bruce Haring. Kirby nodded to Bruce, and he waved back.

"Don't call me 'Ma'am,'" said Darling.

"If I called you by your name," said the young patrolman with a smirk, "there could be some misunderstandings."

"Don't be cutesy and just call me 'Sergeant,'" ordered Sergeant Darling. "Did you talk to Mitch Mandelbaum?"

"He was very forthcoming about the encounter...Sergeant," replied the young patrolman, "in fact, if he had pictures, he'd have shown them to everyone."

"Thank God for small mercies," said Kirby.

"Mr. Haring has a question for you," said the young patrolman.

"How can we help you Mr. Haring?"

"I know you have rules about this sort of thing," said Haring, "but I'd like to know if you're making any progress."

"We can't really comment on an ongoing investigation," said Darling.

"I understand," said Haring, "did you look into her stalker?"

"Her stalker?" asked Darling.

"I mentioned him to that older detective," said Haring, "the one named Spasky."

"You also mentioned him to me," said Kirby. "I feel like an idiot for not thinking about it earlier." This was an honest answer; he really did feel like a Grade A idiot for letting his hunger for a petty revenge against Ashmore distract him from another potential suspect.

"Do you think this stalker may be in town?" asked Darling.

"I don't know," answered Haring, "but I do know that he scared Erica more than she let on and I think it can't hurt to look into it."

"Knowing our luck he was having high tea with the Queen, the Pope and the Dalai Lama," said Darling.

"It still won't hurt to look." said Kirby, knowing that he should have said that much earlier.

"The LAPD have a file," said Haring, "but Erica kept copies of everything she had on her laptop."

"Then let's take a look at that," said Darling.

"It's in her suite," said Haring, "follow me."

"I don't know if this creep followed her to Toronto or what," said Bruce as the elevator chimed their arrival at the Excelsior floor, "but who knows these days."

"It's definitely something to look into," said Darling as she followed Bruce into the hall.

"I wish I had thought of it earlier," said Kirby as he came out of the elevator, followed by Gustav.

"Things have been a little confusing lately," said Darling.

"That's more of an excuse than a cause," said Kirby, giving himself another mental kick in the pants for his stupidity.

Bruce reached into his pocket for the room's key card but froze right in front of the suite's door.

"Were your officers in the room today?" asked Bruce.

"No," said Darling. Kirby stepped aside and saw that the door was ajar. "But there are supposed to be two watching the door. Where are they?"

"Someone popped the lock," said Kirby.

"Stand aside," said Darling, drawing her gun, a 9mm Glock, with one hand and her pocket radio with another. "This is Sergeant Darling," she said into the radio, getting a crackly response from the officers downstairs, "I need back-up on the thirteenth floor, because someone has broken into the Erica Cross suite."

Gustav reached for his holster, but Kirby signalled him to stand down.

Darling nudged the door open with her foot and entered the suite. Bruce stood back, but Kirby followed the detective and Gustav followed him.

Suitcases were lying on the floor of the suite's main drawing room, wide open, and their contents were strewn everywhere. Someone had pulled out the drawers from the little writing desk, turned them over and tossed them aside.

"Oh my..." muttered Bruce from the door.

"Stay here," said Darling as she approached the door to the bedroom.

SLAM!

A figure body-checked the detective and slammed her hard into the wall. Kirby leaped at the figure and while in mid-air asked himself what the hell he was doing, then got the answer when the charging figure slammed him into the other wall. The world spun around Kirby's head as the air rushed from his body, and then he felt the carpet rub hard against his face. It took less than a second for the world to stop spinning. When it finally did, he saw the figure, now transformed into a man with a narrow, rat-like face and thinning hair, his back pinned to the floor by Gustav's beefy arm. The rat-faced man's eyes and mouth were wide open with terror. However, he did have the option of closing his eyes; closing his mouth though was impossible, since the barrel of Gustav's .45 automatic pistol was jammed in it.

"Gustav is a very useful fellow to have around," said Darling as she got up from the floor.

"You have no idea," said Kirby. "Next time, we'll let him go in first, all right."

Kirby carefully unwrapped his cheeseburger, lifted the top bun, peeked at the contents and let out a barely audible grumble.

"Don't you hate that?" said Kirby, looking across the interrogation room table at his subject, "you finally get a chance to eat lunch, after spending half the day running around in circles, you ask them to hold the mayonnaise and guess what, they put mayonnaise on it."

"Lawyer," said the man across from Kirby. Gustav, back in his position of looming doom over the man's shoulder, lowered his own sandwich and gave Kirby a look that reminded Kirby of the time he and Gustav faced a very reluctant informant in London, but Kirby shook his head. He didn't think the Canadian police would allow that sort of thing.

"At least they got the onion rings right," said Kirby, biting one. "These are pretty good, do you want any?"

"Lawyer," said the man.

"That's what Sergeant Darling's arranging," answered Kirby. "But this is not an interrogation. I'm not a cop, I'm just a consultant. I don't even want to be here, I got kind of drafted into this mess, and besides, we already know all we need to know about you."

The man cocked an eyebrow ever so slightly. He wanted to know what they knew, and that was Kirby's opening to find out what this little rat of a man knew.

"We know that your name is Armand Tanzerian," continued Kirby, "you're from North Hollywood, California; you make your living as a paparazzi, selling photos of celebrities to the tabloids. You also have a habit of trespassing on private property, and have just graduated into burglary, assault and assault on a police officer."

"I didn't know she was a cop," said Tanzerian in a mentally rehearsed monotone, "I thought she was a burglar with a gun who was going to kill me."

"A burglar?" asked Kirby. "That's your defence? You thought a woman in a grey suit calling out 'police' was a burglar breaking into a room sealed with crime scene tape and under police guard?"

"I didn't see any guards," said Tanzerian with a faux nonchalant shrug.

"That's right," said Kirby, as he scraped the mayonnaise off his hamburger bun with the otherwise useless plastic knife that came with his lunch. "The policemen guarding the door just happened to be called away to assist hotel security when half a dozen homeless men started causing trouble at the entrance of the convention centre."

"What a coincidence," said Tanzerian.

"We already have the statements of those homeless men," said Kirby, "they were quite eager to say that they were paid by you to cause that trouble. That means you're also on the hook for conspiracy to cause what they call a 'breach of the Queen's peace.' Don't you love the names they give these laws? It's like something out of Masterpiece Theatre."

Tanzerian just sat and stared straight ahead.

"Of course your lawyer can sort all that out," said Kirby. "I wonder if the Canadian lawyers wear the wigs in court like the British ones. I'll have to look into it. Anyway, yours will be quite busy."

Tanzerian sat in silence, Kirby took a bite out of his now mostly mayonnaise free cheeseburger. He chewed slowly and deliberately, letting the time take its toll on Tanzerian's nerves. Then he took a sip of Coke Zero, and turned back to

Tanzerian.

"We took a look in your bag," said Kirby, "and I have to say that it does a really good job of hanging you. By the way, that's just a figure of speech, they don't have hanging here in Canada. Anyway, we found a laptop in your bag that belongs to Erica Cross. Let me guess, you were convinced that she left it to you in her will, and you decided to go get it before any mystery burglars calling themselves cops came and took it?"

No answer.

"Then I guess you'll be using the same defence with all those pairs of her panties we found in your bag?" asked Kirby, trying to be nonchalant himself, and fighting the urge to let Gustav correct this fellow the way he did that irksome informant. "I don't think you got them for yourself. They're not your size. So I'm figuring that you were planning to sell them on the internet as some kind of pervy collectible."

Stony silence. Tanzerian crossed his arms.

"Then again," said Kirby, "maybe you do want them for yourself. Doesn't really matter, this isn't California, juries aren't going to just let you walk away with a fine. You're in a lot of serious trouble, and are looking at some serious jail time."

Tanzerian didn't even blink.

"Do you have anything else to say?" asked Kirby.

"Nice jacket," answered Tanzerian.

"We're done here."


Kirby balled the napkin and tossed it into the wastebasket. It bounced off the rim across the opening, hit the opposite side, and then bounced back and forth along the inside to rest on the crumpled remains of the bag from the burger joint.

Sergeant Darling came into the conference room. "Well," she said, "Tanzerian's booked and the next bus to the city jail is in an hour."

"I didn't learn much from him that we didn't already

know," said Kirby, "other than that he seems to like my jacket."

"I guess it's got a certain retro charm," said Darling, as she studied the jacket, which looked well-worn and dotted with pockets and pouches. "Where did you get it?"

"I got it in a little store in a side street in Geneva," answered Kirby, "it's Swiss Army surplus."

"Let me guess," said Darling, "the sleeves unfold into a bottle opener."

"Gustav said the same joke when I bought it," replied Kirby. Gustav nodded from his seat in the corner.

"What does the patch on the shoulder say?"

"It's a Battlestar Galactica space fighter pilot patch," answered Kirby. "I have a Justice League Trainee patch on the other shoulder."

Kirby's phone rang, it was Molly calling.

"Just a second," said Kirby as he pulled out the phone. "Hello, Molly."

"Hey Kirby," said Molly from the hotel, "have you been able to avoid getting run over again?"

"Yes," answered Kirby, "I'm back at the police station. That guy Gustav caught turned out to be a paparazzi looking for a scoop."

"I was hoping he'd turn out to be Erica's mystery stalker and be ready to confess to everything," sighed Molly.

"He still might be," said Kirby, "the police tech people are going over Erica's laptop and seeing if any of the stalker pictures match anything in Tanzerian's files. The guy literally had at almost four dozen flash drives on him, all full of pictures."

"Almost four dozen?"

"Okay," said Kirby, "I counted forty-three flash drives, but I didn't see all of them."

"Ooh," said Molly, "I've dug some stuff up that might help you."

"Now you're playing detective?"

"I'm sticking with stuff I can find online from the safety

of your suite," said Molly. "Unlike you, I like to keep some distance between myself and the homicidally inclined."

"I'm not sure if 'homicidally' is a word," said Kirby.

"No one likes a know-it-all," said Molly, "besides I did manage to dig some stuff up all by myself."

"Then stop keeping me in suspense and tell me," said Kirby.

"You know about Ashmore's bad contract with MaxCo?"

"Yes," said Kirby.

"Well," said Molly, "I've done some research, and it seems that MaxCo itself is in a similar situation."

"How?"

"Did you know that movies can't get made without some sort of insurance coverage?"

"It's not that big a stretch of the imagination."

"It seems that Max Cooperman has been having some trouble getting insurance for The Vengeance Sisters movie," continued Molly, "he's had a few movies get cancelled before the shooting started and he's cashed out on their insurance. Now his movies won't be covered until after the shooting starts."

"So he has to at least get the movie started," said Kirby.

"After that," explained Molly, "he's in the clear. If something happens to the movie and he's got to shut down after shooting starts he's in a win-win situation. He gets the insurance money, and he keeps the ownership rights over the Atlantic Comics characters."

"That's making me think," said Kirby. "I heard him talking to this mystery man about getting a job done on Tuesday. Maybe the guy got the day wrong? Maybe Erica saw or heard something she shouldn't have? Maybe–"

"Maybe he's just some guy working on the movie?" asked Molly.

"Exactly," said Kirby, "I could be the one misunderstanding everything, and Cooperman may not have anything to do with this."

"I wish we had nothing to do with this," said Molly.

"I wish none of this ever happened," said Kirby, "this isn't the first time, and I worry that it's not going to be the last."

"I should let you go," said Molly, "I've got to kick Mitch's ass for sleeping with that sleazy actress."

"Don't blame Mitch for that," said Kirby, "he's just a man. I'm not saying that you shouldn't kick his ass, because there are lots of other things you can kick his ass for. But you might want to give him a pass on that one."

"You know," said Molly, "when we got back to the suite this morning, I swore I could sense the bitchiness factor in the room rise about fifty per cent. It's like she left a trail behind her."

"Only fifty?"

"My own sweet nature tempered it."

"Temper being the operative word."

"I'm half Sicilian and half Irish," answered Molly, "I'm all temper."

"I really should let you go," said Kirby. "Feel free to abuse the room service, and feel even freer to abuse Mitch, but save some of each for me."

"I will," said Molly. "Goodbye."

"I'll see you in a little while," said Kirby.

Kirby hung up the phone, stuck it back in his jeans pocket and started to take off his jacket. Despite its light weight and the building's air conditioner running full blast, it was starting to feel uncomfortable.

"Is that your girlfriend?" asked Darling.

"No," said Kirby. There were no hooks or hangers for his jacket, so he folded it over and laid it on the counter next to the coffee maker. "It's kind of complicated. No, actually, it's very simple; however we manage to make it complicated."

"I think I know that situation."

"Any word from forensics on the computers?" asked Kirby.

"Mr. Haring got us into Erica's computer without a problem," said Darling, "they're printing copies for us to look at. But it looks like Tanzerian's stuff is password protected, and I don't think he's going to give it to us."

"His password is his birthdate," said Kirby, "backwards."

"Now how the hell do you know that?" asked Darling. "Are you a real mind reader?"

"No," said Kirby, "he's not a very original thinker, so his birthdate is the obvious choice, but he thinks he's clever, so it'll be backwards."

"This I have to see," said Darling as she took out her cell phone and speed dialled forensics. "Hey, Della, it's Liz Darling, did you try Tanzerian's birthdate as his password? ... You did; no dice... Could you try it backwards? ... Yeah, I'll wait... Yes... No way?" Darling cupped her hand over the phone, "It worked. His files are all open." Then she went back to the phone. "Print the ones from the last three days first, and we'll be right down there to see it. Great work."

"We're going to see the forensics lab?" asked Kirby.

"Yes," said Darling, "get moving."

Too many years of crime shows on TV had tainted Kirby's opinion of crime labs. Each time he visited one, part of him hoped for slick, neon-lit, laboratories, populated by equally slick and sexy technicians. Sadly, the flickering florescent lights and sickly bureaucracy-yellow paint of reality always dashed his fantasies.

They were greeted by a short woman in a lab coat and black framed glasses named Della Greene, who resembled Velma from Scooby-Doo a little too much for Kirby's comfort. Once they got past the introductions and the traditional surprise at the appearance of Gustav, she directed them to a computer and stacks of photo prints.

"There's over a hundred photos sent by the stalker," said Della, "almost as many by Tanzerian over the past three days. Some celebrities at airports and some other stuff."

Della Greene then laid out a string of photos that Kirby recognized instantly. They were from the party on Thursday night and showed, like frames from a movie, Erica Cross giving Kirby a peck on the cheek. Kirby also noted that the only one that made it to the internet was the only one that, because of the angle, looked like they were in a full lip lock. Kirby resisted the urge to say 'jinkies,' because he didn't think anyone would get it.

"Can I see the photos the stalker emailed to Miss Cross?" asked Kirby. Della passed them over and Kirby started flipping through them, studying them carefully as they flashed past him, taking in every detail. They were of Erica going in and out of hotels, sitting in make-up chairs, posing for other people's photos, getting her mail, shopping for groceries, having coffee with Bruce Haring at a sidewalk cafe and even doing her dishes as seen from outside via the kitchen window. The settings for the pictures were several major cities in North America and Europe, at different times of year. According to the date stamps on the corner the stalker took them over many months.

"Maybe Tanzerian is her stalker," considered Darling. "We'll have to double check his passport to see if they match up with any of the places in these pictures."

Kirby tucked the photos back into a neat stack and returned them to the work table. He then returned to the stack of Tanzerian's photos. Kirby skipped over the ones featuring Kirby Baxter; because he already knew where and when Tanzerian took those pictures. He set those aside, and he scanned through the others just as quickly as the stalker pictures.

"He's not the stalker," said Kirby, stopping dead at one particular photo and peering at it closely.

"You know that just from looking at the pictures he took from the last three days?"

"Yes," said Kirby, "but I have to talk to him again."

"Okay," said Darling, "but can I at least have some explanation first?"

"Armand Tanzerian is a professional paparazzi," said Kirby.

"Which is a great job for a stalker," said Darling.

"That's good in theory," said Kirby putting the picture

aside and picking up Tanzerian's camera, "but sadly wrong in this case. Tanzerian's camera is high-end, professional grade, with all sorts of fancy lenses and customized extras, like this Bluetooth rig that lets him store back-ups on a separate flash drive even if his camera gets smashed. His pictures show this sort of professionalism. Despite being taken from a distance and with uncooperative, if not hostile subjects, they are carefully composed, with lots of extra shots to make sure he gets the one that's just right."

"It's not that big a stretch," said Darling, "he is a professional photographer."

"The stalker pictures are done by a mid-range, off the shelf digital camera," explained Kirby. "The kind with a built in auto-zoom that doesn't go as close as Tanzerian's camera." Kirby picked up one of the stalker photos. "Look at this shot, it was taken from a distance, and it's fuzzy around the edges. The focus isn't as sharp and the composition isn't anywhere near as clear. This stalker is an amateur and doesn't really know anywhere near as much about photography as Tanzerian."

"So Tanzerian is a scumbag," said Darling, "and probably a creepy pervert, but he's not our stalker, and is probably not our murderer. So why do you want to talk to him again?"

"I need to talk to him about this picture," said Kirby, holding up one of the photos from Tanzerian's stack.

"What is that?" asked Darling, narrowing her eyes to study it closer.

"This is a picture of our murder weapon," said Kirby.

"Sorry," said the uniformed officer as he led Tanzerian into the conference room, "but Narcotics need all the interrogation rooms."

"Just sit him there," instructed Darling, pointing to a chair next to the conference table. The uniformed officer took Tanzerian to the chair and the photographer sat down. Gustav took his usual position in the corner behind Tanzerian.

"I want a lawyer," said Tanzerian.

"This isn't about your case," said Kirby. "This is about the murder of Erica Cross."

"So I'm not a suspect anymore?" asked Tanzerian.

"You are a lot of things," said Darling, "but Mr. Baxter here is convinced that you're not her murderer."

"Well," said Tanzerian, "isn't that just wonderful."

"I'm not completely convinced," added Darling, "but I'll give him a chance to show off."

"All I want to know," said Kirby laying a single photograph on the table, "is where you took this photo."

"This picture," said Tanzerian. "It's a dumpster full of garbage."

"But you focused on a specific bag in that dumpster," said Kirby. "Why?"

"It stood out," said Tanzerian. "Actually, it 'smelled out' if you know what I mean. I caught a whiff of it as soon as I opened the damn thing."

"That's why you opened this bag and took this picture?" asked Darling.

"I thought it had to be something funky," said Tanzerian. "Maybe it was a new kind of drug or something like that."

"But you didn't find drugs," asked Kirby, "did you?"

"You can see the picture," said Tanzerian, "it's some sort of mangled fruit salad in there."

"A salad would have more than one kind of fruit," said Kirby, "this bag is full of apples. Apples that look like they've been gutted and torn apart next to broken glass and what look like the parts of a hot plate."

"Yeah," said Tanzerian, "I'm more of a grape man myself."

"Where did you take the picture?"

"It was at the Waterloo Hotel," said Tanzerian, "right under the chute for the trash from the Excelsior floor. Even their garbage gets special treatment."

"I knew it," said Kirby.

There was a knock at the door. A young detective stood

there with a manila folder in his hand.

"Sergeant Darling?" asked the young detective.

"What is it?" asked Darling.

"We have a possible ID from Mr. Baxter's sketch," said the young detective, "I put together a photo line-up for him to look at."

"Okay," said Darling, before turning to the uniformed officer, "keep him here until I say, all right?"

The uniformed officer nodded. Kirby, Darling and Gustav then followed the young detective into the main bullpen. The detective then opened the manila folder, revealing six photographs, all of men of the same build and facial features. It took Kirby less than a glance to spot the one he saw in the bathroom.

"Number five," said Kirby, without hesitation or doubt.

"His name is Laval," said the detective. "Montreal police has him as a suspected arsonist and muscle for some of their local gangsters, but he's managed to avoid getting pinched in the last five years."

"Any idea where he is now?" asked Darling.

"I checked with his parole officer," answered the detective, "and she told me that he's in the movie business now. He's working security at Northern Star Studios."

"Let me guess," said Kirby, "that's where they're filming Max Cooperman's latest movie?" The detective nodded.

"We better check this out," said Darling. "Care to come along?"

"Yes," said Kirby. "But we should hold on to Tanzerian until we get back. I still want to know everything he knows about those apples."

"What is it with you and those apples?" asked Darling. "She wasn't beaten to death with a sack of fruit."

"It's not what's in the bag that's got me freaked out," answered Kirby. "But what wasn't in the bag."

"All right," said Darling, "I'll bite. What wasn't in the bag oh great detective?"

"The seeds," answered Kirby. "All the seeds were gone."

"What's so special about the seeds?"

"If you know a little chemistry," answered Kirby as they headed to the door, "or can find the right recipe off the internet and can get enough apple seeds, you can kill someone."

"How?"

"Apple seeds contain cyanide."

Tanzerian's eyes drifted along the walls, taking in the posters warning of the dangers of drunk driving, intravenous drugs and life as a runaway on the mean streets of the big city. His eyes then drifted to the coffee maker.

"So," said Tanzerian, "how long do I have to wait?"

"You'll wait until Sergeant Darling gets back," said the uniformed officer. "Then she'll decide what to do with you."

"Fine," said Tanzerian. "Are the handcuffs really necessary?" he asked, half raising the hand that the policemen had cuffed to the leg of the conference table.

"I think so," said the uniformed officer. Tanzerian let his eyes wander some more. Baxter's jacket hung on a hook. A ball point click pen lay on the table, next to a scattering of half a dozen staples.

"I'm a little thirsty," said Tanzerian. "Do you have anything to drink?"

"We have some coffee in here," said the uniformed officer.

"I'd kill for some tea," said Tanzerian. "That's just a figure of speech, not a confession."

"I figured that out for myself."

"Can I get some tea?" asked Tanzerian. "With just a little milk in it."

"I'll see what's in the break room," said the uniformed officer.

"You're a saint," said Tanzerian, watching the uniformed officer leave, then waiting a beat, before reaching for the pen, and the staples.

ISSUE #13
NO BUSINESS LIKE SHOW BUSINESS

"Do you have a pass?" asked the guard at the gate of Northern Star Studios with the name tag saying his name was Arthur.

"This is my universal pass," said Darling, taking out her badge and sticking it out of the window. "I need to see your supervisor."

"It's Saturday," said the guard, "she's at home, but I'm sort of the supervisor on weekends."

"Then let us in," said Darling. "We need to talk."

"Are you all cops?" asked Arthur the guard/supervisor pointing to Kirby in the passenger seat, and Gustav looming in the back of the grey sedan.

"That's strictly need-to-know," answered Darling.

"No skin off my nose," said Arthur as he raised the gate and waved them in.

As she drove in Darling leaned out the window and asked: "Where can we find a security guard named Pierre Laval?"

"He's not a studio guard," said Arthur.

"What do you mean?" asked Kirby.

"Only six guys work directly for this facility," explained Arthur as he stepped out of the booth. "We just make sure no one enters the studio complex. The producers using the individual sound stages are in charge of their own security. They either bring in their own people, or they subcontract to a local security firm."

"Do you at least have a record of him coming in and out

of here?"

"Sure," said Arthur, reaching into his booth and pulling out a clipboard. "Do you know what company he works for?"

"MaxCo Films," said Kirby, "he's working on The Vengeance Sisters movie."

"That narrows it down," said Arthur flipping through the pages. "According to this, he's on duty right now at sound stage thirty. You just go straight down there, and turn left. It's the big grey building with the number thirty painted on it in big red letters."

"Thank you," said Darling.

"So let me get this straight," said Darling as they got out of the car in front of the massive grey block of a building with the number thirty painted on the side in massive red letters. "Max Cooperman could actually make money if this film doesn't get made?"

"If he times everything just right," said Kirby, "he could cash in the insurance and retain control of the Atlantic Comics characters, even if he never actually finishes making the film."

"The movie business doesn't make any sense," said Darling.

"You're preaching to the choir," said Kirby.

"Do you think he's willing to kill to get this scam to work?" asked Darling as they walked to the door.

Kirby shrugged.

"The timing is all off," he answered. "None of the things he needs to happen will go into effect until Monday at the earliest when shooting is supposed to begin."

Darling tried the door.

"It's locked," she said. "Do you think we should knock, or should we keep our element of surprise?"

"I'm all for surprise," said Kirby. "Can you claim exigent circumstances since we have a potential murder suspect inside?"

"I'm sure we can justify popping the door," said Darling, "but it's steel and I don't think the studio's owners will appreciate me using a battering ram."

"Battering rams are unnecessary," said Kirby. "We can be subtle."

"How subtle?"

"Gustav," asked Kirby, "do you think you can handle this?"

The big man nodded, positioned himself in front of the door, knelt and took a small black package out of his jacket, and from that package he took out a small thin metal tool. He slipped it into the lock, turned it, and it clicked." Gustav smiled, put his tool back in its package, and put that back into his jacket pocket.

"What do you know," explained Kirby, "the door just spontaneously unlocked itself, thank you for discovering that Gustav."

Gustav nodded and stepped back from the door.

"Ladies first," said Kirby, "since you are the designated cop."

Darling drew her pistol, Gustav followed suit and gestured for Kirby to get behind him. Kirby obeyed and slipped behind the big man, after his rough encounter with Tanzerian he remembered that he preferred to illustrate heroes rather than be one.

Darling entered the sound stage.

"Pierre Laval," she ordered, "Toronto Police. Come out with your hands up."

No answer, Darling cocked her head to signal Gustav and Kirby to follow her.

"Now I know this movie is bullshit," said Kirby after seeing the inside of the sound stage.

"What do you mean?" asked Darling.

"Look around," said Kirby. Darling looked around, to her it looked like a cave decked out like a mad scientist's lair. Various strange machines and metallic scaffolding lined the faux rock walls, and a massive metallic V stood in the centre of it all. "Can you see all that's wrong here?"

"It looks like the Batcave from the old TV show," said Darling.

"Exactly," said Kirby, "it's supposed to be The Vengeance Sisters headquarters, but their headquarters is on the top of a tower overlooking the city. Trust me; the fans are militant nitpickers about such stuff. When I drew a crossover issue with my Shadowknight book, I got all kinds of snark in the fan forums about getting the shape of the windows wrong. The fanboys are going to look at this and carve this movie a new one before it's even released."

"Will that affect the box office?" asked Darling, re-holstering her pistol at no sign of Pierre Laval.

"If the book's core fans are doing nothing but crapping on a movie," said Kirby, "the general audience is going to be turned off from wanting to see it. The moment pictures of this set get on the internet, the movie's going to be branded a turkey before it's even released."

Gustav touched a wall, and it started to rock.

"I know that movie sets aren't supposed to be very substantial," asked Darling, "but I don't think the walls are supposed to rock like that."

"Especially when the trades are saying MaxCo spent over two million on this set alone," said Kirby. Then he froze.

"What?"

Kirby put a finger to his lips. Darling held her breath and heard footsteps in the distance, footsteps that were coming from behind a fake rock wall.

Darling drew her gun, and cocked her head to signal Gustav to follow her. Gustav drew his own pistol and stepped in behind her.


They walked in silence along the edge of the set. Carefully treading on the concrete floor to avoid making any noise. The trio approached a door marked STAGE OFFICE. Light seeped out from under the door, and Kirby could see the shadows of moving feet, and hear something coming from inside.

"Do you hear it?" asked Kirby from behind the wall otherwise known as Gustav, which experience taught him was the safest place to be.

"Sounds like someone talking."

"Singing," corrected Kirby. "I think it's ABBA."

Darling touched the doorknob, it was unlocked, and she swung open the door and stepped inside.

"Toronto Police!" she barked.

Kirby looked around Gustav and peeked into the room. Laval was sitting at a table, his back to Darling, a pair of chunky old school headphones on his head. That same head was bobbing up and down as he tunelessly sang along to his favourite Swedish pop quartet. He was working on something, Kirby could smell a soldering iron, and he assumed it was something to do with wiring.

Darling reached up and yanked off Laval's headphones. The man leaped to his feet, his old school portable CD player fell to the floor with a clatter.

"Toronto Police!" Darling yelled as she swung him around and slammed him against the wall.

"Tabernac!" barked Laval as he hit the wall.

"Pierre Laval, you're wanted for questioning in the murder of Erica Cross," declared Darling as she handcuffed Laval. She then turned to Kirby. "You can be subtle when you have to be, and I can be rough when I have to."

"Uh," said Kirby staring at table, "Houston, I think we have a problem."

"What problem?" asked Darling turning to look at the table. In the centre of the table was a contraption of metal pipes, wires and a digital clock. Something from inside the mass of wires was emitting a strange blue smoke. "That's a bomb."

"I suggest running," said Kirby.

"Good suggestion," said Darling, passing off Laval to Gustav, who more or less tucked the handcuffed man under one arm, and all four of them ran like hell for the exit.

"I think diving in the grass was a little excessive," said Darling. "The bomb hasn't even gone off."

"Damn," said Kirby from his spot on the grassy verge on the edge of the parking lot, "I was sort of going for the 'leaping away from the fireball action star' look."

Laval was cursing in French from his position pinned between Gustav's arm and the trunk of Darling's car.

Kirby sat up. "That had to be a bomb. I haven't seen many bombs in my life, but that sure looked like one."

"I'm calling the bomb squad," said Darling, pulling out her cell phone. "We better not take a chance."

Kirby stood up, brushed the grass from his jeans, and realized that he forgot his jacket at the police station.

"This is Sergeant Darling," she said, "We need the bomb squad at Northern Star Studios. We have a possible explosive device."

BOOM!

Kirby felt the shock wave tackle him across his chest and toss him like a four-hundred-pound linebacker in mid-steroid rage. The world spun, and he saw his sneakers backed by a clear blue sky. Then he felt pavement slam into his back, and the air stampede from his lungs. Everything went grey for a second. He waited for the roar to fade before he attempted to sit up.

"Is everyone okay?" he asked.

Darling sat up and nodded. Gustav gave them the thumbs up as he rose from the asphalt, Laval, who was beneath him, just cursed some more in French.

"It's not a possible explosive device," he said before coughing, "it's a definite." Kirby looked and saw that the rear half of the sound stage was now a heap of smoking shattered concrete.

"Now you'll never get your chance to try out your action star leap," said Darling.

"Definitely," answered Kirby. "Reality has terrible timing."

# VOLUME THREE

# THE DORK KNIGHT RISES

ISSUE #14
BUSTED / FLUSHED

"I want a lawyer," grunted Laval from his chair in Interrogation Room One, "and I want another doctor."

"Another doctor?" asked Darling. They had only just got back to the station after getting the 'all-clear' at the Emergency Room. Aside from a few bruises and scrapes to their bodies and egos they were all deemed fit for duty.

"I think that goon," growled Laval pointing at Gustav in the corner, his accent making it sound like 'I dink dat goon,' "cracked one of my ribs."

"He did save you from the explosion," said Darling.

"I got nothing to say about no explosion," said Laval.

"Fine," said Darling, "you know the drill. A lawyer will be obtained for you but remember, you were caught in the act of making a bomb. We can make a case for terrorism."

Kirby watched Laval's eyes widen in surprise.

"What are you talking about?"

"As far as we know," added Kirby, catching the hint and playing along, "you could be working for Al Qaeda, ISIS, or maybe the FLQ is making a comeback."

"Bullshit," muttered Laval, sounding like 'bool-sheet.'

"It's your funeral," said Darling, rising from her chair. "The crime scene unit called me from the scene while we were at the Emergency Room. The collapse of the building buried a lot of evidence, but buried evidence is pretty easy to dig up. They've already found a lot of bomb-making materials—"

"That's just common household stuff," said Laval with a shrug.

"The jury isn't going to hear that," said Darling, "not after months of the press calling your little back room a 'terrorist bomb factory.'"

Darling sat back, Kirby saw that it was his turn to talk.

"Do you know what catches people who make bombs?" asked Kirby.

Laval just shrugged.

"They get sloppy covering their tracks," said Kirby. "If they do it enough times they start to assume that all the evidence, like fingerprints and DNA are just going to be burnt up or blown up. The problem is that the labs these days have caught up to all that."

"But that's just small change really," said Darling.

"That's right," added Kirby, focusing on Laval's eyes, "there is the murder charge."

"What murder charge?" asked Laval. "Nobody got killed by that bomb! That's bullshit!"

"We're talking about Erica Cross," said Darling.

"Who the hell is that?" asked Laval.

"She's the young woman you murdered," declared Kirby.

"I have nothing to say without a lawyer," said Laval.

"Have it your way," said Darling, "the clock is ticking." Then she and Kirby rose from their seats, Kirby signalling Gustav to join them.

As they reached the door Kirby turned and asked: "Do you think a rich, pampered, Hollywood producer like Max Cooperman is going to be as tough as you under questioning?"

Laval folded his arms and lowered his head. It was an attempt at defiance, but Kirby knew he had him.

As the door clicked shut behind him Kirby said.

"He'll be ready to make a deal on the bomb, but I don't think he killed Erica."

"Did you read his mind?"

"Don't be silly," said Kirby, "it's just that all of his cues show guilt toward the bomb, and some shady business with Cooperman, but things were totally different when we mentioned Erica's murder. All of his little signals showed that he really didn't know who she was or what we were talking about."

"Not knowing who she was doesn't get him completely off the hook," explained Darling.

"Good point," said Kirby. "There is room for error, and there could be a whole unrelated reason for him to have done it."

"Excuse me," said a man with grey hair in the uniform of a police captain. "Sergeant Darling, can I have a word with you in private?"

Darling gave Kirby a signal to 'hold that thought,' and followed the captain around a corner. Kirby pricked up his ears, hoping to catch something, but all he got was some low muttering, then a very audible "What the hell?" from Darling, followed by something akin to a snake hissing.

Darling returned.

"My captain told me to take you back to your hotel and tell you to stay out of the investigation," said Darling.

"You did explain my status as a consultant to him?" asked Kirby.

"He knows all about it," said Darling, "but the explosion at the studio has made him worry about the optics of the situation."

"I've been almost killed twice today," said Kirby, "if anyone should want out, it should be me."

"Let me get to the end of my story," said Darling, "Because the captain told me something else."

"What?"

"Tanzerian escaped," answered Darling.

"How the hell does someone escape from a police station?" asked Kirby.

"It looks like he got the cop watching him to leave the room for a little over a minute, in that time he picked his handcuffs and walked out wearing your jacket."

"The bastard," said Kirby, "I loved that jacket."

"The captain became more reasonable about your involvement when I told him how certain members of my family wouldn't be too happy to hear over Sunday dinner tomorrow about a murder suspect escaping under his watch."

"Tanzerian isn't a murder suspect anymore."

"You know that, I know that, but the captain doesn't."

"Who is in your family to scare him so much?"

"I thought you'd have figured all that out already?"

"Even I have limitations," answered Kirby.

"You were right with that thing about my family; my dad retired a deputy chief, but his younger brother, my uncle, is the current deputy chief in charge of personnel," answered Darling. "The sort of person who would bust a captain down to meter maid for letting a prisoner escape."

"I like your style," said Kirby. "Oh, I should call Molly, make up some story about being nowhere near the explosion before it hits the news, or you'll have another murder to investigate."

"I'll warm up Cooperman for you," said Darling. "He's already got a lawyer."

"Good," said Kirby, as he took out his cell phone, "keep him and Weatherby separate this time. There's something there I can't quite put my finger on, and I need to keep them apart."

"No problem."

"Oh," said Cooperman looking Kirby over as he walked in the door of the interrogation room, "it's you."

"Yes," answered Kirby as he took a seat opposite Cooperman, "it's me."

"You brought your gorilla with you too," snarled Cooperman.

"My client was only calling your...uh...associate, a gorilla in the spirit of good humour," said Thurston, Cooperman's lawyer. "He means no offence."

Kirby looked over to Gustav, and the big man gave him a slight nod.

"I can speak for Gustav and say that none was taken," said Kirby.

"Mr. Cooperman was just telling us his theory on Mr. Laval," said Darling.

"Really," said Kirby, "why don't you tell it to me?"

"You're not really a cop," said Cooperman, "but you can consult on this. It's all about the unions."

"The unions?"

"Yeah," said Cooperman. "I'm doing The Vengeance Sisters movie without them and they got all pissy about it."

"Pissy enough to blow up the studio?"

"That's what I've been telling Sergeant Preston of the Yukon here," declared Cooperman. "They've been threatening me and the production since day one."

"But there's nothing in Laval's record to show that he works for any of the film related unions," said Kirby.

"The guy's probably a goon for hire," explained Cooperman.

"We can provide you with some emails and recorded phone messages that clearly illustrate union members threatening my client," added Thurston.

"The problem I have with your theory," said Kirby, "is that the union gets nothing from shutting down your production. Meanwhile you get quite a lot if something were to happen. Something like, let's say, that bomb going off on Tuesday, possibly in the wee hours of the morning before the day's work begins."

"What are you accusing me of?" asked Cooperman, his eyes narrowing to little black dots.

"You did tell Laval that it had to be Tuesday," stated Kirby as he watched Cooperman's left eyebrow twitch.

"My client doesn't know how to answer that question."

"If that bomb went off on Tuesday, the second day of shooting," said Kirby, studying the volcano bubbling beneath Cooperman's skin, "then you could shut down the production, collect the insurance, and blackmail Continental Pictures and Atlantic Comics into getting you and your company out of debt by rebuying the movie rights to The Vengeance Sisters and all the other Atlantic Comics characters."

"All this consultant of yours is doing," said Thurston "is slandering my client with innuendos and outrageous conspiracy theories."

"What went wrong?" asked Kirby, his eyes burning a hole into Cooperman's. "Were you planning to kill her all along, and Laval got the timing wrong? Did she see or hear something she shouldn't have?"

"You don't know what you're talking about," hissed Cooperman.

"Laval is a career criminal, he knows the score," said Kirby, "he'll save his own bacon from a life sentence before falling on his sword to save you."

"You fucking piece of shit!" bellowed Cooperman as he leaped to his feet, only to have Gustav's massive hand clamp down on his shoulder.

"I need some time to talk to my client!" cried out Thurston, leaping to his own feet and throwing an arm across Cooperman's chest.

"Sure," said Darling. "We need to talk to Laval again anyway."

Gustav had only just closed the door behind them when two tall men in matching haircuts and dark blue suits intercepted them in the hallway.

"Sergeant Darling?" asked one of the men, his voice with a subtle Georgia drawl. "We need to speak to you, as well as Mr. Baxter and Mr. Gustav?"

"You're FBI," said Kirby.

"Wow," said the FBI man, "you're living up to your reputation. How did you know?"

"Your accent," said Kirby, "is from Virginia, plus you have a little FBI crest on your tie clip."

"Oh, well if you haven't already deduced my name, I'm Special Agent Stewart Granger," said the FBI showing them his ID card and badge, "this is Staff Sergeant Bentley Fraser, of the RCMP."

"Pleased to meet you," said Fraser. "Can you come with us to the conference room?"

"All right," said Darling, "but we are in the middle of a murder investigation."

"We're actually here to help," said Granger. "Keep you from chasing red herrings up a blind alley."

"Or mixing metaphors," added Kirby.

"Just come with us," said Fraser. "He's in the conference room."

"Who is he?" asked Darling, getting an answer when the door opened.

Karl Weatherby sat at the table sipping a cup of coffee.

"Hello Sergeant Darling, Mr. Baxter," said Weatherby.

"Why is my suspect here?" asked Darling.

"Because he's been working for them all along," said Kirby.

"Our mutual friend from Scotland Yard was right," said Granger, "you do seem to read minds."

"Just an educated guess," said Kirby, taking a seat across from Weatherby. "I wouldn't mind hearing the whole story."

Granger nodded to Weatherby, who sighed with the inevitability.

"My family's bank is heavily invested in MaxCo Films," explained Weatherby. "We own some shares but our biggest investment is that we hold most of the company's debt. Recently we got worried that Cooperman was playing fast and loose with the numbers, and I'm talking way beyond the usual Hollywood accounting games. Production budgets didn't make any sense, he'd overspend on buying independent movies, then he wouldn't release them, but he'd still claim them as collateral for more loans."

"Let me guess," said Kirby, "he'd claim that the high price he paid was the real value of these movies?"

"Exactly," said Weatherby. "Put that with the company's inability to release a movie people might actually pay money to see, and it was a recipe for disaster. We decided to protect ourselves."

"You went undercover, so to speak," said Darling.

"Getting a job as Cooperman's assistant was easy," said Weatherby. "Before me he went through assistants like Kleenex. Staying his assistant was trickier, despite him owning my family a fortune; I still had to eat a lot of shit."

"You also got the police involved?" asked Kirby.

"I managed to look at some of MaxCo's finances," said Weatherby, "and it scared the hell out of me. I think just looking at them counted as a felony. I talked it over with my family, and our attorneys, and we decided to get the FBI involved."

"I'm with the interstate fraud division," added Special Agent Granger, "and since a lot of Cooperman's movies were shot here in Canada we called in the RCMP."

"I soon realized that Cooperman had no intention of finishing The Vengeance Sisters. He was arranging for something to happen during the second day of principal photography. It turned out to be a bombing by Laval, and Cooperman was hoping to frame the unions for it. In fact, he was deliberately picking fights with the unions to throw suspicion their way."

Sergeant Darling shrugged, "You're not exactly convincing us that Cooperman didn't have Erica Cross killed."

"We're getting to that," said Fraser. "Mr. Weatherby wore a wire, and arranged for us to tap Mr. Cooperman's phones as well as bug his hotel room."

"You had him under surveillance at the time of the murder?" asked Kirby.

"He was on the phone with his brother in Hollywood between one and one fifty-five on the night of the murder," answered Fraser. "They were laying out plans to extort money from Atlantic Comics and Continental Pictures and then hide it from their shareholders and creditors."

"At the same time Laval was caught on camera shoplifting junk food from an all night grocery store," added Granger, "and Mr. Weatherby was with us, being debriefed on the situation."

"They all have alibis?" asked Kirby.

Granger nodded.

"Could they have involved someone else?" asked Darling.

"Not without popping up on one of our tapes," answered Granger. "We had Cooperman and his associates pretty well wired for the past year."

Kirby rubbed his eyes, and cursed to himself.

"Back to square one."


Kirby scratched "What do I know?" on the white expanse of his sketch pad. The hustle and bustle of the detective squad room was just a low hum to him now. All of his attention was on that damn blank white page. His pencil touched paper, but instead of drawing he made a list.

1. The killer murdered Erica Cross with cyanide. (Autopsy should confirm it)

2. The scream puts the time of Erica Cross' death at approximately 1:35 a.m. Friday night.

Who are the suspects:

1. Armand Tanzerian – Scumbag paparazzi. Unlikely killer.

2. Max Cooperman – Alibi – Planning another crime.

3. Karl Weatherby – Alibi – Ratting out Cooperman at time of murder.

4. Chaz Healey – Ex boyfriend. Alibi – Too dumb to use cyanide.

5. Pierre Laval – Alibi – Committing another crime at time of the murder.

Kirby tapped his chin with the eraser end of his pencil.

Unanswered questions:

Killer may have made cyanide from apple seeds.

1. What does that person need to know in order to do that?

2. Why did they go to so much effort?

3. Who is Erica's stalker?

4. Where is the stalker?

5. Is the stalker even involved?

6. What if everything I think I know is wrong?

Kirby slumped in his seat and rested his head on Darling's desk. For a moment, doubt started to nibble at the edges of his confidence. What if I was all wrong? What if I didn't really smell cyanide on Erica's body? Darling was using all of her connections to get the autopsy and toxicology tests rushed through, and there was the very definite possibility that first impressions were right after all. Erica Cross may have really tripped, fallen, and somehow trapped herself in the freezer full of dry ice. It could all be just an insane Wile E. Coyote style accident after all. That could be the reason why Kirby was finding all sorts of crimes, but so far, no murderer, and maybe not even a murder.

"You cocksucker!" bellowed a voice from across the room.

Kirby looked up and saw Max Cooperman charging across the squad room like an enraged rhino, his arms outstretched, and his hands ready to strangle Karl Weatherby who retreated, leaping over a detective's desk like a terrified lemur. Half a dozen cops, both plainclothes and uniformed leaped in to tackle the charging Cooperman. Gustav put himself between Kirby and the chaos, blocking his view of the fracas.

Kirby could hear Cooperman let out a combination howl of rage and anguish, while his lawyer yipped and yapped about police brutality, only to have a policemen tell him to shut it. Gustav stepped aside and Kirby saw a flurry of heads, arms and legs, heading toward the holding cells.

"You don't see that every day," said Kirby.

"Are you all right?" asked Darling, her hair a bit disheveled from the fracas.

"Yeah," said Kirby. "I think I need to call it a night. Go back to the hotel, get some dinner and maybe some peace and quiet."

"Sounds like a good idea," said Darling.

Kirby was glad to see Molly waiting for him in the lobby of the Waterloo as he and Gustav entered. He was glad to take a second to ponder how cute she looked in the black minidress with the white polka dots, even though when she drew closer he could see that the white polka dots were, in fact, little cartoon skulls. He was even glad to see Mitch rising from his lounge chair, even though part of him was tempted to clip him on the ear. Molly just silently hugged him, but Mitch had to say something.

"When Molly told me about you getting blown up," said Mitch, "I thought you got lucky in a completely different way."

Kirby gave into temptation and swung for Mitch's ear, but the little man was quick and all Kirby got was some air.

"Are you finally done with this business?" asked Molly.

"I think I'm done," said Kirby. "I think I did enough damage."

"I'll say," said Mitch, "you got to blow up a building."

"I didn't blow it up," said Kirby. "That was done by a malfunctioning bomb. I didn't even get a chance to do my action star leap."

"Do you think Cooperman and the goon killed Erica?" asked Molly.

"I don't know what to think now," answered Kirby. "In fact the only thing I do know is that I'm tired, I'm hungry—"

"Your jacket's missing," added Mitch.

"It got stolen in the middle of a police station if you can believe that," said Kirby. "I say that we go back to the suite, have some room service and raid the minibar."

"I can support that," said Molly, finally letting Kirby go.

"Damn straight," said Mitch.

"I think we should avoid the convention floor," added Molly, "there are reporters sniffing around, looking for you."

"Crap," muttered Kirby, as he turned to the elevators, his

arm draped on Molly's shoulder.

"Now Gustav," said Molly, "I want you to promise me that Kirby will stay out of trouble from now on."

Gustav shrugged.

"Gustav knows that he can't make those kinds of promises," said Kirby as he hit the elevator call button. "But we'll definitely try."

"I guess that's the best I can ask for," said Molly. "I don't have to like it, but it'll do."

The elevator chimed, and Kirby heard: "Hold that elevator, please!"

Kirby looked over his shoulder, and saw Henry Hack and his wife Andi crossing the lobby and waving to them. Gustav put his hand in the door, keeping it open while they rushed in.

"Thank you," said Henry.

"You're a lifesaver," added Andi.

"What's up?" asked Mitch.

"We just couldn't stand being cooped up in our suite all day," said Andi as the door slid shut.

"And I couldn't do anything since my entire show is currently locked up as a crime scene," said Henry, patting the camera case slung across his neck, "so we went out and tried to play tourist for the day. Hopefully put some the past few days behind us, if only for a little while."

"Didn't really work," said Andi. "Did we hear right that you're helping the police?"

Kirby shrugged. "I got kind of roped into it because of some stuff that happened in Europe."

"He just helped them bust Max Cooperman," piped in Mitch.

"Cooperman killed Erica?" asked Andi.

Kirby shook his head. "Fraud," he answered. "It looks like the entire Vengeance Sisters movie was just one big scam."

"Ashmore will be happy," said Molly, "he's now free from that contract and can sell the company."

"But who killed Erica?" asked Henry.

Kirby shrugged. "I really can't comment on that part of the investigation."

"Yeah," said Andi, "I understand. I've seen enough detective shows."

The elevator chimed, the door slid open and they were home, more or less, on the Excelsior floor. "Perhaps you'd like to join us for dinner?" asked Kirby.

"I think we need some time alone together," said Andi, wrapping a delicate arm around her husband before they stepped out onto the floor, "but thanks for the offer."

Molly screamed.

Kirby turned to see a dead body wearing a Blue Jays baseball cap and Kirby's army jacket. The body was flat on the floor in front of the door of Kirby's suite, two bullet holes in the back of the jacket.

"Tanzerian?" asked Kirby, already knowing the answer.

ISSUE #15
OTHER VOICES OTHER ROOMS

Kirby felt Molly tremble in his arms. Though he had known her for years, he never really saw her as fragile. Her personality always made her seem bigger beyond her mere physical presence, but right now she seemed small, and scared. Gustav had put himself between them and the cluster of crime scene technicians at work down the hall, being better as a sheltering wall than as a window.

"Two goddamn bodies," she muttered, her head pressed against his chest. "Two goddamn dead people."

"This is officially the worst convention ever," said Mitch. "Cons aren't supposed to have body counts."

Kirby nodded in agreement.

"I mean sure I tapped a Hollywood starlet," said Mitch, "but all these murders, attempted murders and explosions are really going to put a cramp in my future bragging."

"One second," whispered Kirby to Molly, before letting her go just long enough to flick Mitch across the ear.

"Ouch!" Mitch winced. "Was it something I said?"

"Silence is golden," said Kirby, holding Molly tighter.

"Excuse me," said Mitch. "Not everyone gets to be the hero you know. Some of us have to settle for what they have."

"You call sleeping with a Hollywood star 'settling?'"

"I wouldn't use that term," replied Mitch, "we didn't sleep at all. Ouch!!" After that second flicking, Mitch stepped a couple of paces out of range.

A moment passed with only the shuffling and murmuring of the crime scene techs down the hall to keep them from total silence.

"So," said Mitch.

"So what?" asked Kirby.

"Who do you think will play us in the movie about all this?" asked Mitch.

"They'll never make a movie out of this," said Kirby. "It's all comic book characters now."

"We have comic book characters involved," said Mitch.

"Yeah," said Kirby, "but it's about people who make or buy comic book characters. That's boring business crap, movie studios want superheroes tossing buses at each other and tearing down buildings. Not a bunch of geeks stumbling around like idiots."

"Knowing our luck it'll probably end up a TV movie," said Mitch.

"A cable TV movie," pondered Kirby aloud. "Maybe on Lifetime."

"That channel will replace you with a plucky female reporter," continued Mitch, "who is always in peril until rescued by a square jawed detective who doesn't shave but never gets beyond a day's growth for some unexplained reason."

Kirby suppressed the urge to laugh.

"That would probably be my luck," said Kirby.

"Amanda Seyfried," said Molly.

"What?" asked Kirby.

"I want Amanda Seyfried to play me in the movie," said Molly.

"Why her?" asked Mitch.

"Why are you asking why?" asked Molly, annoyed at the question.

"Well," said Kirby, "she's a lot taller, blonder, and...um..." Kirby wanted to find a way to say 'bigger breasted' in a way that wouldn't result in him having a tiny fist slamming into his jaw.

"That's why I want her to play me," answered Molly, "I want my self-delusion on the screen, not reality."

"Can't argue with that logic," said Kirby, "at least you're not going to be replaced by a plucky female reporter." He then turned to Mitch and asked: "Why was I replaced by a plucky female reporter in peril anyway?"

"You're a very hard role to cast," answered Mitch.

"Why do you say that?"

"Face facts," said Mitch, "you're no George Clooney, and I think Thom Bray is retired from acting."

"Thom Bray?" asked Molly.

"He played a nerdy scientist on the show Riptide," said Mitch. "It was a PI show from the eighties, you can catch the reruns on cable sometimes."

"I remember him," said Kirby, "but that's only because I have an eidetic memory and I remember everything, even reruns I saw on Croatian television."

"You don't remember to call your friends sometimes," said Molly while pinching Kirby's side.

"Ow," said Kirby, "I said I was sorry and moved you into the most expensive suite in the hotel. Is that not enough penance for you?"

"A suite with a dead body by the front door," said Molly.

"That wasn't in the brochure when I booked the room," said Kirby. "I can't win with you people. You're a rampant perfectionist, and Mitch is digging deep into the black hole of pop culture to insult me."

"I did not insult you," said Mitch, "I merely brought up an actor that you might possibly resemble."

"And he was the best actor you could come up with to play me?" asked Kirby.

"No," said Mitch. "The best I could come up with was a plucky female reporter in peril."

"You could have picked that kid from Freaks & Geeks," suggested Molly.

"Why does it have to be someone who was in Freaks & Geeks?" asked Kirby. "Why can't I have my self-delusion fantasy version of myself cast in this movie like Molly?"

"That would break the rules," said Mitch.

"What rules?" asked Kirby.

"How the hell should I know!" answered Mitch.

"At least I'm not the comic relief sidekick," said Kirby.

"That's Gustav's job," said Mitch. "Isn't that right big guy?"

Gustav just looked over at Mitch with about as much emotion as a rock.

"Okay," said Mitch, "I'll admit that I am the comic relief sidekick. I'll probably get some hack comedian with a bad haircut playing me. However, I think poor Gustav will probably be written out of the movie."

"Why?" asked Molly.

"Too unbelievable," said Mitch. "No offence Gustav, but I still find you hard to believe and you're standing right in front of me."

"I can't believe we're having this conversation just feet from a murdered man," said Molly.

"True," said Kirby, "It's partially a coping mechanism, but since I actually met him, and he stole my favourite jacket, he might have magically turned me into a callous asshole."

"When I saw him sprawled out on the floor wearing your jacket and the ball cap I thought it was you for half a second," said Mitch, "even though you were standing right next to me. That was a freaky-ass half a second."

"Do you think he was mistaken for you?" asked Molly. "The killer saw the jacket and just opened fire?"

"I don't know," said Kirby. "Tanzerian probably had a lot of enemies, so it's wide open."

Sergeant Darling came from down the hall, followed by Bruce Haring. They exchanged hellos with Bruce, who expressed his shock and sympathy to them over the discovery of a second body.

"How are the Hacks?" asked Kirby.

"Once we finished getting their statements Henry Hack hit the minibar," said Darling, "and his wife retired to her room with what she called a 'me-grain.' I think she's got some aromatherapy candles burning in there. Smells like a bakery."

"I suggested to Sergeant Darling that you come down to Erica's old suite," said Bruce. "Since you can't get into your own room until the police are done here."

"Is that okay Sergeant?" asked Kirby.

Darling nodded. "We have your statements and there's no reason for you to hang around here in the hall anymore."

"I think we could use the privacy," she said.

Erica's former suite was in a lot better shape than the last time they saw it. The clothing and personal items that Tanzerian had scattered in all directions were gone, neatly packed in a quartet of suitcases stacked in a corner of the main sitting room. It was smaller and simpler than Kirby's own much more lavish suite. Just a simple sitting room with a small dining table in the corner, and two adjoining bedrooms. Gustav headed straight for the broad plate glass window and drew the curtains to blot out the glare of the setting sun.

"I managed to get the place straightened up with the help of the maids," said Bruce. "I have to ship all this stuff back to her folks on Monday. Then I head back to Los Angeles on Tuesday to find another job."

"Where's the bathroom?" asked Molly.

"Right through that door," answered Bruce. Molly slipped from under Kirby's arm and went into the bathroom.

"This must really be upsetting for her," said Bruce.

Kirby nodded. "You never really get used to it."

"Have you discovered anything new about Erica's murder?" asked Bruce.

Kirby shook his head. "It looks like we found evidence of everything else but."

"Do you know anything more about the stalker?" asked Bruce.

Kirby shrugged as he picked up a copy of the room

service menu and passed it to Mitch. "It wasn't Tanzerian, or Chaz Healey, the type of camera used by the stalker is all wrong."

"Chaz is definitely not the stalker," said Bruce, sitting down on one of the dining table chairs. "He lacks the attention span."

"The forensic people here in Toronto," said Kirby as he sat on the sofa, "are going to consult with the forensic people in LA, to see if they can figure out the make and model of camera from some bits of digital code that came with the email attachments."

"How will that help?"

"I don't know," said Kirby. "I'm sorry to say that, but I'm at a bit of a loss right now."

"I understand," said Bruce, unable to hide a hint of disappointment. "She was just such a nice person. One of the few truly nice people I've ever worked for."

"We're trying," said Kirby, "it's just not as easy as it looks on TV."

"Nothing ever is," added Mitch.

Someone knocked at the door. Gustav went straight to the door, crouched a bit to look in the peephole, and then opened it. It was Stevens, the Waterloo's concierge, with a look of grave, and actually sincere, concern on his face.

"Hello Mr. Baxter," said Stevens, "I just came to see if everything is all right and to hope that you won't judge this hotel and the city by this rather horrible experience."

"Thank you," said Kirby.

"I discussed things with Sergeant Darling," added the concierge, "and they should be finished with their work in about two hours and you will be able to go back to your suite shortly after then. If you wish to change your rooms, the Waterloo would gladly assist you in finding someplace new."

"I don't think that will be necessary," said Kirby. "Just out of curiosity, does the hotel have any security camera footage of the shooting?"

"I'm afraid not," answered the concierge with a careful shake of his head. "We take the privacy of our guests very seriously, and the security cameras only cover the elevators and the stairways."

"Do you have any footage of anyone coming or going around the time Tanzerian was shot?"

"Not until your party and the Hacks arrived."

Kirby rested his elbows on his knees, and his chin on his hands.

"What are you thinking about?" asked Mitch. "You have that deep in thought look on your face."

"I'm thinking of the blatantly obvious," answered Kirby.

"Why don't we get something to eat," offered Mitch. "You can't think on an empty stomach, so I'm thinking pizza with the works for everyone."

"The Waterloo will gladly provide that," said Stevens.

Molly stuck her head out the bathroom door.

"Kirby," said Molly, "can you come in here for a second?"

"What is it," asked Mitch, seeing an opportunity for fun with the only person he knew who was shorter than him, "is the towel rack too high for you to reach?"

"Put your mouth to good use," said Kirby as he got up from his seat and headed toward the bathroom, "and work out what to put on the pizza. You know the rule."

The "rule" was 'no pineapple,' and it was strictly enforced.

"Sure," said Mitch, "as the comic relief sidekick I know my place."

"What is it?" asked Kirby as he came into the bathroom.

Molly put her finger to her lips and closed the door behind Kirby. "Listen," she whispered.

Kirby listened. He could hear his own breathing and Molly's breathing, the low hum of the toilet tank refilling. When the tank finished filling up he heard something else.

Voices?

"You hear it," mouthed Molly.

Kirby nodded. Where was it coming from? Kirby scanned

the room, which was entirely comprised of gleaming white tile, with accents of Moroccan style floral patterns along the edges. A little vent covered with a row of tightly closed flaps sat in the upper right-hand corner of the wall behind the toilet. He could make out two voices, but even his keen ears couldn't quite make out what they were saying. Kirby crouched down and looked under the counter, a tiny plastic footstool was under there, just like the one in his suite's bathroom. It wasn't much, but it was enough for Kirby to reach the vent.

Kirby slid out the stool, wedged it against the wall under the vent and stepped up on it. The voices were clearer now, and he could make out the occasional word, but it wasn't perfect. Kirby found a tiny metal tab sticking out of a slot in the side of the vent and nudged it upwards. He did it carefully and slowly, making sure not to make any untoward noise.

"There is no problem," said a voice that Kirby instantly recognized because he could now hear it as clear as if they were in the same room.

"I know that voice," said Molly, covering her mouth as soon as she realized how loud she said it.

"What?" said the voice from the vent. "I thought you said something, sorry. Listen, Kirby Baxter will not be attending the auction because he's had some sort of falling out with Dick Wilco a few years ago. I don't know the details, the old guy is pretty close-mouthed about that sort of thing. Besides, you don't need Baxter to authenticate the artworks. Dick Wilco himself has flown in from Utah to authenticate the work himself. Trust me, the old bastard's taking a chunk out of my commission for the privilege, but getting the artist himself is a much bigger coup."

Kirby heard what sounded like a knock on the door through the vent.

"I gotta go," said the voice through the vent, "someone's at my door. I'll see you at the auction. Don't forget it's in two hours in Room Three Sixteen."

Kirby heard a phone hang up and footsteps heading to a door. He slid the tab down, closing the vent.

"I thought I heard your name," whispered Molly, "then I realized that I could hear someone talking in the next suite. Then you opened the vent and—"

"It was Jim Madden," added Kirby.

"He was talking about Dick Wilco coming," said Molly, "is the man himself really coming here?"

"He was talking about more than that," said Kirby, "he was talking about a motive for murder."

"So," said Mitch, to Gustav who sat stone-faced in the corner, "do you know what they are doing in there?"

The giant man shrugged.

"I mean I know that women go to washroom in pairs," said Mitch, "but I never heard of a woman inviting a man to join her." Gustav didn't react at all this time. Part of Mitch wished the concierge had stayed, at least he responded instead of just sitting like a human mountain. "I know that Molly's always sort of had a thing for Kirby, but you know this is sort of a strange time, and stranger place, to show it. You know what I mean?"

Nothing.

"Try to contain your excitement," said Mitch, "you might actually show some sort of expression."

Everything went silent, which Mitch just couldn't bear.

"What's Kirby paying you these days?" asked Mitch. Gustav didn't answer, just looked straight at, and then through, Mitch.

"Do you have health insurance with your job?" asked Mitch. "I think that would be important with all the crashing cars, exploding buildings and people getting murdered everywhere you go."

Gustav didn't even ignore him.

"Dental is a must these days," said Mitch. "Do you belong to a union of any kind? Is there a union for whatever it is they call your job?"

Silence.

"Okay," said Mitch, "I can understand you wanting to play things close to the vest and all that."

The door to the bathroom swung open, Kirby leaped out of the bathroom and went straight for the exit. He opened the door and called out: "Darling! We need you!"

"Now it's just getting kinky," said Mitch, less than second before Molly's hand smacked him across the back of his head.

ISSUE #16
THE BIDDING

Grant Upton cleaned his horn-rimmed glasses for the twelfth time that night. They were brand new, and unlike the pair he had owned for almost a decade he noticed every smudge or fleck of dandruff that dared to touch their pristine lenses, no matter how small. He had to make this trip from California alone, no assistants, no secretaries and no communication with anyone about where he was going or what he was going to do when he got there.

He felt naked without his Blackberry, his Android smartphone, his iPhone, his iPad and the laptop that he always carried in a custom-made leather shoulder bag, for the sake of not missing anything going on anywhere. Sure most of the time he ended up going over reams of memos discussing everything from the number of company pens, to company cars, but Upton desperately needed to know everything going on with his software company, no matter how trivial. He also desperately needed to wash his hands twenty-five times a day whether they needed it or not, tap his right foot three times and his left foot twice every time he sat down, and only wear blue coloured underwear. You be the judge.

Upton had to go completely incommunicado for this trip, using only one of those pre-paid cell phones provided by Madden and only for talking to Madden, as well as avoiding anyone who might interfere with the auction. That meant that Madden pulled him off the convention floor, scolded him, and threatened to blackball him from the auction just for taking a peek at the convention and trying to talk to Kirby Baxter.

Upton didn't think he had committed anything that egregious, and had half-expected Baxter to participate in the auction. Everyone considered Kirby Baxter the authority on Wilco and his work, and word was, thanks to a lottery ticket, Baxter had the money needed to be a bidder. Madden just told him that Baxter had some sort of falling out with Wilco and wanted to screw up the auction as some sort of revenge.

Upton really didn't understand that, but then again, he really didn't understand people, their personal operating system just didn't add up sometimes.

"Your taxi is ready Mr. Upton," said the concierge of the Royal York.

"Thank you," said Upton, folding that curiously analog relic called a newspaper, and putting it on the little side table next to his lounge chair.

A moment later he was telling the back of the cab driver's turban to go to the Waterloo Hotel and Convention Centre. Then he leaned back, squirted out some hand sanitizer and rubbed his hands together, working it all between the fingers and up past the wrist. The fact that he stopped this ritual at just past the wrist was a personal triumph, not just for Upton, but also his therapist Dr. Lowenstein.

The lights of the city slipped passed Upton's window as he fidgeted in his seat. He wondered who else was going to be at the auction, how hot the bidding was going to get and if Wilco would sign his autograph book. That would be almost as big a coup as getting his freshly sanitized hand on all that original art.

"We're here," said the cab driver. Upton pulled a couple of Canadian twenty dollar bills and passed them over the back of the front seat. He pulled a paper napkin out of his pocket, wrapped it around the handle of the cab door and stepped outside. He took a deep breath of night air laced with car exhaust and cigarette smoke, tossed the napkin into a trash can, re-sanitized his hands, again, and charged into the hotel.

"Hello," said a familiar voice. Upton turned to see the familiar and slightly unwelcome face of Richard Imahara. Imahara's business was online search engines, and his hobby was outbidding Upton at every auction. "You must be here for the auction."

"I am Richie," said Upton, knowing that it really bugged the snobbish Imahara to refer to him by what he called the low class 'trucker' version of his name. "I'm assuming they made you play all Secret Squirrel about this too."

Richard Imahara nodded. "Will Blaylock is here too, he's getting an elevator." Blaylock was from Greenwich Connecticut, a big wheel in the hedge fund business and an even bigger player in the rarefied world of high-end comic book art and memorabilia collecting.

"Madden's left no stone unturned," said Upton.

"It should make the auction interesting," said Imahara. Upton could sense that his rival was sizing him up.

"The most interesting thing to me," said Upton, trying to sound casual about his desire for those beautiful pages, "is getting to meet Dick Wilco himself."

"I'm sure it is," said Imahara, nodding.

Will Blaylock waved from the bank of elevators. "Hey, guys," called Blaylock, "I got an elevator! Haul your asses!"

"Let the games begin," said Upton.

Madden washed his hands, scrubbing a little more vigorously this time and going farther up his arms than usual or necessary. He leaned in on the bathroom sink, rinsing his hands and arms up to the elbows. For a second he paused, wondering why he was imitating a surgeon getting ready for an operation or if he was turning into LaGuardia who spent most of the past few hours going back and forth from the bathroom, leaving only a sliver of hotel soap for Madden.

Baxter was dead and gone; he wasn't going to crash their auction, or their plans. If anyone asked, he'd just say that it was a terrible loss, but he heard that the dearly departed was meddling in a murder case, and must have crossed the wrong person. The cops made everyone on the Excelsior floor stay in their suites and give statements to some female detective with rat blonde hair and a sense of surrender when it came to her appearance, accompanied by a dull-eyed uniformed constable. Madden's statement was simple, he didn't hear anything, or see anything, because of a well-timed nap in his bedroom, followed by a series of business calls. They then asked a flurry of dumb questions like: Did you know the deceased? Yes. How well? Casual acquaintance, usually at conventions and similar industry events. Blah-blah-blah, yadda-yadda-yadda.

This seemed to satisfy the female detective, who apparently slept her way up the ranks because the dull-eyed cop called her Sergeant. She left, and LaGuardia crawled out from under the hotel bed when Madden told him that the coast was clear.

An hour later, a crime scene cop showed up and told them that they were now free to leave their suite and move freely. Madden muttered something about it being 'about time' and made his way to Room 316, with LaGuardia following as soon as the cops had left. They got to the room just a half-hour before the auction, giving them little time to prepare. Madden set up the chairs, while LaGuardia took the artworks out of their case and laid them across the long table.

Madden then went to the bathroom to empty his bladder, and was just finishing washing his hands and thinking about what happened that day when LaGuardia knocked on the bathroom door.

"Wilco is here," said LaGuardia through the door.

"Get him a chair," said Madden, drying his hands and arms.

When Madden came out of the bathroom his Wilco was sitting in a chair by the long table. He was in his mid-seventies, tall, thin, with a narrow face and just a fringe of snow white hair over his ears. His suit was grey and baggy and rumpled, just as Madden ordered. "How are you doing?" asked Madden, not really caring about the answer.

"I heard there was a second murder in this hotel," said Wilco.

"We heard that too," said Madden, "you've got nothing to worry about. We'll be done with all this in less than an hour. Then you can collect your money and go home."

"Spooky," said Wilco, rocking slightly in his seat.

"Yeah," said Madden, "spooky as hell." A quick exchange with one of the bellboys who brought the chairs told Madden that guests had been fleeing the hotel all evening when word got out of there being second murder in as many days. The death of Erica Cross hadn't had that same effect. It happened in the adjoining convention centre, and it involved a celebrity, things that put a psychological wall between the event and the everyday folks staying in the rest of the hotel. But this second murder was different, it may have happened on the rich person floor, to a rich person, but it happened inside the hotel proper and it involved some nobody the average person had never heard of. If it happened to someone famous like the last one, the hoi polloi would put a few bricks in that imaginary wall between them and the victim. This new victim tore down that imaginary wall, telling them that anyone and/or everyone could be next. That scared the royal piss out of the other nobodies, and those nobodies were fleeing in droves.

Three knocks on the door.

"Who is that?" asked LaGuardia, he was scratching his hands again and Madden figured it had to be nerves.

"It's the bidders," answered Madden as he went to the door. He looked through the peephole first, just in case, and confirmed he was right. Then he opened the door.

"Come in gentlemen," said Madden as the bidders paraded in. Blaylock made a point to come in first, shaking Madden's hand with a grip capable of cracking concrete. Grant Upton entered second, he didn't shake hands, preferring to squirt some more sanitizer. Richard Imahara followed him, and was himself followed by a few newbies from Asia and Europe. "Please take a seat. Can I get anyone a drink?"

Most shook their heads, and took their seats in an arc in front of the table displaying the artwork.

"Could you please stand up?" Madden asked Wilco and the old man rose from his chair.

"As you may know," said Dick Wilco, his voice frail, "things are in a bit of upheaval at my old employer the Atlantic Comics Company. There are rumours of a takeover by the Continental Pictures movie studio, and the company is seeking to avoid any expensive litigation from creators like me. They figured the best way to settle with artists like me is to let us have some of our original artwork. A few months ago I agreed to settle in exchange for the original artwork from my book Answer Man number one."

On cue, LaGuardia lifted up the framed sheet of paper containing the inked cover page, revealing the ominous form of the mysterious Answer Man, complete with trench coat and slouch hat, looming over a pair of particularly shady looking criminals.

Despite their status as the jaded elites of the collector market all let out a little gasp of awe. Most of them already owned a copy of the first edition of Answer Man #1, and had paid through the nose for it, but here was the closest thing to a holy grail they could expect to see in their lifetimes. It was the original artwork itself, presented and authenticated by the man himself.

"I was hoping to hold onto it for a little while," said Wilco, his head hanging low, "but my wife's been ill and you know how the bills tend to pile up, and don't get me started on the tax man. Anyway, long story short, I'm selling these pieces right now, in the only way I can where I won't violate the confidentiality agreements they made me sign. I hope for a good auction, and may the best, and by that I mean the highest paying, man win."

The group let out a little laugh as Wilco took his seat.

"Okay," said Madden, "I'll give you all a moment to look over the artworks, and then we can start the bidding."

The bidders rose from their seats, walked to the table and started looking over the art. All were intimately familiar with the final published product and searched for the slightest discrepancies. Grant Upton, always a stickler, even took out a magnifying glass and leaned in like he was Sherlock fucking Holmes searching for Moriarty's fingerprints, or the Sign of the Four, or maybe even the Red Headed League, Madden didn't care. They weren't going to find anything untoward, LaGuardia made sure of it.

Madden gave them ten minutes, then he beckoned them all back to their seats.

"All right," said Madden, "please return to your seats, we'll start the bidding at five hundred thousand dollars, American."

"Five fifty," said Blaylock.

"That's a good start," said Madden, "but it's just a start."

"Six hundred," said Upton.

"Six fifty," said Imahara.

"Do I hear seven hundred?" asked Madden.

Someone knocked on the door.

"Who the hell is that?" asked LaGuardia.

"Why don't you go see?" ordered Madden.

LaGuardia headed to the door, then Madden heard the latch click, someone had unlocked the door.

LaGuardia froze when he heard the latch click and saw the door start to open. Then all he saw was the immense black hole of a gun barrel. Seconds later LaGuardia felt a rough hand grab his shoulder, then the carpet against his face.

All LaGuardia could hear were the boots stomping on the floor, shouts of "FREEZE!" "POLICE!" and "PUT YOUR HANDS UP!" LaGuardia felt the cop snap metal handcuffs on his wrists, and rolled him over to his side. He could see the bidders dropping to their knees, their hands up. Looks of terror on their faces. Dick Wilco leaped to his feet, screaming: "This isn't in the script!" Two burly cops in black body armour cut the scream short when they tackled him to the floor.

Madden went down on his knees, his hands on his head. His expression was blank, and LaGuardia knew that meant he was angry enough to kill someone. Gloved hands pulled LaGuardia first to his knees, then to his feet and turned him to the door.

The hall seemed full of uniformed Toronto police officers, and they all parted like the Red Sea before Moses, and LaGuardia had to consciously fight to avoid pissing his pants.

"Kirby?" asked LaGuardia, staring at the impossible. "Kirby Baxter!"

"Yes," said Baxter, with a nod, and that massive bodyguard by his side, "the reports of my death were greatly exaggerated."

"Who–"

"Don't say a fucking word!" ordered Madden. "Not one fucking word!"

"James Madden and Kevin LaGuardia," said a woman with dark blonde hair. "You are under arrest for suspicion of murder, fraud and conspiracy."

"I want a lawyer!" screamed Madden. "A lawyer!"

LaGuardia didn't know what to say, because the only thing he knew was that he was in way over his head.

Back in Interrogation Room One. Kirby was starting to feel more at home in this plain grey room than in the very expensive suite he had paid for back at the Waterloo.

"Hello Jimmy," said Kirby, as he took his now usual seat next to Darling and Gustav moved to his usual spot looming over Madden's back like impending doom.

"You're looking a lot better than the police let on," said Madden. "If you're here, then who–"

"My client has nothing to say," said Madden's lawyer.

Kirby thought the arrest of Jim Madden had dragged the attorney from a late night pool party considering he smelled faintly of chlorine and beer, and was wearing a t-shirt and a pair of shorts. "And can't this wait until tomorrow?"

"It'll be tomorrow in thirty minutes," said Darling. "We can wait until then."

"What's your story?" asked Kirby.

"I have nothing to say," said Madden.

"Okay," said Kirby, "I'll tell you your story. You, Kevin LaGuardia and the actor you hired to play Dick Wilco were going to defraud some collectors by selling them bogus artwork."

"I have nothing to say," said Madden.

"I got suspicious when I heard about this auction," said Kirby, "and wasn't invited to attend. Dick Wilco literally taught me how to draw and, thanks to my lottery win and some lucky investments, I have lots of money, so you think that I'd be the first guy to invite. I was going to look into that, but I got distracted with other things, but then I heard you say that Dick Wilco had flown in from Utah for the auction."

"You bugged my phone?" asked Madden.

"If you didn't have a warrant—" said the lawyer, but Kirby cut him off.

"We didn't bug your phone," said Kirby, "and how I heard that isn't important at this moment. What is important is that the moment I heard you say that, I knew your whole auction was a fraud."

Madden shifted uncomfortably in his chair.

"You probably want to know how I knew," said Kirby, "well, I knew Dick Wilco when I was growing up, and I learned a lot about the man. I learned was that Dick Wilco had his faults in the form of some pretty odd prejudices. Two of his biggest prejudices were airplanes and Mormons. There isn't any way the real Dick Wilco would have flown in from Utah."

"The actor you hired has already talked," said Darling,

"and it was one heck of a story he told. He said you told him it was all part of a prank you were going to pull on a friend, and that everyone but this one friend was supposed to be in on it."

"I don't know what he's talking about," said Madden. "I'm the victim here. Kevin LaGuardia said that he and Dick Wilco had some original art from the archives at Atlantic Comics that they wanted to sell. I agreed to help facilitate the sale, in good faith, thinking LaGuardia had real art, and that man was the real Dick Wilco. Remember, I don't know Wilco from Adam. You're the only one who had seen the man in years."

"That's your story?" asked Kirby.

"That's my story," said Madden. "I didn't have any part in any fraud, and I certainly didn't shoot Kirby Baxter, because he's sitting right in front of me."

"At least one part of that statement is true," said Kirby. "You didn't shoot me. You just shot a man who stole my jacket and was probably trying to break into my suite."

"I didn't shoot anyone," declared Madden. "You can't prove I shot anyone."

"It's not much of a stretch," said Darling. "The security cameras—"

"Don't cover the floor," said Madden, "guest privacy."

"Let me finish Mr. Madden," said Darling. "The security cameras cover the elevators and the stairs. They don't show anyone coming to or leaving the Excelsior floor at the time of the murder."

"They didn't show Kevin LaGuardia coming and going," said Madden, "because he was hiding in my room when the cops came to ask questions. I'd tell you the whole story, but I need a deal where I go for a walk straight out of here, or I'm not going to tell you anything."

Interrogation Room Two. Kevin LaGuardia sat alone, his court appointed lawyer hadn't arrived yet. He fidgeted in his seat, his eyes scanning the shape of every brick.

"Shall we go in?" asked Darling watching LaGuardia through the one-way mirror.

"Yes," said Kirby Baxter, nodding his head. "But we should let Gustav walk in first."

"Why?"

"Kevin LaGuardia was never very good at handling stress. Right now he's terrified beyond anything he's ever felt before," answered Kirby, "there's a chance that we can use that fear to get him to talk. Let me tell you, Gustav can give a stink eye that would make Lee Marvin wet his pants. With the state LaGuardia's in now, one look and he'll tell us if he's wearing women's underwear."

Darling looked over to the large man and he nodded.

"Whatever works."

Gustav opened the door and went in. Darling followed the big man into the interrogation room, though she couldn't see the look Gustav was giving LaGuardia, she could see the flash of absolute terror on LaGuardia's face, and the way his fists clenched on the table.

"Hello Kevin," said Kirby.

"Hello Kirby," said LaGuardia, "I'm glad to see you alive."

"Are you ready to make a statement?" asked Darling as she took her seat, followed by Kirby.

"Should I wait until I get a lawyer?" asked LaGuardia, glancing over his shoulder at Gustav taking his position in the corner.

"We could wait," said Darling, "but it's late on a Saturday in the summer. We might have to wait until tomorrow, or even Monday, and until then we'd have to put you in general population in the city jail... Besides, if you did nothing wrong, there's no problem."

"I think I should tell you something," said Kirby, "it's about the hotel."

"What about the hotel?"

"The garbage chute on the Excelsior floor goes to a different dumpster than the others," continued Kirby. "That means the cops won't have to wade through tons of garbage to find the gun. In fact, I'll bet dollars to donuts that they've found it already and are rushing it back here as we speak. I'm talking about the gun that you tossed into the chute."

"How did you–?" asked LaGuardia, his eyes wide with surprise.

"I know you weren't the shooter," said Kirby. Now Darling was looking at him in wonder. "Madden did it, and he made you toss the gun down the chute."

"I don't believe this," said LaGuardia. "I'd seen you do those tricks, but I thought they were just tricks..."

"Right now Madden is in the next room," said Kirby. "Now you can wait for a lawyer to come, if you choose to not waive your right to an attorney we will be forced to end this right here. But I have to tell you that Madden already has a lawyer, and he's already talking about making a deal, a deal where he puts the whole thing on you."

LaGuardia slumped and laid his head on the table.

"I'll waive," he said, not raising his head off the table.

"I drew the pictures," said LaGuardia, still not raising his head. "But it was all Madden's idea. At first we thought about just forging art and claiming that it was coming out of the Atlantic Comics archives. But if we did that, folks might ask how we got it legally. So Madden came up with the idea of Atlantic Comics making a secret deal with their old artists to avoid any lawsuits that might screw up the sale to Continental Pictures. But most of the hardcore collectors know most of the artists that are still alive and would want them involved to verify the provenance and all that shit."

"So you needed someone that no one knew," said Kirby.

"Exactly," said LaGuardia raising his head and staring straight up at the subtly flickering florescent lights above. "Nobody had seen Dick Wilco in decades, nobody knows where he lives, or what he looks like now. He has no family, and you were the only friend anyone knew about, and you were gone into the wild blue yonder. It seemed a perfect way to get a little something for ourselves. The plan was for me to fake up the pictures, Madden was to hire an actor to play

Wilco and set up the auction. The bidders were told that they had to keep everything secret for five years because Wilco was forced by Atlantic to sign some confidentiality clauses and the actor was told some bullshit about it being a prank being played by some rich men on other rich men."

"He told us about that," said Darling.

"No one was supposed to get hurt," said LaGuardia, rubbing his face with his free hand.

"But someone was hurt," said Kirby, "in fact, he's dead."

LaGuardia faced his interrogators. "It was because of you Kirby. You showed up after two years of being God-knows-where and Madden started to panic because you could screw up the deal."

"Madden was the one that tried to run me over?"

LaGuardia nodded.

"You were going around asking questions," answered LaGuardia, "you almost stumbled on our actor on the convention floor. He was there to do 'research on his character,' which was strictly forbidden. But you asking all those questions and running into Grant Upton was the kicker. Madden decided that you had to go."

"Did he buy the gun here," asked Darling, "or did he smuggle it into Canada?"

LaGuardia shrugged. "He just whipped it out, I don't know where he got it. Then this guy appeared in the hall wearing your jacket and sniffing around your door, and Madden started blasting. Then he shoved the gun in my hands and told me to dump it. Bastard was wearing gloves."

"So only your prints are on the gun?" asked Darling.

LaGuardia nodded.

"But if you check my smartphone," said LaGuardia, "you'll find a video file labeled 'convention video.' I filmed the son of a bitch doing it, because I knew he was going to screw me eventually."

"We'll look into that," said Darling.

"How did you know?" asked LaGuardia.

"Know what?" said Kirby.

"Know that I dumped the gun down the garbage chute?"

Kirby Baxter shrugged. "Your hands are swelling."

Darling looked down to see LaGuardia's hands were slightly swollen with alternating patches of red and white skin.

"I remembered that you were allergic to the washroom soap at Atlantic Comics," said Kirby, "which is very similar to the soap in the rooms at the Waterloo. The amount of swelling shows that you scrubbed both hands hard with a brand of soap that you know you're allergic too. The only reason I could think of for you to do that was that you were trying to wash off gunshot residue and/or garbage."

LaGuardia nodded, "Damn," he said, "I thought you really were a mind reader for a second there."

"Why was Erica Cross killed?" asked Kirby.

LaGuardia shrugged, "I don't know."

"Are you saying that you had nothing to do with it?" asked Darling.

"Yes," said LaGuardia, "because I did have nothing to do with that."

"You didn't know she could hear everything happening in Madden's suite from her bathroom?" asked Kirby, leaning in, his eyes narrowing.

"I haven't got a clue what you're talking about!"

ISSUE #17
TOSSING & TURNING

As Kirby and Gustav stepped out of the elevator he took some relief that there wasn't another body lying by the door to his suite. The police had been extremely thorough, removing the patch of bloodstained carpet where Armand Tanzerian had breathed his last. The hotel staff had been even more thorough, replacing the missing patch with one that was only a slightly deeper shade of beige than the rest of the hallway.

It was almost two in the morning, Kirby struggled to keep his eyes open and was tempted to just toss self-respect into the dustbin of history and ask the big man to carry him into the room. While Kirby yawned Gustav unlocked the door and opened it for him, allowing him to keep a scintilla of dignity.

"Kirby," said Molly, rushing to the door and giving Kirby a big hug.

"You didn't blow up this time?" asked Mitch.

"How did everything go?" asked Henry Hack.

"Did they confess?" asked Bruce Haring.

"What happened?" asked Andi.

Kirby took a second to take in the scene. The large living room area of his suite was almost full with people. Molly was hugging him, Mitch was sitting on one of the easy chairs. Andi and Henry Hack were sitting on one of the sofas clinging to each other, and Bruce Haring was standing up by the antique Art Deco writing desk.

"Okay," said Kirby making his way to the other sofa, guided by Molly, "one at a time."

"I think I can speak for everyone," said Andi Hack, "when I say that we hate to bother you, but we really need to know what's going on."

"Long story short," said Kirby, taking a seat, with Molly sliding in next to him. "We have Jim Madden and Kevin LaGuardia dead to rights on killing Armand Tanzerian in the hallway. LaGuardia recorded it with his phone, either to protect himself, or blackmail Madden, it doesn't really matter now."

"What was going on?" asked Mitch. "When you left here with Darling you were a little lacking in the explanation department."

Kirby took a moment and explained to them how he heard Madden talking through the air vent in Erica's bathroom, how it led to the bogus art scam, the fake Wilco and the raid on the auction.

"But are they responsible for Erica's death?" asked Andi.

Kirby shrugged. "I don't think so," he answered, "when I hit them with them being overheard by Erica, neither of them had a clue. If they're not lying, and they don't show any of the usual signs of lying, then my theory of them killing Erica because she overheard them talking about their scam kind of goes out the window."

"Can you make a circumstantial case?" asked Molly.

"I don't know," said Kirby, "they were coaching their fake Wilco at the time of Erica's death. Since he's just an actor who didn't even know he was involved in a scam, he doesn't really have much to gain from lying to protect them from a murder charge."

"So you're back at square one?" asked Bruce, taking his seat by the writing desk.

"I'm afraid so," said Kirby.

"Maybe it was the stalker?" asked Bruce.

"That's a little far-fetched," said Andi.

"It's not the first time a stalker killed someone," said

Bruce.

"But I don't think this moony-eyed fool was dangerous," said Andi, "and I don't think Erica took it that seriously, or she would have at least mentioned him to me."

"What about the fire?" asked Bruce.

"What about this fire?" asked Kirby, his mind cloudy from sleep. "I need the details."

"She told me it was caused by bad wiring in her garage?" said Andi.

"That's what she said so you wouldn't worry," answered Bruce. "What really happened was that someone stuffed a rag in the gas tank of her lawnmower and set it on fire. The lawnmower blew up, but the fire failed to spread to the house."

"So it was definitely arson?" asked Kirby.

"Definitely," said Bruce. "The police thought Chaz Healey did it, but he had an alibi for that night."

"Let me guess," said Kirby, "he was off getting wasted with some nightclub bimbos."

Bruce nodded.

"I just thought that Erica would have come to me if she was really frightened," said Andi, a hint of tears lingering in the back of her voice. "I could have helped her then."

"I don't think there was anything you could have done," said Henry, holding his wife tighter. "It's not your fault, really it isn't."

"I could have warned her that something like this could happen," said Andi. "The poor girl had the most dreadful luck with relationships. They always ended with lots of anger and yelling and all kinds of accusations. It was only a matter of time before one of them went over the edge."

"The police are giving the stalker pictures a second going over," said Kirby, "they think they might be able to decipher some traceable data from the emails and the attached photos, but that's the sort of technical stuff I'm no good at."

"You think your work on this case is done?" asked Molly.

"I think it is," said Kirby, "my position as a 'police

consultant' is tenuous at best. It's only a matter of time before someone in authority decides that having an American interfering in a Canadian homicide case is a little too much to take, and not give a crap about the endorsement of Interpol."

"You must be exhausted," said Andi, rising from her seat. "Maybe we should stop wasting your time."

"You're not wasting my time," said Kirby, "but I am exhausted. Let's all get some sleep, and maybe we can talk all this over in the morning."

"That sounds like a capital idea," declared Henry, rising to join his wife. "I think we all need to get some sleep. Maybe in the morning one of the people the police have in custody will confess to being the stalker and the killer. Then maybe we might be able to put this nightmare behind us."

"I'll miss Erica though," said Andi, squeezing her husband's arm.

"We will all miss her," said Henry, "she was a beautiful soul."

Everyone rose from their seats, said their goodbyes and headed for the door. Bruce was the last to leave, pausing in front of Kirby to give him a package.

"This is Erica's iPhone," said Bruce. "Turns out she kept copies of everything to do with the stalker on a cloud server you can access with it. Perhaps if you look them over in the morning, with a clear head you can...well, figure something out. I mean you've solved over half a dozen crimes already this weekend, and everyone really needs you to solve this last one."

Kirby took the small black phone in his hand. Physically it was featherlight, but emotionally, it felt like a lead brick.

"I'll do what I can."

"That's all I ask."

The bed was soft and inviting, but once Kirby got there, the slumber party just wouldn't start. He couldn't turn off his brain and it kept jumping around in his skull, bashing against

the sides like an angry lion in a cage. Bits of information –
what the old time detectives in old time novels called clues –
zipped around like fleas on that angry lion, irritating the hell
out of it. He couldn't sleep because he was thinking too
much, and he couldn't think straight because he was too
damn tired.

Kirby sat up and looked over at his bedside table. Erica's
iPhone sat by the lamp, staring at him like a big black eye.
He picked it up and turned it on. He scrolled through the
files, found the link connecting to her stalker files and
opened it. There were dozens of them, the email and social
network accounts were all with different free webmail
providers, but they all had variations of the same username
of True-Lover. He opened the earliest ones, which were
saved on screenshots of Erica's Facebook fan page. The only
harm done by these messages was to the art of love poetry.
They were overlong rambling attempts at capturing the
beauty of her face, her figure, her heart and her soul. All
those elements of Erica escaped those attempts, but it didn't
stop the variations of True-Lover from keeping on trying.

Trying at least until Facebook did one of their celebrity
clients a favour and blocked anyone with any variation of the
True-Lover username from having any communication with
Erica Cross in any form, let alone poetic.

As Kirby waded through the files he saw that the ban by
Facebook lead to the first emails. The messages themselves
didn't give any clues as to how this guy got Erica's email
address. The messages also shifted from poetry to eerily
detailed descriptions of Erica's day to day activities. What
she had for breakfast, telling her that she didn't need to diet.
To her exercise regimen, to descriptions of the people she
worked with at photo shoots, and even that low budget
horror film she appeared in.

True-Lover's emails dripped with jealousy over any man
who showed the slightest attention to her. Telling her that
they were not worthy of her perfection, and how all they
wanted was her body, while he adored her soul. Erica had

made notes and attached them to each email, recording where she was while her anonymous paramour was watching her. The locations went all over the world, from Los Angeles, to London, to Paris, Milan, Beijing and Tokyo.

Kirby thought back to what Andi told him about bitter ex-boyfriends. None of these messages had a whiff of bitterness and/or rejection directed at Erica. The messages were all kittens and unicorns, dripping with the hope of a relationship to come, not the resentment of one that ended badly.

While it went against his better judgment, he made a mental note to get a list of ex-boyfriends from Bruce and Andi. Maybe one might turn out to be delusional and have accumulated a hell of a lot of air miles over the past two years. Kirby's eyes were feeling heavy, the iPhone slipped from his hand and the room faded to black.

Molly turned over, again, then rolled the other way, again. She just couldn't sleep. It wasn't the strangeness of sleeping wrapped in sheets with a thread count similar to the population density of Bombay, nor was it the fact that the room was so quiet. Molly couldn't hear pipes rattling in the walls or her roommate, Dora, snoring in the next room, or any of the other familiar noises that surrounded her apartment at night.

What was keeping Molly awake was that she felt like a total and complete idiot.

Kirby Baxter was just across the living room, alone. That condescending cow Zoë was long gone, in what was probably the worst case of break-up timing ever known, and Kirby looked like he really needed someone. He looked like he needed someone in particular, someone who might be named Molly Prudence Garrett, though she thought it best that she leave her middle name out of the equation for now.

Molly thought back to the first time she met Kirby Baxter. It was at a convention in her native Philadelphia, and she was already a huge fan of his work. They had conversed a few times via social media, but it was their first face to face meeting. He was actually pleased to meet her, and they spent that afternoon talking over their favourite characters and stories. He even introduced her to Nick Pappas, then Smiling Sam Ash's right-hand, which helped land Molly her first job in the industry as an assistant to Simone Galen the editor and head writer of The Vengeance Sisters book.

That first meeting gave her a career. It also put her in regular face to face contact with Kirby and the more she got to know him, the more she found out she loved him. At first she wrote it off as a childish infatuation, and tried to suppress it and act solely as a friend and professional colleague. It was a mask but, thanks to Kirby, she was in the business of people who wore masks.

The mask almost slipped three years ago at the Atlantic Comics Halloween party. That was the night Kirby debuted his relationship with Zoë, AKA 'The Condescending Cow.' Zoë was kind of pretty in an 'I hate my daddy that's why my hair is purple' kind of way, but her beauty really was just skin deep. She worked at a used bookstore Kirby frequented while living in a Tribeca condo that her hedge fund managing daddy bought for her. Zoë was on her fifth year working on her doctoral thesis about the social and political implications of the work of Sylvia Plath, knew nothing about comics and wanted to know even less than nothing about comics. She latched onto Kirby when she found out that he was an 'artist' who owned a seaside farm on Long Island. Molly could tell Zoë was disappointed when she found out that Kirby was just a comic book doodler who only barely held on to that seaside farm by renting the grazing rights to his land to the rich hobby farmers who lived on either side of him. When Kirby lost his job he lost the one thing that set him apart from the pseudo-academics and trust fund brats that Zoë normally hung out with, a respected position in a creative industry.

Of course Molly knew how it all turned out in the end. Zoë dumped Kirby, and then Kirby got really rich really fast.

Then Kirby Baxter disappeared, leaving Molly to spend two years reading about his adventures in Europe on the roughly translated websites of European tabloids. He hadn't called her, in fact, he hadn't called anyone during that time. Kirby's silent absence left Molly sort of emotionally paralyzed, however Mitch finally tracked down Kirby to share the rumour that Dick Wilco might be coming to OmniCon. Although Kirby did eventually expose that rumour as part of a massive fraud, the thought of reuniting with his childhood mentor was the perfect way to remind Kirby that there was a place where he had friends, a career and people who still cared about him even though his life had changed rather drastically.

She didn't think her feelings would come back so strong when she saw him again in front of the convention centre. He was still a goof, a rich goof now, but still a goof and those feelings had gone beyond what she thought was a girly little crush. However, she kicked herself for needing a belly full of tropically flavoured booze to work up the nerve to say anything about it. Only to have that anything drowned out by that damn scream.

Molly pulled herself up into a sitting position and turned on the bedside lamp. The light stung her eyes, and she wondered if she missed an opportunity. The moment that little bastard Mitch mentioned Kirby meeting a model, she had to choke down the urge to scream. It was her nightmare that Kirby would leave their cozy little comfort zone and become one of those rich playboys forever pursuing younger and younger bimbos who often looked more sexually fantastical than the characters Kirby used to draw for a living.

Molly admitted to herself that she was burning with jealousy when she first heard about Erica Cross, but that blaze went down to a simmer when she saw her and Kirby in action. Kirby found her attractive; it was stupid to deny that, any man would, but Molly got the feeling that Kirby knew that a real romantic relationship between them was most likely impossible.

She meant that it had to be impossible. Girls like Erica didn't go off and live happily ever after with geeks like Kirby Baxter. They marry them, cheat on them and clean them out in a messy, scandal plagued divorce. Molly knew that Kirby understood that, at least she hoped that Kirby understood that.

Molly hated to admit that once the horror of Erica's murder faded she felt a wisp of relief. It was wrong, but inevitable when you're a mere mortal competing with a scarlet haired goddess for the attention of Kirby Baxter. Even though she was dead, Erica Cross had an even stronger hold on Kirby's mind now. Erica was no longer an object of fantasy to Kirby, but a victim, someone screaming from beyond death for justice. Molly knew Kirby couldn't let something like that go, he didn't have a choice, she read all about it in the European papers. Molly didn't want Kirby to know just how closely she had followed the news of his life in Europe, because she felt kind of embarrassed about it. It made her feel like a little girl caught clipping pictures of her teen dream out of back issues of a fan magazine. All of her research, coupled with her personal knowledge of Kirby Baxter as a human being told her that there was no way Kirby could let such an injustice go.

Now he was on the opposite side of this massive suite, alone, his inability to find a solution to this mystery eating at his mind and soul. Molly wanted to go to him, to hold him, to kiss him and tell him it was going to be all right, because she loved him.

Instead she curled up in her bed, tears streaming down her face.

"Check it out."

"Andi?" asked Kirby sitting up and looking around. In the dim light he could see that there was no one in the room with him. Now Kirby was confused, he could have sworn he heard Andi Hack's voice telling him to check something out.

The bedside clock told him it was three forty-five in the morning. So where did the voice come from?

Was he dreaming?

"Check it out."

It was Andi Hack again. This time her voice sounded more muffled. Kirby looked down and saw the faint glow of Erica Cross' iPhone lying face down on the bed. He picked it up.

"Check it out," said Andi Hack again, and this time he saw her on the phone's monitor. It was an app, titled 'Andi's Fashion Alerts' on the top of the screen, and it showed a video of Andi Hack holding a glowing button marked PRESS.

Kirby pressed it with his thumb, and a list of Toronto area stores cutting prices on high-end clothing appeared. Pressing on the listings for individual stores got catalogue pictures of clothing, accessories, and shoes. All the while a little digital Andi Hack offered approval from a little box in the corner.

Kirby logged off the app, figuring he probably turned it on by accident when he rolled over, and powered down the iPhone. He placed it carefully on the bedside table, pulled up his sheets and stumbled uneasily back to sleep.

Kirby looked up from the Tiki Bar and saw that he was at the base of the old lighthouse at Charlatan's Cove.

Except it wasn't a lighthouse.

It was a clock tower now.

"What time is it?" asked Molly from her seat next to him at the Tiki Bar.

"Check it out," said Andi Hack from his other side, her head literally buried in her now massive purse.

Kirby looked up the clock tower. The digital clock at the very top read one thirty.

"The clock is wrong," said Kirby, because it couldn't be one thirty in the morning, because they were in the middle of a sunny day.

"It has to be right," said Molly.

"Check it out," said Andi's purse, lying alone on the counter.

"That bitch has to be right," said Max Cooperman from behind Kirby.

"Why does it have to right?" asked Kirby.

"Because it's my alibi," said Cooperman.

"Mine too," said Ashmore, standing behind the bar.

"Check it out," repeated the purse this time with Henry Hack's voice.

"In comedy," said Cooperman, "as in life, timing is everything."

"She had a beautiful soul," said Erica Cross from the behind the bar, "does anyone want another drink?"

"I'll have a Mai Tai," said Molly, holding up her hand.

"One Mai Timing coming up," said Erica, her image growing fuzzy around the edges as she passed a bottle to Molly.

"Delicious," declared Molly, somehow able to speak while chugging the contents of the bottle.

"Does anyone want anything else?" asked Erica, now growing transparent.

"I'll have a beautiful soul," said Henry Hack sitting on the bar where his wife's purse was just a second ago.

"One beautiful soul coming up," said Erica, almost completely insubstantial, passing a bottle over to Hack.

"Why are you here?" asked Bruce Haring as he emerged from the lighthouse turned clock tower. "You have work to do!"

"What work?" asked Kirby. "I'm not a cop. I'm just an idiot with really screwed up luck."

"You're supposed to find out who killed me," said Erica, now just a few wisps of mist hanging in the air behind the bar.

"But—"

"No buts," said Mitch as he and Sandra Doyle stumbled past.

"This is not my job!" declared Kirby as he stood up and

stepped away from the bar. "I draw pictures for a living, I don't solve murders!"

"But you're so good at it," said a wisp of Erica as it floated by. "Can't you do it for me?"

"Can you do it for me?" asked Molly.

"But I can't!" said Kirby. "All I'm doing is making everything worse!"

"Why?" asked the wisp of Erica, as everything around him started to fade, everything but the lighthouse turned clock tower.

"Because the timing is all wrong!" yelled Kirby.

"The timing is all wrong..."

"All wrong," muttered Kirby as he snapped awake.

A phone was ringing.

This time it was Kirby's phone, he sat up and grabbed it.

"Hello," he muttered.

"Did I wake you?" it was Darling.

"Yes," said Kirby, "but it's okay." He looked over at the bedside clock, it read seven thirty in the morning. "What's up?"

"There's a lot of strange stuff going on," said Darling.

"What do you mean?"

"Cooperman just got bail."

"How did he get bail in the middle of a Saturday night?"

"Technically it was on a Sunday morning," corrected Darling. "It seems a judge showed up at the jail and called a special emergency hearing. The crown prosecutor had to get out of bed and drive like a maniac to make it there on time. This judge seemed very adamant that Cooperman get bail, but the crown was able to get it bumped up to five hundred thousand and have Cooperman surrender his passport. Then someone sent by Cooperman's brother arrived, paid the bail, and he just walked out."

"I don't know much about the Canadian justice system," said Kirby, "but this seems highly unusual."

"It is extremely unusual," answered Darling, "I put a tail

on him, and the tail says that he's heading back to the hotel as we speak."

"What about Weatherby?" asked Kirby.

"Weatherby," is in a safe house with his handlers. They say his family's preparing to seize control of MaxCo on Monday morning," answered Darling. "But that's not why I called, it's because I'm concerned about him going after you."

"I saw the fear in his eyes when he saw Gustav," said Kirby, rubbing his eyes, "it was the only sincere feeling I got from him. I don't see him doing anything that stupid, but he might try to run for it. He's already pretty much lost everything, becoming a fugitive is not that big a stretch right now."

"There's some other news," said Darling. "We got the autopsy results."

"What are they?"

"I want to tell you face to face," said Darling, "with everyone taping and filming everyone else I've become convinced that someone's listening in on us right now."

"An epidemic of buggery?" asked Kirby with a half-smirk.

"That's a new definition of that word," answered Darling.

"Have you eaten yet?" asked Kirby.

"I barely slept," answered Darling.

"Okay," said Kirby, "come and join us for breakfast, because I have something to tell you too."

"You do?"

"Yes," said Kirby, "I just realized that Erica was already dead when we heard the scream. That means that everything we thought we knew about alibis and evidence is all wrong."

Something that smelled really good hit Darling's nose as Gustav opened the door to the Royal Suite. Of course, since the last thing she ate was half a half-stale bran muffin over ten hours earlier, anything edible would have smelled good.

"Sergeant Darling," said Molly Garrett, dressed in an oversized black bathrobe, her hair wet. "We weren't sure what you liked, so we asked the hotel to send up a buffet kind of thing, and it's got everything."

Molly was not exaggerating, lined along the wall next to the dinner table were three long carts, bearing heated serving trays. The trays were so full they were almost tipping their shiny silvery lids.

"You weren't kidding," said Darling.

"The concierge even said it's on the house," added Molly. "I guess they lost a lot of guests and are just grateful to anyone willing to stay."

Marvin Mitchell Mandelbaum came out of his room, clad in a red t-shirt with a logo featuring a yellow lightning bolt in the centre of a white circle, dark blue jeans and lime green socks.

"Good morning Sergeant," he said.

"Good morning Mr. Mandelbaum," replied Darling.

"Call me Mitch," replied Mitch, "grab a plate, fill it up and grab a seat, Lord Peter Flimsy will be joining us shortly."

"'Lord Peter Flimsy?'" asked Baxter as he came out of his room, dressed in a plain black t-shirt and matching jeans.

"The rich amateur sleuth," said Mitch, as he scooped up a spoonful of scrambled eggs from one of the heated trays. "I thought it was fitting. I even thought about buying you a monocle."

"Sometimes you amaze me Mitch," said Baxter as he approached the improvised buffet, getting in line behind Darling and saying, "good morning Sergeant Darling."

"Good Morning Mr. Baxter," replied Darling.

"Just call me Kirby," said Baxter, "it's easier that way."

"I like to think that I always amaze everyone," said Mitch getting back on his favourite topic, which was himself.

"Not always," said Kirby as he got a plate and loaded on some bacon, French toast, and real Canadian maple syrup. "But sometimes you do succeed at being amazing when you can dig up a pun from the nineteen twenties, and it's still fresher than your Thom Bray reference."

"Who is Thom Bray?" asked Darling, not having a clue what they're talking about.

"He's not involved in this case," said Kirby.

"At least not yet," said Molly.

"The day is young," added Kirby, "but for now he's just a bit of flotsam from the bottomless vault of trivia that we call Mitch's brain."

"I'm going to toss some clothes on, save something for me, I'm starving."

"I'm not making any promises," said Mitch, as he squirted some ketchup on the side of his plate.

Gustav filled glasses of orange juice and placed one by each place setting before getting himself a plate of two eggs, bacon and toast, and sitting down across from Darling and next to Mitch.

"I guess we should get down to business," said Kirby.

"You better not whip out any autopsy pictures from that file," said Mitch. "Not that I'm the type that gets queasy easily. I'm just concerned about Molly."

"You're truly chivalrous," said Kirby.

"That's duly noted," said Darling, putting her zippered

leather folder on the floor by her seat. "Don't worry, I won't be too graphic."

"That's good," said Molly as she re-entered the room. Her hair was still wet, but she was now dressed in a dark purple t-shirt and blue denim shorts. "Mitch is the sensitive type. He can't even watch CSI."

"I guess I should start with the cause of death," said Darling, dribbling that real maple syrup on her waffles.

"It was cyanide," said Kirby.

"Yes," said Darling, starting to slice up her first waffle into neat squares. "You were right all along."

"Were there any needle marks?" asked Kirby.

Darling shook her head, not wanting to talk with her mouth full.

"But that's not the odd thing," said Darling after swallowing.

"What's the odd thing?" asked Kirby.

"Erica Cross was a virgin," said Darling.

"No needle marks," said Mitch, "and she was virgin. I guess she never–"

"Gustav," said Kirby, "do me a favour."

Gustav's meaty finger flicked Mitch across the ear.

"Ooowww!" howled Mitch almost falling off his chair. "That almost took my ear off." Then he said to Darling: "That's assault."

"I think it's justified as self-defence," said Darling.

"Sheesh," said Mitch rubbing his sore ear.

"I think that remark needs a matched set," added Molly, flicking Mitch across the other ear.

"Ouch!" screamed Mitch. "That hurt even more."

"The sharp fingernail has many uses."

"Can we get back to business?" asked Kirby.

Darling agreed, followed by Gustav and Molly. Even Mitch agreed, grateful for using his ears for hearing, instead of target practice.

"So the cyanide had to have been in something she either ate or drank," said Kirby as he cut up his French toast.

Darling nodded, realizing that someone in the Waterloo's vast kitchen had somehow managed to make the greatest waffle she ever ate. She swallowed and asked Kirby: "So what's your theory about time of death and alibis and all that?"

"I read somewhere that cyanide acts very quickly," said Kirby.

"That's right," replied Darling. "The coroner looked at the amount in her blood and thinks it took a little more than ten seconds to kill her."

"She also wouldn't have been able to scream." Kirby took a sip of his orange juice, "which is why I think the scream we heard was some sort of distraction engineered by the killer."

"But it sounded like her," said Molly.

"There are ways to fake that," said Kirby, "Erica was in a horror film last year and she told me that her role was just a lot of running around and screaming. It doesn't take much technology or know-how to swipe a scream from a movie and play it back at just the right moment. Like when the killer is supposed to have an alibi."

"But you think she was already dead then?" asked Darling.

"I think she was killed at the party," said Kirby. "Remember that she left the Friday night party early, but no one saw her leave."

"Oh my God!" gasped Molly. "She was in the freezer while we were dancing."

"That's what I think happened," declared Kirby.

"That means everyone's alibis are worthless," said Darling.

"Exactly," said Kirby, "no one was dancing in the area behind Henry Hack's stage. The killer somehow lured Erica behind the stage, gave her something to drink and then slipped the body into the freezer, which wasn't even locked at the time, because who would steal dry ice."

"Now we have to reinterview everyone," said Darling.

"And trying to retrace their movements at a party where everyone's mingling," said Kirby, "and milling around in a dimly lit room filled with loud music will be next to impossible."

"Our killer may have committed the perfect crime," thought Darling aloud, "by doing it in a room full of people."

"Nothing's perfect," said Kirby, "there's a trail to Erica's killer."

"And how do we find this trail?"

"We follow the scream."

"All right," said Darling, "and how do we do that?"

"I haven't figured that out yet," said Kirby. "Let me do a little thinking while I eat."

"I could get used to this," said Darling as she stepped out onto the Royal Suite's expansive balcony.

"It does have its perks," said Kirby crossing over to the carved marble Art Deco railing and looking down at the street below. There was a crowd at the entrance to the convention centre. Kirby looked over what looked like a mass of ants and wondered how many were there for the convention, and how many were ghouls looking for the morbid thrill of being close to the site of so much murder and mayhem, and how many were reporters sniffing around for a scoop. When he talked to the concierge about breakfast Stevens warned them that reporters were starting to call, looking for information on him. They agreed that none should get through, but Kirby knew that the media had ways of getting what they wanted. Once they did, getting the time to think straight would be impossible, and this whole damn mess could remain unsolved. "But it seems to come with its own baggage."

Gustav slid out an elegantly formed metal chair for Darling to sit in.

"Thank you," said Darling.

Molly came out onto the balcony carrying her laptop. "The sun feels great."

"Yeah," said Kirby pulling over a long outdoor chaise lounge, "why don't you sit down and join us, we're just going to brainstorm for a bit."

"Don't mind if I do," said Molly, lying across the piece of high-end patio furniture and barely taking up any space on it.

Kirby pulled up a chair and sat down.

"How do we follow the scream?" asked Darling.

"That's the tricky part," said Kirby. "Everyone who heard the scream heard it coming from different directions. What does that tell you?"

"The PA system," said Darling.

"Exactly," said Kirby, "except that there are half a dozen ways to access the PA system, especially when the hall is pretty much empty."

"I'll call the tech guys and ask them to look it over," said Darling, taking out her cell phone.

"Just a second," said Kirby, sitting up straight. "Do you have the information on when the pictures were taken?"

"Yeah," said Darling, picking up her leather binder and unzipping it. "I have a printout that has all the dates and locations."

"Molly?" asked Kirby.

"What is it?"

"I need you get on the internet," asked Kirby, "and look for Henry Hack's website."

"What are you thinking?"

"Of something blindingly obvious," said Kirby taking the printout from Darling.

Molly typed and clicked.

"I found it," said Molly, and Kirby could hear tinny techno music playing on the laptop's tiny speaker.

"Check to see if he's got an archive listing past performances and public appearances," asked Kirby.

"I think I see where you're going with this," said Molly.

"Can you pass me the laptop?" asked Kirby, and he took the machine from Molly.

"Well?" asked Molly.

"I hate being right," said Kirby. "When musicians do a tour they try to lay out their schedules along a simple predictable pattern. You start at one city, go the closest one next and then the next closest, it's all to save money and time – do you see what I'm getting at?"

"But Hack's not a musician," said Darling, "he's some sort of celebrity DJ, doesn't he have to go wherever the celebrity parties take him?"

"One thing I learned about being a rich person," said Kirby, "is that the other rich people act a lot like migrating birds. They move in groups, from place to place, depending on the time of year. These movements, like music tours also follow predictable patterns."

"But Hack's appearances don't follow these patterns?" asked Darling.

"They are all over the place," said Kirby. "He's skipping some key markets to zigzag halfway across the world to places that are out of season, or never in season."

"But they're all places and times that put him near Erica?"

"Not all," said Kirby, "but I figure that three quarters of his 'tour dates' coincide with the dates and locations of the stalker photos. Erica does a fashion shoot in Berlin; Hack plays a small nightclub in Berlin. Erica appears in that low budget horror movie in Vancouver; meanwhile Henry Hack does a dance show at a nearby ski resort, even though it's in the fall and the ski season hasn't started yet. I'll bet dollars to donuts that if we do some digging over all his other travel, like business trips and holidays, he'll pop up in all the other places. What brand of camera did the tech boys say was used by the stalker?"

"There are some data markers in the pictures," answered Darling, "that say it's a mid-range digital camera, the brand is Canon, but they can't get more specific."

"Hack owns a mid-range Canon digital camera, and if we let your tech boys look at it they'll find that if it isn't the stalker's camera then it's got a twin."

"We'll need a warrant for that," said Darling, "and warrants are harder to get than bail these days."

"I know where we can get you what you need," said

Kirby, "and you already have a warrant to search it."

"Where's that?"

"We're going to need Mitch," said Kirby, rising from his seat, "where is he?"

"He said something about putting ice on his ears and sulking in his room," answered Molly.

"Gustav," said Kirby. "Could you get Mitch to come out here, please?"

Gustav nodded and slipped back into the suite.

"What do you need Mitch for?" asked Darling.

"Mitch is very good at using Macs," said Kirby, "and Hack just happens to have one left in the middle of our crime scene and it's hooked up to the PA system."

"I see where you're going," said Darling.

"But I can't see where I'm going!" said Mitch from his place slung over Gustav's right shoulder.

"Mitch," said Kirby, "what the hell are you doing there?"

Gustav turned around to let Mitch look up at Kirby.

"He let Molly ride on his shoulder," said Mitch, "so I asked if I could get a piggy back ride to make up for the ear flicking, and this was his answer."

"Put him down Gustav," said Kirby, "feet first, we need to pick what's left of his brain."


They came to Room B by the small 'Staff Only' door at the back of the room, because reporters were out sniffing for stories on the convention floor. The cop watching the door tipped his hat to Sergeant Darling as he opened the door for this strange looking ensemble.

"I think we should let the tech boys look at this first," said Darling.

"Relax," said Molly, pulling out a compact little video camera, "I got Mitch's camera and I'll record the whole thing to preserve your chain of evidence."

"Thank you 'CSI,' now everyone thinks they're an expert."

"Can you do something with this?" asked Kirby as he and Mitch went up onto Hack's DJ platform.

"It's a Mac," answered Mitch, "I've used Macs my whole life. The question is what I'm supposed to be looking for."

"It's a sound file," replied Kirby.

"It's a DJ's sound system," said Mitch, "it's nothing but sound files."

"I'm looking for a sound file that is between three to five seconds in length."

"Ah," said Mitch as he booted up the computer, "I have no idea what it is, but I think I know how to find it."

Mitch punched some keys, clicked the mouse.

"There's something here," said Mitch, "a file marked EC-100. The duration is only four seconds."

"Can you play it for us?" asked Kirby.

"Sure," said Mitch clicking the mouse, "it's all pretty straightforward."

Erica's scream echoed across Room B, and throughout the whole convention centre.

"I wanted it played only in this room," said Kirby.

"Then you should have been more specific," said Mitch.

The door leading to the convention centre opened and a uniformed police officer stuck his head in.

"What the hell was that?" asked the uniformed cop. "Everybody out here just jumped half out of their skin."

"Technical glitch," said Darling. "Get someone out there who knows what they're doing to announce that the scream was just a malfunction with the sound system or something."

The cop nodded and slipped back into the convention centre.

"I swear," muttered Darling, leaning against the platform's railing, "that if we don't close this case soon, your little Scooby Gang will put me in the hospital next to Spasky."

"This is almost over," said Kirby, "because I don't see Henry Hack explaining that away. Especially with his iffy alibi."

"Since I helped you crack this case in my own little way," said Mitch, "I just have one request."

"What is it?"

"When you arrest the killer," said Mitch, "can you ask him to say: 'I would have gotten away with it, if it weren't for you meddling kids'?"

"Do you really want to get hurt?" asked Kirby.

"I can't believe it," said Mitch as they went down the hallway, "I came this close to sharing my Freezie Pops with a killer."

Kirby shrugged, "It sure looks that way."

"I got some officers meeting us at the Excelsior floor," said Darling, pocketing her cell phone. "When we get there I want all of you to go to your suite and stay there, while we do the arrest."

"No arguing here," said Molly.

"I'll gladly step aside," said Kirby.

They were passing the manager's office on their way to the elevators. The door was open, and Kirby couldn't help hearing a woman's voice saying: "Someone broke into the utility closet and stole the hose from my vacuum cleaner."

"Why would someone–?" replied a man's voice.

The company turned a corner, and they came face to face with Max Cooperman coming out of the elevator.

"Whoa there sheriff," said Cooperman, "you can't arrest me, I'm out on bail. I'm here legally."

"We're not here for you," said Darling, "we're here for the elevator."

"Fine," said Cooperman, "but you really shouldn't be talking to me without my lawyer."

"Then don't talk, just go," said Kirby, and on cue Gustav cast Cooperman a stink-eye that would have made King Kong step aside.

Cooperman stepped aside.

"Far be it for me to interfere with police business," said Cooperman.

"Don't leave town," added Darling as the elevator door closed.

"While I'm sure I'll be milking the stories from this

weekend for years to come," said Molly, "I'm actually happy to have the end in sight."

"Hack might try to run for it," said Mitch.

"Let's not dwell on what might happen," said Kirby.

"He could try to shoot his way out," added Mitch.

"That's a happy thought," said Darling. "There's no sign he's armed."

"Madden didn't show any signs that he was armed either," said Mitch, "but we still found a dead body on our front door."

"Mitch," said Kirby.

"What?"

"You're not helping anymore," added Kirby.

"I'll send in the guys with the vests first," said Darling.

"Sorry," said Mitch, "my mouth tends to run on."

"Admitting you have a problem is the first step," said Kirby,

"The second step is to shut up," said Molly.

"I stand corrected," said Mitch. "Not all of us can be strong silent types like Gustav."

"Why do people keep saying that?" asked Kirby.

The elevator chimed and they stepped off onto the Excelsior floor. The first thing Kirby noticed was the door to the utility closet hanging slightly ajar, the wood around the lock splintered. Two uniformed police officers were waiting for them.

"You two are with me," said Darling to the officers, "the rest of you should get back to your suite."

"My work here is done," said Kirby, raising his hands and turning to join the others.


It was only two minutes later that someone knocked on the door to Kirby's suite.

"I'll get it," said Kirby, because Gustav was making a fresh pot of coffee for everyone in the suite's kitchen. Kirby peeked into the peephole and saw a uniformed cop. He opened the door.

"Are you Kirby Baxter?" asked the cop.

"Yes," said Kirby.

"Sergeant Darling told me to tell you something," said the cop, "she said your work is not done yet."

"Guys," said Kirby, "I'll be back in a minute."

He hadn't finished the sentence when he realized that Gustav was standing right behind him.

"And don't worry," he said to Molly, who poked her head out of her bedroom, "Gustav's coming with me."

"I'll finish making the coffee," said Mitch. "I'll make extra so there will be enough for the cops."

Kirby thanked Mitch and followed the cop out into the hall. Sergeant Darling was standing in the door of the Hack's suite waving to Kirby.

"What is it?" asked Kirby as he reached the door.

"Hack is gone," said Darling, her voice low. Over her shoulder Kirby could see Andi Hack perched on the edge of a black leather sofa, wiping her eyes with a tissue. Andi looked up at Kirby, her expression pleading for him to help.

"You have to help me," said Andi, "he's gone off, and I'm scared he's going to get hurt."

Darling stepped aside and let Kirby enter the suite.

"What do you mean?" asked Kirby as he approached Andi, crouching down.

"I picked up his laptop," said Andi, "because the battery was dead in mine, and I—"

Andi blew her nose.

"What happened next?" asked Kirby, placing a hand on her free hand and letting his fingertips rest on the wrist.

"I picked up his laptop," continued Andi, "and tried to get on the internet, but I must have clicked on the wrong thing or something... I found a file."

"What was in the file?" asked Kirby.

"It was pictures," said Andi, "of Erica. Hundreds of them. And love letters, emails really, all to Erica."

"Then what happened?" asked Kirby.

"I asked him about the pictures and the emails,"

continued Andi. "He got defensive. Then I started getting suspicious."

"Of what?"

"Of my husband!" cried Andi. "I knew he was lying, I just knew it. Then I asked him about that mysterious phone call to Australia at the time of the murder... That made him angry."

"He got angry?" asked Kirby.

"Very angry," said Andi. "I thought he was going to hit me. Then he just stormed off. About thirty seconds later Sergeant Darling appeared."

"We have his laptop," added Darling. "We're getting a warrant to do a completely legal search of the thing."

"You can search this suite," said Andi. "I need to know the truth of what's going on here."

"Thank you," said Sergeant Darling.

"Do you think he killed her?" asked Andi, her hand clamping on his. "I know you're helping the police, you must know something!"

Kirby shrugged. "His guilt or innocence is not for me to decide, all I can do is look at the evidence and see where it takes me."

"Please do something for me," pleaded Andi, "I'm begging you."

"I'll do what I can," answered Kirby.

"Please don't let him get hurt," begged Andi, tears streaming down her sculpted cheeks. "Please."

"I'll do what I can," repeated Kirby.

Andi rubbed the side of her head.

"I'm sorry," said Andi. "I'm getting a migraine."

"I think we could do something about that," said Kirby. "Sergeant Darling, I think we should take her someplace quieter."

"Yes," said Darling before turning to signal a policewoman standing by the door.

"Take her to my suite," said Kirby, "we have lots of space there, and Molly can find you someplace quiet."

Darling whispered some instructions to the officer.

"Could you please go with the officer," said Sergeant Darling, guiding Andi from the sofa to a uniformed policewoman standing by the door. "If you feel you need a doctor, feel free to ask and, if you're up to it, we'd like you to make a formal statement."

"Please help him," said Andi, squeezing Kirby's hand tightly one last time before letting go. "I'm so scared that something bad will happen to him."

"Put on an Amber Alert," ordered Darling into her police radio. The radio replied with some static that even Kirby's keen ears couldn't understand at that distance, but Darling fully understood. "I know it's not a missing child, just put the hotel and the convention centre on lockdown. There's a chance he might still be in the complex."

Kirby stepped away from Darling and toward the opposite end of the suite. The policewoman took Andi Hack to Kirby's suite to make a formal statement while Darling and her colleagues searched the suite she shared with her husband. The place was much smaller than his, less than half the size, and had only two bedrooms connected to the main living room area. The style was more high-modern than the classically elegant Art Deco of Kirby's suite. With stark white walls decorated with geometric shapes in primary colours.

Kirby looked into the first bedroom and saw a set of dark blue luggage stacked next to the bed. Despite the window being open the air smelled faintly of cigarettes and chemically processed flowers. He looked into the wastebasket. A can of floral scented air freshener lay spent in the wastebasket, an empty pack of French cigarettes with an elaborately filigreed and unreadable label crushed underneath it. An iPod connected to a set of high-end headphones lay on the bed, next to a notebook, the paper covered with rough scribbles and a felt tip pen wedged into the wire rings. He went over to the closet and looked over the clothes. All were high-end, custom-tailored, and from top designers and tailors from all around the world. Two years earlier he wouldn't have been able to tell any of them from each other, but his experience at living on the fringe of high society gave him a few lessons in the basics. He didn't wear those types of clothes, partially because the ghost of a parsimonious ancestor would vigorously smack him on the back of the brain whenever he considered it, reminding him that everything he wore was eventually going to get ink, or worse, all over it. The floor of the closet featured a row of sneakers, and dress shoes, the cheapest among them cost about a month's rent on his first apartment.

Kirby stepped out of the bedroom and crossed the living room to the other bedroom. Powder blue luggage was stacked in the corner.

"They had separate bedrooms," said Darling from the door.

"Henry's a smoker," said Kirby, "and judging from the smell of this room, I don't think Andi is a fan of the smell."

"My grandmother got migraines," said Darling, "she couldn't stand the smell of cigarettes when she was sick. Really couldn't stand the smell of anything when she was having a migraine. Or the sound of anything either."

"Do you smell that?" asked Kirby.

"I told you it smells like those really fancy scented candles in here," said Darling. "Probably trying to ward off the smell of the cigarettes from across the way."

Kirby looked around, his eyes scanning every inch of the room. "Yes," he said. "Hack is using a rental car, isn't he?"

Darling nodded.

"Find the receipt," asked Kirby. "Call the rental company; most have GPS systems installed."

"I've already got somebody on that," said Darling.

"I think we really need to find Henry Hack," said Kirby, "and find him as soon as possible."

"That's good," said Darling into her cell phone, "thank you."

"Good news?" asked Kirby while Gustav hit the button for the elevator.

"The rental agency's GPS says that the car is still in the hotel garage," answered Darling.

"That could mean that he took a taxi," said Kirby as a chime announced the arrival of the elevator, "or the bus."

"The first thing is that none of our people or hotel security saw Hack at any of the exits before the lockdown," said Darling.

"Excuse me," said Fred Ashmore as the elevator door opened.

"Oh," said Kirby, "hello Freddie."

"I see you're still around," said Ashmore, adjusting his horn-rimmed glasses.

"I'm still helping the police with their inquiries," said Kirby, "can you get out of our way?"

"Sure," said Ashmore, sidestepping around Kirby and Gustav, "I should be looking for a new editor because of you, but that's someone else's problem now."

"The sale's final?" asked Kirby as he and the others went into the elevator.

"The papers are going through on Monday," said Ashmore, a smug grin on his face. "Things worked out just fine for me in the end."

The elevator door closed.

"Douche," muttered Kirby as he reached over and hit the button for the garage level.

"You really hate that guy?" asked Darling.

"You don't know how much," said Kirby. "The man has an incredible gift for screwing up and still coming out on top mostly because of his family and the work of other people."

"So he's the proof that shit floats," said Darling.

"Yes," said Kirby, "what's your proof?"

"Proof of what?" asked Darling.

"That Henry Hack didn't make a run for it on foot?" asked Kirby.

"What?" replied Darling.

"You said that the first thing was about him not being seen around any of the exits, which usually means that there's a second thing."

"Right," said Darling. "My train of thought got a bit derailed there. The second thing is that the rental agency's GPS says that the car is running. I think he's sitting there thinking about running the gate, which is closed and guarded."

"Could they tell you where it is in the garage?" asked Kirby, because the Waterloo's parking structure was three levels, two of them underground, and each level had the square footage of a football field.

"No," said Darling, "but I have a dozen cops coming in, it won't take a minute."

"I think we might already be too late," said Kirby.

"Why do you think that?"

"Something about a vacuum cleaner," answered Kirby.

"Now you're getting all strange and obscure again," said Darling. The elevator chimed to announce their arrival on parking level three. "I want the two of you to stick with me," she added, "this man is a killer."

The elevator door opened and they stepped into the dim grey world of the parking garage. The walls were concrete, clad in shades of grey, with numbers painted in reflective yellow matching the stripes on the grey concrete floor. In the distance the floor started to angle upward, turning into a ramp that took drivers up to level two. Two uniformed police officers appeared on that ramp, one waved a flashlight at Darling, and she took a small metal flashlight from her own pocket, turned it on and waved it back.

"Good," said Darling. "Our back-up's here."

Darling's radio crackled to life.

"Darling here," she said into the radio.

Kirby inhaled deeply through his nose.

"There's no sign of Hack or his car on level one," said a voice over the radio. "We're sweeping level two right now."

"Keep me informed," said Darling before turning to Kirby. "What are you doing?"

"I smell car exhaust," said Kirby.

"We're in an underground garage," answered Darling, "the place reeks of it."

"I also hear a car running," said Kirby starting to run to the far end of the garage, "this way."

Gustav and Darling followed Kirby. Darling only paused to signal to the other cops to follow.

"Damn it!" muttered Kirby. "Damn it! I've been so goddamn stupid!"

"What are you talking about?" asked Darling, then she saw the answer.

Henry Hack's rental car was nestled in a far corner of the grim cavernous garage. The rental car's engine ran on a low purr, a vacuum cleaner hose connected the exhaust pipe to the back driver's side window. The interior of the car was an opaque grey cloud.

"Oh hell," said Kirby, he had to stop and cough, the air around the car was toxic. He pulled his shirt up over his face, in a vain attempt to filter out the carbon monoxide pouring out of the car. Darling covered her face with her sleeve and tried the driver's side door.

Gustav held a handkerchief over his face with his right hand and drew his pistol with his left. Gustav signalled Darling to step aside, gripped the pistol by the barrel and in one swing smashed the driver's side window into a thousand little pieces. Toxic exhaust gushed from the busted window as Gustav unlocked and opened the door and leaned over to turn off the engine.

"The back seat," said Kirby, seeing a shape in the back of the car. Darling opened the back driver's side door and Henry Hack flopped out of the car. Only Darling's quick reflexes kept him from hitting the garage's concrete floor head first.

The other cops arrived.

"Call an ambulance," ordered Kirby.

"But–?" asked Darling, checking Hack's pulse.

"Just call the ambulance," ordered Kirby.

"–and that was the last time I saw Henry," said Andi Hack.

The uniformed policewoman nodded, and scribbled down some notes. Andi studied the policewoman's face; it was a severe face, which Andi thought was aged beyond its actual years by cigarettes, stress, and a total and complete lack of style of any kind. She wondered what she could do to fix that face, maybe fix was too strong a word, perhaps upgrade it a little.

"Henry Hack has made no attempt to contact you since he left?" asked the policewoman.

Andi shrugged.

"No," she answered, trying to hide her annoyance at such an obvious question, "I've been with police all this time and my phone hasn't rung once."

The policewoman nodded. There was a knock on the door.

"Come in," said Andi.

The door opened and Molly stuck her head in.

"There's some fresh coffee in the dining area," said Molly, "would you like me to bring you both a cup?"

"I'd love some," said the policewoman, "but I need to type up this statement."

"The detectives have finished setting up their computer in the living room," added Molly. "You can type it up there."

"I think I'll have coffee on the balcony," said Andi, "I'm feeling a little cooped up, even in here."

"Sure," said Molly, "come with me."

Andi's trip through the Royal Suite to the wide balcony reminded her of the sort of luxurious suites she used to stay in during her glory days. Back when she was number one, there was always some oil baron, or stock market billionaire, trying to impress her with their wealth, status and power. Yet she didn't get that vibe from Kirby Baxter's presence here. With his decidedly unpretentious entourage of an oversized employee, friends and police using this suite as their headquarters he really did seem to need the space.

"How do you like your coffee?" asked Molly as they reached the door to the kitchen. Andi could see the concern in her large brown eyes.

"Do you have soy milk and some of that fake sugar?" asked Andi.

"The concierge made sure we had everything," said Molly, "so I'm sure I'll find some. You head on outside and I'll get your coffee."

A uniformed policeman opened the balcony door for her. Andi thanked him and stepped out into the sunlight. A hot dry wind caressed her face, but the glare stung her eyes. Andi reached into her voluminous purse for her sunglasses. Her hand trembled slightly as she unfolded them, and she almost poked herself in the eye as she put them on.

"Steady," she whispered to herself.

She looked over the railing of the balcony, and counted four police cars on the street below. It was only a matter of time before they found him.

"Andi," said Molly bringing in a cup of coffee.

"Thank you," said Andi, taking the cup. It smelled delicious.

"We had the soy milk and everything," said Molly.

"It's good," said Andi.

"I'm sure Kirby will sort this whole mess out," said Molly, Andi could see that she was trying to be comforting, sympathy radiated from those huge brown eyes. "He's surprisingly good at this sort of thing."

"I read something about it on the internet," said Andi.

"He tends to keep things to himself," added Molly, "and that's really annoying, but he's really a good person and he's going to do everything he can to...well...fix things."

"I think my husband might be a murderer," said Andi, her upper lip stiffened.

"Need a hug?" asked Molly.

Andi shook her head. "I'm a little too British for that right now. Maybe later."

Mitch stuck his head through the door.

"Andi!" said Mitch, he looked surprised and excited.

"What is it?"

"Kirby just called, they found your husband. This is going to be a shocker but–"

Andi put her hand over her mouth.

"–he tried to kill himself," said Mitch, "but don't panic, they got him out of the car in time. He's alive."

"Oh my God," gasped Andi.

"He's inhaled some carbon monoxide," continued Mitch, "and Kirby says he's a mess, but the convention's first aid people got him some oxygen and he's going to be okay."

"I have to see him," said Andi.

"I have to warn you," said Mitch, "that Kirby told me that the first aid people think he took some drugs because he's talking crazy."

"He's talking?"

"Mostly nonsense that no one understands," said Mitch. "Sergeant Darling's hoping that you'll get him to calm down in time for the paramedics."

"Where is he?"

"Henry's in Room B," said Mitch. "One of the officers will take you there."

Andi hugged Mitch.

"Thank you," said Andi. "I feel that everything's going to be all right."

The ringing of his cell phone made Max Cooperman jump, his stubby fingers fumbled the phone out of his pocket and dropped it on the bed, sparking a flurry of curses as he picked it up.

"What is it?" snapped Cooperman.

"It's Thurston," answered a voice over the phone. It was his lawyer.

"Where are you?" asked Cooperman, the man was supposed to meet him, and at two hundred and fifty bucks an hour, with time and a half on Sunday, the bastard better be on fucking time.

"I'm outside the hotel," answered Thurston. "They have the whole building on lockdown."

"Why?"

"I asked the cop," replied Thurston, "they said that they were looking for the suspect in the murder of Erica Cross."

"Goddamn that bitch," grumbled Cooperman, "she's a bigger inconvenience dead than she was alive."

"At least it looks like they're not looking for you," said Thurston, "unless you're hiding in a closet somewhere."

"I am not hiding in a closet," snapped Cooperman, "that's not funny!"

"Relax," said Thurston. "You'll live longer."

"Why should I relax?" demanded Cooperman. "I'm looking at hard time here!"

"And I'm trying to work out a deal for you," said Thurston, "you will have to do some time, but I think I might be able to swing it so that you do minimum security."

"That's the fucking best you can do?"

"Need I remind you," said Thurston, "that the FBI and RCMP have recordings and copies of almost every meeting, phone call and email you have been involved in since you hired young Master Weatherby? Every single one of those recordings and copies is evidence of you committing multiple felonies. The FBI wants a big white collar pelt from Hollywood to mount on their wall, your friends in

Washington are steering clear, and it looks like their indictment's going to be the size of a phone book."

"Dammit," muttered Cooperman.

"I was also talking to your brother," added Thurston. "Weatherby's family is already making moves to start a hostile takeover of MaxCo and force the both of you out."

"Fuck them," barked Weatherby.

"I think the correct term," said Thurston, "in your vernacular, is that they are fucking you."

"Shit."

"Your best bet is right here in Canada," said Thurston.

"What do you mean?"

"I'm talking five years in minimum security," said Thurston.

"Five goddamn years!"

"That's the best they've offered so far," added Thurston.

"What do they want?"

"They know that you've done business with certain people in Montreal—"

"Fuck no!"

"Hear me out."

"No way," said Cooperman. "Those bastards will skin me alive."

"Something's happening," said Thurston.

"Is there another offer?"

"No," answered Thurston, "the cops are talking among themselves. I know a couple of them, so I'm going to see what's happening. Hang on."

Cooperman sat on his bed for an eternity and a half, hearing only some muffled voices from the other end.

"Okay," said Thurston, "I have some news."

"What is it?"

"They have Henry Hack," said Thurston, "he's your neighbour in the hotel."

"I met him," snapped Cooperman, "why do they have him?"

"From what I was able to gather," said Thurston, "Hack's

their prime suspect for killing Erica Cross. They found him trying to kill himself, and there's something about him rambling all crazy about being forced to do something–"

"He's talking?"

"Apparently," said Thurston. "They have him waiting for an ambulance in Room B, and they don't think he can threaten anyone else so they're calling off the lockdown. I'll be with you in a minute."

"Fuck that," barked Cooperman, "you go back to that Crown Persecutor–"

"He's the Crown Prosecutor," corrected Thurston.

"That son of a bitch is persecuting me, so I don't fucking care what other people call him," roared Cooperman. "Go back and get a better deal where I don't have my ass carved up by bikers."

"Fine," said Thurston. He was billing him for the trip to the hotel anyway, might as well bill him for another pointless trip to the prosecutor's office.


"Can you hold that elevator!" called out Ashmore as he rushed down the hall toward the elevator.

"Sorry," said Molly Garret as the elevator door slid closed. "The police are using it."

"What?" said Ashmore.

"Trust me," said Molly, "I wouldn't even put you in that elevator right now."

"Why?" asked Ashmore, knowing that Molly Garret wasn't exactly his biggest fan, and that there weren't too many places Molly wouldn't put him in.

"The woman riding that elevator," whispered Molly, "is going to see her husband before he's arrested for murder. That ride would be beyond awk-ward."

"Did he kill Erica Cross?" asked Ashmore. Ashmore himself had been on his way to make the formal announcement of the sale of Atlantic Comics to Continental Pictures, but he was willing to wait. They couldn't start without him, he wanted to know what Molly Garret knew, and plus, an extra few minutes in this hallway meant an extra few minutes before he had to face the exhausted goat smell that all convention floors got on their last day.

Molly nodded.

"He tried to kill himself," said Molly, "but they caught him before he finished the job, now they're waiting for an ambulance to take him away."

"The killer is still in this building?"

"Don't be scared," said Molly, a sliver of sarcasm in her tone. "Kirby said that he's in pretty bad shape and there are a dozen cops and Gustav watching over him."

"How bad?"

"Ranting and raving mostly," said Molly. "Kirby says he's talking about being forced to do it or something like that. Sounds crazy but then again he's a nutcase stalker, so crazy's to be expected."

The elevator chimed.

"This is my ride."


The ride down from the Excelsior floor passed in silence. It really wasn't the place for small talk and, for some reason, Andi had to choke down the urge to attempt to make any such small talk with her police escort. For some reason she had the urge to talk about the weather, the local sports team, whoever they were, or even if the cop had a spare cigarette hidden somewhere in his body armour.

The elevator chimed to announce their arrival on the ground floor, and the door slid open. Just as they stepped out into the lobby the cop's radio crackled to life, calling for Unit Seventy-Three.

The cop spoke into the radio mounted on his shoulder and got what sounded to Andi like a few muffled bits of static and chatter in reply.

"I'm going to need you to stay here," said the cop. "A brawl broke out at one of the panels." The cop then turned back to his radio and said: "Unit Seventy-Three Bravo, is en route to Room A."

The policeman then ran down the hallway to the convention centre, leaving Andi standing next to the reception desk. Andi felt like an idiot just standing there. Another elevator chimed, a door slid open and that fellow, what's his name, Fred Ash-something stepped out, squeezing between a gaggle of cosplayers, dressed either like superheroes or hockey players, she didn't know the difference. He looked like he was concentrating on something as he headed into the convention centre.

Andi turned when she heard the door to the stairs open. This one she knew, it was Max Cooperman, his face was red, and he was sucking air like a beached fish. He clutched a briefcase to his chest, and he too ran into the convention centre.

Andi started getting pissed. It looked like everyone was going into the convention centre, her husband was lying there, injured and delirious, and she was expected to just stand by the reception desk and wait like a stupid mannequin. To hell with what the copper said, she was going to see her husband and she didn't care if there was a full scale nerd riot going on, because nothing was going to stop her.

The killer opened the rear door to Room B just a crack. The killer then poked in their head, studying the room. Henry Hack lay on a table, an oxygen tank nestled next to him and a breathing mask on his face. The lights were low. The killer stepped in, carefully closing the door behind them.

Kirby watched the whole thing, from atop Henry Hack's DJ platform, but stayed crouched behind the equipment to remain unseen. He turned on the microphone, then he turned on the lights. The killer froze, just feet from the stricken form of Henry Hack.

"Hello Mrs. Hack," said Kirby as he rose from behind the control console.

"My friends call me Andi," said Andi Hack, one hand inside her voluminous purse.

"I don't think we can call each other friends," said Kirby, "not anymore."

"What's going on?" asked Andi.

"We're alone Mrs. Hack," said Kirby, "the cops are all handling the brawl in Room A. We can speak freely. I must tell you that what you're planning is not necessary."

"What is not necessary Mr. Baxter?"

Kirby Baxter sighed from his perch on the top of the platform, his thin face was grave and he kept his hands behind his back.

"The weapon you have in your purse," said Kirby, "my guess is that it's a small syringe with some leftover cyanide. It's not necessary; your husband is already dead."

"You must really be psychic," said Andi as she drew her hand from her purse, revealing a small syringe filled with clear liquid, "I did have some left over."

"I'm not psychic," said Kirby, "I just notice little things most people ignore."

"Is this where you amaze me with how clever you are by gloating about how you exposed my evil scheme?" asked Andi.

"I'm not going to gloat," said Kirby. "I've been too stupid for that."

"Really?" asked Andi.

"I didn't trust my instincts," said Kirby, "I saw the hatred bubbling beneath your oh-so-perfect surface the night of the party. Maybe I should have said something, or done something, maybe warned Erica... I don't know."

"I don't think warning her would have worked," said Andi, "she was a trusting kind of idiot."

"I guess this is where I tell you what you did," said Kirby.

"Who am I to break a long running tradition," said Andi.

"Killing your husband was one step too far," said Kirby taking his hands out from behind his back, revealing a piece of paper inside a clear plastic evidence bag, "you got sloppy."

"Why don't you tell me what I did wrong?"

"It'll be my pleasure," said Kirby. "You told us that he had left minutes before we arrived, but the vacuum hose you used for the faked suicide had been stolen long before that. So either he had the intent to gas himself before your alleged argument and you failed to notice that he was carrying a fifteen-foot-long plastic hose, or you had drugged him and stuffed him into the car long before we even arrived. Then there's this."

Kirby unfolded a sheet of white paper in a plastic police evidence bag, it read: I KILLED ERICA, FORGIVE ME, printed in the Arial Black font.

"Sloppy," said Kirby, "because you said that you were using his laptop and his printer's attached to it, so how did he print this?"

"What can I say," said Andi, "it was a rush job. He realized that I was framing him for Erica's murder and I had to do something fast that still made him look guilty. I was just hoping to muddy the waters long enough for me to get out of the country."

"Erica's death wasn't a rush job though," said Kirby, folding the piece and putting it in his back pocket. "That took a lot of planning and a lot of time, months even. You wanted her dead and your husband framed. You took a digital copy of Erica's scream from that low budget movie she did, hid it on your husband's computer, then you copied the program he used to use control his sound system with his phone and put it on yours. It shouldn't have been that hard, since you're smart enough to program your own app."

"I was always good with that sort of thing," said Andi, "it was surprisingly easy."

"You also studied a little chemistry," said Kirby, "probably from the internet, in order to make cyanide out of apple seeds."

"Now how did you figure that out?"

"The paparazzi Tanzerian took a picture of a bag of apples in the dumpster," explained Kirby. "They had all their seeds removed. I also smelled apples when the maid took them out of your suite, and then I caught some residual smell in your bedroom. Most people assumed the smell was from scented candles, but you didn't actually have any fancy candles in your room."

"I also had to mail hundreds of seeds to a rented mailbox," added Andi. "It takes a lot of apple seeds to make enough cyanide to kill someone. Even then I overdid it and made too much. I must say that you really are good at this."

"Not good enough," said Kirby. "Or I would have figured it out earlier."

"Well, you did have a lot of distractions going on," said Andi. "That was a problem for me too. It took you so long to connect Erica and my sack of shit husband, he ended up figuring it all out himself."

"I guess I should finish this up before we get too far ahead of ourselves," said Kirby. "You talked her into going behind this platform with you, slipped the poison in her drink and, when she died, you stuck her into the dry ice tank. Death by cyanide has very similar symptoms to suffocation by carbon dioxide, so it would look like an amateur trying to play clever."

"That was almost perfect all by itself."

"Especially with the alibi you created," said Kirby, "there you were, in a room full of people, me included, when we heard the scream, your husband was alone, trying to talk long distance to Australia, no doubt with a bogus caller."

"He spent all that time talking to a recording of static and a voice asking if they could hear him," said Andi. "The beauty of it was that he was trying to talk to his own laptop. Something I was hoping the police would find when they searched it, as well as the recording of Erica's scream on his main computer."

"You spent what had to be months planning and arranging the murder of your best friend, your own alibi and the framing of your husband," said Kirby, leaning on the railing. "The only thing I haven't figured out yet was why?"

"It's because the truth is," said Andi stepping toward the base of the platform, "that she wasn't my best friend. Friends don't take everything that matters from other friends."

"What did she take from you?"

"First it was my career," said Andi, "but that wasn't deliberate, she did it just by showing up. Before I even knew what happened I was out and she was in."

"What came second?" asked Kirby.

"The bitch then went and took my husband," snarled Andi as she walked back toward the dead body of Henry Hack and put the syringe back in her purse. "He wasn't much, but he was mine and she couldn't have him."

"You think they were having an affair?"

"My husband was screwing that bitch!"

Kirby sighed.

"You had it all wrong," said Kirby, "he wasn't screwing her. He was stalking her!"

"What?"

"Your late husband was stalking your best friend," answered Kirby. "She didn't even know it was him, and it was terrifying her."

"I don't believe you!"

"She wasn't having sex with him," added Kirby, "we have evidence, hard medical evidence, that she wasn't having sex with anyone."

"What the hell are you talking about?"

"She died a virgin," said Kirby. "The medical examiner has a term for it, but this really isn't time for a science lecture."

"You're lying," declared Andi, "her sex life was all over the tabloids. She went through men like they were candy."

"And you believed the tabloids?" asked Kirby. "Personally, I believe the medical examiner over them."

"You bastard!" said Andi, slowly realizing that Kirby wasn't lying.

"I'm the bastard?" asked Kirby. "Do I have to remind you that you did murder two people?"

"I think I might as well go for three," snarled Andi.

"That's not a good idea," said Kirby, "because you should have clued in that an unarmed man like me wasn't going to meet a double murderer alone."

Gustav emerged from behind the platform, in his hand was a gun that looked like a cannon to Andi.

Andi stopped cold as the big double doors opened behind her, revealing Sergeant Darling and two more uniformed police officers, their guns drawn. The rear exit swung open, and two more cops appeared as if out of nowhere.

"Freeze!" said Darling.

"Did I mention that this whole conversation was being not only recorded, but listened to by the police?" said Kirby. "And the story about the brawl was just a distraction we concocted, for you to think you had an opportunity to finish off your husband."

Andi Hack's entire body went rigid.

"You bastard," she hissed, as tears began to roll down her face.

"The cyanide's in a syringe in the bag," said Kirby.

"Put down the bag," ordered Sergeant Darling.

"All for nothing," said Andi, her voice cracked. "All for nothing."

"Put down the bag," said Kirby, "it's over now."

"Yes it is," said Andi, her hand dove back into her big purse.

"NO!"

Andi winced; the purse strap slipped from her shoulder and fell to the floor, revealing her hand, the syringe driven deep into her palm.

"Oh God! No!" called Kirby. Darling leaped toward Andi, but wasn't fast enough.

Andi drove the plunger of the syringe into her hip, her whole body arched back, and she looked up at the ceiling, her mouth open wide and gasping. Then she fell to the floor, dead.

"Damn it," said Kirby his hand slamming the rail, "not another damn body."

ISSUE #20
KIRBY BAXTER'S FINEST HOUR

Kirby Baxter watched a sliver of Monday morning sunlight peeking from between the high buildings from his place on the Royal Suite's broad balcony. The street below was quiet, for now. The convention had closed the night before, trying to maintain some semblance of normalcy, despite the police activity. The media was already all over the case. TMZ's headline was SUPERPSYCHO SUPERMODEL, and most of the more respectable outlets weren't much better.

The door from the suite opened.

"You're out here," said Molly. She was wearing only a Scott Pilgrim t-shirt that would have been loose on Gustav, but was big enough to be a long dress on her.

"Yes," said Kirby. "I thought I could use some fresh city air."

Molly rested her head on his shoulder and wrapped her arms around Kirby's chest.

"Damn you are one skinny bastard," said Molly.

Kirby had to chuckle.

"Yeah," he said, "I guess I am."

"Are you still flying out today?" asked Molly.

"The cops think it's for the best," answered Kirby, "I made all the statements they need, and I can always fly back if the coroner needs my testimony for the inquest."

"Have the press started calling?"

Kirby shook his head. "Lucky for me, they got a little distracted."

"Distracted," asked Molly, "by what?"

"You didn't hear?"

———

"Hear what?" asked Molly.

"Max Cooperman took a run for it while we were confronting Andi Hack," answered Kirby. "He's not in his room and he's not answering his phone, which he conveniently dropped in the back of a garbage truck. Right now the press is busy speculating on connections that don't exist, which will buy me enough time to get the hell home. But enough about me, what about you? Are you still flying back with the others?"

"Obviously you didn't hear my news yet," said Molly.

"All right," said Kirby, "what is your news? It better be good, because I need some cheering up."

"The Continental Pictures people are flying the senior staff back to New York on their company jet," said Molly.

"Senior staff?" asked Kirby, turning to face Molly.

"Do you know who Continental Pictures is putting in charge of Atlantic Comics?" asked Molly.

"Kevin LaGuardia?"

"No," said Molly, "he's not available; the new boss is our old friend Nick Pappas."

"Really?" said Kirby, at what could only be great news. Nicholas "Big Poppa" Pappas went from sorting fan mail, to become Smiling Sam Ash's right-hand man and everyone expected him to take over running the company when Sam retired, because he managed to keep it afloat during Sam's last chaotic years at the company. Instead the Ashmore family replaced Smiling Sam with his great nephew, Frowning Fred, whose first act was to fire Nick Pappas. Marvel Comics immediately snatched up Pappas to be a senior vice-president, but Kirby surmised that Continental Pictures made him an offer to come home that he couldn't refuse. "But what's all this about senior staff."

"While you were with the police acting as the Great Mouse Detective," said Molly, "Nick Pappas called, and offered me the job as editor of The Vengeance Sisters."

"That's great," said Kirby, turning to hug Molly, and finally admitting to himself how comfortable it felt.

"I will finally be able to afford my own apartment," said Molly, letting Kirby go to pull up a chair next to his. "It will still be in the ass-end of Brooklyn, but it's a start."

"You do know," said Kirby, "that Brooklyn's only a short train ride from a little town on the ass-end of Long Island called Wahegon Bay."

"And the Wahegon Bay train station's just a short hop from a little farm called Charlatan's Cove," added Molly.

"That's right," said Kirby. "I'm no good at this kind of talk—"

"Don't stop trying," said Molly.

"I'm going to settle down there for the foreseeable future," said Kirby, "and I'd like to see you... Damn it, I am really bad at this..."

He was going to try to say more, but he couldn't speak with Molly's lips pressed on his.

"Dude, you really are bad at this," said Molly when her lips released. "So let's just skip the prologue."

"I could go for that."

"Good," said Molly, "because I expect you to spoil me rotten."

"You do?" asked Kirby with a smile.

"Of course," said Molly, "you're cute and being rich doesn't hurt, but all these murder cases you get involved in are definitely a big minus. This will require you to lavish attention, expensive gifts and luxury trips on me."

"So that's your price?"

"I think it's reasonable," said Molly with an impish grin.

"Well I have to say," explained Kirby, "that the odds of me getting involved in another mess as bad as this are pretty damn slim. They have to be."

Molly slipped off her chair and onto Kirby's lap.

"I could go for that," she said.

Kirby held her tight, and together they watched the sun rise.

"So you and Molly are an item now?" asked Mitch as took

his suitcase from Gustav and put on the cart.

"Why do you need my confirmation?" replied Kirby. Mitch had walked in on them dozing in each other's arms on the balcony. The flapping of his swim fins, as he tried to sneak past them to the pool, woke them up, leading to some sharp words from Molly.

"All I have to say is that it's about time," said Mitch as he put the last bag on the cart. "It's my duty to note such things as your official mooch."

"Thank you official mooch," said Kirby.

"I finally got a t-shirt with that title printed on the front at the Con," said Mitch. "The printer got a really cool font too."

"You can wear it when you're raking leaves at the farm," said Kirby.

"Wait a minute," said Mitch, "I'm the official mooch, not the official slave."

"Okay Gustav," said Kirby, "we'll meet you at the gate after you return the rental."

Gustav nodded and returned to the car.

"Let's check in," said Kirby.

They reached the security gate twenty minutes later. Kirby showed the security staff his Interpol card, they checked it out and once it got the all clear, they waved straight through. Mitch had to show them his passport, put everything he had into a plastic tray, go through the metal detector, and then he head to remove his Superman belt buckle and go through the metal detector again.

"How do I get an Interpol card like that?" asked Mitch.

"All you need to do," said Kirby, "is get stabbed by a deranged heiress with a steak knife."

"You got stabbed?" asked Mitch.

"It was just a scratch," said Kirby, "but I would prefer that Molly not hear that story until we've had some quiet, crime free, time."

"How much time?" asked Mitch.

"Let's give it a few years," answered Kirby as they walked

into the international departures area.

"Can I at least hear the story?" asked Mitch. Up until now his friend's adventures had been one big blank slate with only a few mysterious tidbits of information to go on. That wasn't enough for Mitch.

"I'll tell you," said Kirby, "but after that it's a case of zipped lips for everyone."

"I will be as silent as Gustav," said Mitch.

"Why do people keep saying that?" asked Kirby.

"You never noticed?" asked Mitch.

"Speak of the devil," said Kirby, nodding toward Gustav, who waved to them as he entered the departures section.

"This is almost a comedown," said Mitch, "just a boring flight, and boring drive back to Queens."

"I'm actually looking forward to boring," said Kirby. "Then I might be able to get some work done. Let's find our gate."

Kirby and Mitch led the way to the gate, while Gustav followed, carefully scanning the world around them. They didn't have to go far, and managed to find some available seats, near the gate.

"I never flew first class before," said Mitch, "I'm kind of disappointed that the flight's going to be so short."

"Good," said Kirby, "it'll keep you from getting too used to it."

"As your official mooch I expect to be flown first class everywhere."

"Maybe I can get the airline to classify an 'official mooch' as a pet," said Kirby leaning back in his chair, "and get you stowed with the luggage."

"Now you're hurting my feelings," said Mitch.

"I'm pretty sure Gustav can fit you in a pet carrier," said Kirby, as Gustav leaned over, sized up Mitch, and nodded.

"Now you're scaring me," said Mitch, with a laugh.

Kirby yawned and stretched in his chair. His plan was to sleep on the plane, then sleep in the car on the way to Charlatan's Cove, then crawl into his bed and sleep until the next weekend, hopefully by then the media would find something else to obsess about, and then he would pick up Molly from the train station for her first visit to the cove as his official girlfriend. After that, he didn't have any plans, and he liked it that way.

"Quite a crowd," said Mitch. Kirby scanned over the groups of people clustered around the gates. The crowd was a diverse sampler from all over the world. There were students dressed as the pseudo-hippy interpretation of explorers, going off like their thousands of predecessors to backpack around exotic places as if no one else had done it before. Kirby could smell the patchouli oil even at a distance. There were middle-aged tourists heading home to their various nations after a summer touring Canada. Down by the gate for the flight to Mexico City, there was even a Greek Orthodox priest, thanking an attendant for helping him with his carry-on luggage with a blessing performed by his right hand.

Kirby leaned forward, his attention zooming in on the priest, a stout fellow dressed in a long black cassock, and sporting a black beard that would impress a member of ZZ Top. Something very familiar lay beneath those distractions.

"Mitch," said Kirby.

"Yeah," said Mitch.

"Would you like to be a hero?" asked Kirby.

"What do you mean?"

"I'd like you to go down to the security desk by the juice bar," said Kirby, "and tell security that the fugitive Max Cooperman is at gate thirty-seven waiting to board the flight to Mexico City, and that he's dressed like a Greek Orthodox priest."

"You've gotta be–" then Mitch looked at the priest in question "–Holy shit, it is him."

"Here's my last Canadian twenty," said Kirby.

"You want me to tip them too?"

"I want you to get me a small orange juice, a medium pomegranate for Gustav, and get yourself something while you're there."

"You're being way too casual about this," said Mitch as he took the money, "because of that I will take your money, and I will spend your change on junk food."

"That's a good idea," said Kirby, "I'd like some chips too. The rippled ones."

Father Cooperman had taken a seat with his back to them, giving no sign that he had seen them, or that he noticed anyone being able to see through his elaborate disguise. That didn't stop Mitch from skulking off like he was a ninja on a mission.

"Jeez Mitch," moaned Kirby. Gustav gave him a look, one he didn't need to interpret. "Relax Gustav, I know Cooperman's annoyed you, but let the airport police handle it, we've done our part."

Gustav nodded and leaned back in his seat.

Five minutes later Mitch returned, carrying a little cardboard tray loaded down with paper cups filled with juice, and tossed Kirby a bag of chips.

"I dropped the dime," said Mitch.

"Are you trying to speak in code or something?" asked Kirby.

"I went to the coppers and they looked at me and said 'what's the rumpus?' so I told them I was your finger man and dropped the dime on Father McFatfuck over there."

"You're the 'finger man?'" asked Kirby. "Is that your new superhero? Because I don't want to know what superpowers come with that name."

"I'm trying to talk like an old school detective," said Mitch.

"You're failing."

"Screw you."

"Here are the real cops," said Kirby.

"Oh, this is exciting." Mitch took his seat and pulled out his camera. "I have to record this show for posterity."

Three airport security officers and a Toronto city policeman approached the gate where Max Cooperman was sitting. Suddenly, the big man's head shot up, and he leapt to his feet.

"Stop!" ordered a security officer. "Police!"

Cooperman turned and leaped over his row of seats with an agility that belied his bulk, and started running from the gate with surprising speed.

Gustav looked at Kirby, a plea in his eyes.

"If it will make you happy," said Kirby, waving him on.

Gustav passed Kirby his pomegranate juice and shot out of his seat like a rocket. Max Cooperman saw the great wall of Gustav heading straight for him, and tried to sidestep away from him. The fat man nimbly avoided Gustav's body, but he failed to avoid Gustav's outstretched right arm, which crossed Cooperman right across the cassock.

"Ooh," said Mitch, wincing, but keeping his camera on the action.

Cooperman's fake beard went straight up, while the rest of him went straight down. Airport cops had him surrounded in less than a second, pulling him to his feet and snapping handcuffs on his wrists.

"You!" Cooperman gasped as his eyes met Kirby's.

"Hi Mr. Cooperman," said Kirby, "or can I call you Max now, I feel like we're getting to be old friends?"

"I'll kill you!" howled Cooperman as he struggled to break free from his captors.

"Do you know this man?" asked an airport security officer. He had to do it loudly to drown out Max Cooperman's howls of rage.

"I helped the police catch him the first time," said Kirby.

"It's getting to be a bit of a habit with you," said the security officer.

"Before you take him away," said Mitch, "can I make a request?"

Even Cooperman paused in his writhing wrath to look at Mitch.

"Mr. Cooperman," requested Mitch, holding his camcorder out to get both himself and Cooperman in the frame, "can you please say into my camera: 'I would have gotten away with it, if it weren't for you meddling kids.'"

Cooperman didn't fulfill the request, instead he let loose a stream of obscenity that tested the vocabulary and imagination of even the most perverse longshoreman. As the security officers dragged him away Mitch called out: "This is why nobody likes Hollywood anymore! You don't give the audience what it really wants!"

THE END

Also by Duncan MacMaster...

Video Killed The Radio Star

Hack

Printed in Great Britain
by Amazon

75455777R00173